The
Unlikely
Samaritan

By

Jolie Mae Miller

Book Two of The Good Samaritan Series

Books by Jolie Mae

The Good Samaritan Series

Contents

Authors Note

As an independent (aka "indie" author), I can tell you it's not easy! We are 100% responsible for all facets of our books. In other words, we don't have big publishing houses helping us. The previous page discussed the legal terminology of copyright protection. In layman's terms, books are pirated through "sharing" sites, therefore, stolen, every day. If you obtained this book through channels other than reputable retailers, PLEASE delete it now and purchase through legitimate sources. Authors spend countless hours working to provide you with entertainment and we put everything into our books. In the scheme of things, the cost is minimal. PLEASE adhere to the law.

On a more fun note, indie authors NEED your assistance by supplying feedback/reviews wherever possible. If you enjoyed it, TALK ABOUT IT! On Facebook, Twitter, Goodreads or anywhere you're asked about a good romance or book boyfriend. Word of mouth is a powerful tool and is the only way we indie authors can survive!

Thank you! End of rant... now on to the sexy part. ♥

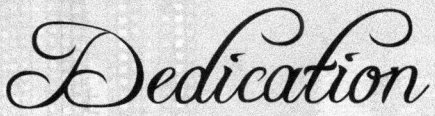

Dedication

To Deena Harrison Schoenfeldt,
the baddest of ALL the Badass Book Bitches!

I thank God every day that you survived,
and that my little book played a part
to ensure you'll be around for a long time to come.

Synopsis

In book one, the *Loving* and *Macintyre* families, faced hardships caused by those closest to them. Left to pick up the pieces, they're unable to shed the painful experiences, from a life they wish to leave behind. In book two, their entwined histories become the platform for a hopeful future.

Multimillionaire, *Jack Loving, Jr.*'s romantic obsession with *Lizzie Macintyre*, was immediate. While present on her darkest day, he vowed to save her, making her part of his life—helping others as good samaritans.

After her exposed secret led to personal tragedy, Lizzie, consumed with guilt, moves on. Taking steps to further secure her future and others, she forms new secret alliances, putting everyone she cares about, at risk.

Forces converge, led by the couple individually, and others with hidden agendas, creating great harm to their future. Will they survive, finding forgiveness for Lizzie's secrets which have the power to destroy them personally and professionally? Is Jack keeping secrets of his own? Prepare for an unexpected ride to discovering the most *unlikely samaritans*, in this very explicit, suspenseful, contemporary erotic romance, in Book Two—The Good Samaritan series.

Chapter One

Raindrops and Broken Spirits

Lizzie

*H*ave you ever really watched the rain hitting a window? It makes random splotches, with no known pattern. Before the drip falls, it bulges seemingly about to burst, then trickles down the window. You can never really tell which direction it will flow or whether it will join up with other drips preparing to fall. The randomness must be nature's way: always changing, always keeping us guessing. Kind of like the mystery of a seashell or a snowflake. Just like life, we never know what's going to happen or if we're about to be derailed. Or dead. Just like Jeremy.

It's been two months since he died—today is Valentine's Day. Two months that I haven't taken a breath. I'm a walking zombie who is barely existing. This is a day couples are happy. They're excited about young love, reminiscing about old love. I hate this day. It just reminds me of how circumstances took my happiness away. Alcohol ruined a once, good husband and father. The kids are suffering, and I know it. I try to be a relevant influence in their lives right now, but even they know: *I'm a failure*. Every time my beautiful daughter, Hope, looks at me, she has this look in her eyes: desperation. She needs me to be the mom, but reality is, we've had a role reversal. At only ten-years-old, she has taken on the traditional mom role, making breakfast and packing their lunches. Oftentimes for dinner, I'm comatose and she makes us grilled cheese sandwiches. Yep, I totally suck.

Everyone is worrying the shit out of me. The endless, daily phone calls, and the repetitive knocking on my door… the ones where they knock for fifteen minutes and NEVER get the idea to leave me the hell alone. The meals left on the doorstep, plus the piled-up mail on the countertops, are all signs of me not coping. I know this has to stop. I'm not completely a basket case. The problem is, my desire to pick myself up and move on, is not stronger than my desire to lay in bed all day. Of this, I absolutely know. Besides, I've made some progress today. I actually moved to my chair, which is where I'm at presently. Staring out the window, I'm focused on these damn raindrops, trying to ponder the patterns and mysteries in nature. I took a bath two days ago, which is major progress for me. I'm scared to admit how many days it's been since I washed my hair. Considering I keep it in a bun, on top of my head, no one sees the long beautiful, *change that—dirty stringy tresses*, generally flowing down my back. I'm just existing, and I don't give a shit about anything right now, because the truth is, the guilt is so strong. It overshadows any good that I might rightfully feel. I don't deserve to feel good because I'm here breathing oxygen. Jeremy isn't. He can't, because it's kinda hard to do that when you're dead. Right? Thanks to me, my kids have lost their father.

The sound of the door opening alerts me to the fact that Hope and Ethan are coming home from school. My ever faithful neighbors, show sympathy to the widow, causing them to walk the children to the door, every afternoon. I know at some point, I'll need to seriously kiss some ass to make up for all the kind deeds done on our behalf. Everything from finding bags of groceries, magically arriving on my doorstep, *every morning,* at 10:00 a.m., to notices posted on my door: "rent paid," that month. Again. *No doubt by the good-hearted Mark, who I have intentionally, and repeatedly, ignored.*

"Mommy?" I hear through the crack in my bedroom door.

"Yeah, sweetie?" I reply.

The door opens and my sweet baby, Ethan, walks in. At eight years old, he's not literally a baby, and he is mature for his age. Since he's the youngest, he'll always be my baby. Having an alcoholic father, generally causes the only other male in the house, to take on a leadership role. Even if it is unfair, and incomprehensible, for a boy of eight years, to fill a man's duties. These last few months have been horrendous, but Ethan has demonstrated a level of strength, far beyond his natural age. Unfortunately, he had practice even before his father's death, helping me take care of his alcoholic dad. Disgusting scenes: constant bouts of vomit left around the apartment, our personal possessions ripped to shreds. All in Jeremy's effort to find objects of value, easily pawned. It still crushes me when I think of my jewelry, stolen by Jeremy to support his habit. Or, my precious antique jewelry box smashed to bits—an insignificant barrier between him, and cash I set aside to pay monthly bills. Ethan's face, always bright, is my oasis. My sweet angel. "Hi, mommy. I just wanted to see how your day was today."

He looks at me expectantly, and I always feel the guilt each day, when this exact scene plays out. Hope in his eyes, begging for me to say something—anything, hopeful. But, today, like days gone by, I'm again *not* hopeful. I'm *not* positive. I'm seriously lost in my sea of negativity. Just sitting in my chair, watching raindrops, thinking about their structural properties. Wishing I could release the weight of seven thousand elephants, laying on my chest. Unable to find the path free of guilt, enabling the proverbial, *snap out of it.* Problem is, I don't know how to even begin to feel anything, other than guilt. The boding sense that I deserve this stifling pain. An ocean of constrictive guilt. I didn't find a solution for Jeremy's problems. My problems—our problems. I was his wife—his partner, it was *my duty.*

I should have tried harder, insisting on finding the answer to his drinking. He was so down on himself when he originally lost his job. The seismic shock, receiving marching papers from a company you envisioned retiring from, threw him off axis. When you make a six figure salary, and suddenly it's gone, you can't just get a job at the local 7-11. Replacing that kind of salary, when the country is in recession, is tough. Before we even realized it, he joined many other Americans in the ranks of the long-term unemployed. Prior to his job loss, we were extremely happy, living well amongst others. We had a country club membership and contributed to charitable children's causes. Our dream home, which Jeremy lovingly designed, became an anchor around our necks. Unwilling, then unable to sell it, we held onto it entirely too long. We used savings to pay the sizable mortgage, eventually losing everything. It was shocking, how quickly our rainy day fund, disappeared. Jeremy was incapable of rational thoughts, especially when his daily goal was single-minded: *getting blitzed.*

Forcing a grin, which is more habit than genuine, "I'm okay, but today would have felt better if you were home. You know I always miss you at school."

Looking down with a bashful smile, he walks quickly to me. Reaching around my neck, his hands squeeze me tight. All the love this little boy has for me, flows like electricity, straight to my soul. The sweet crushing feeling on my heart, takes control of me, causing my eyes to fill. No matter what is wrong in the world, during these moments, all I feel is the power of love exuding from my child. It's similar to rechargeable batteries. He fills me with the strength to get through another day, when I'd rather be in a ball, under my bed's comforter. Sensing my emotions, he squeezes harder. Dishing out strength in abundance. "I love you, Mommy."

Pulling away, I kiss his little cheek and watch his eyes as they carefully inspect my face. Taking inventory of my emotions, he decides if I need more of his affection. "I love you more, Ethan." Peering around the corner, Hope watches us. Always accessing the world around her, deciding if she should give us uninterrupted quality time. Under her watchful eye, I draw strength. Hope behaves motherly towards Ethan and me. She obviously has matured in recent years as well. Developing a distrust and frustration with her father's selfishness, has hardened her personality somewhat. I'm always fearful of the lasting effects of Jeremy's alcoholism on Hope's future relationships with men. "Hope? Did you have a good day at school?"

Shaking her head affirmatively, she walks gingerly into my room. Her eyes moving over all the surfaces, she can easily tell that I've made little progress today. "Ethan, you need to go to your room and start your homework," she instructs. Without hesitation, Ethan gives me another loving squeeze, and quickly exits following his sister's direction. I can't help but wonder the oddity of an eight-year-old boy accepting his ten-year-old sister's orders without complaint. It just reaffirms the role reversal which has taken place. Sadly, I'm not entirely ungrateful because I know I'm a mess. "Mom, I checked the fridge and noticed there's food from some restaurant called Greek On Cary? I'm confused is it the same diner on Cary Street we like so much?"

"Yes, sweetheart. You're so smart. They changed the name from Basilis."

"Oh… well I like the old name."

Inwardly laughing at the marketing evaluations of my smart, little girl. "Well, it's definitely exacting to their location."

She harrumphs, "Whatever. What time do you want to eat tonight?"

Shrugging in response, "I'm not particularly hungry sweetheart. Just warm it up whenever you're ready."

"Do you think you will come out to the living room tonight? You need to get out of this room, Mom."

It's hard to hold back my exasperation, but I realize she just cares deeply for me. "I'll think about it, but I'm not sure yet."

Reaching into her back pocket, she pulls out a familiar looking notecard. "This was on the door when we came home." After gently placing it on my bed, she looks at me with her steely eyes and leaves me alone.

Seeing another of Mark Chesney's messages brings about multiple feelings. Initially, there's a rush hearing from him. He is, without doubt, an amazing person. It's not the sex appeal that exudes from him and leaves you panting, or the way he makes you feel cherished in his presence. It's his heart that makes him the most attractive man I've ever met. Deciding I'm not ready to hear from him, I add it to the growing pile of unopened notes on my dresser.

My friendship with Mark began, when I answered an advertisement for a job, as an escort. Our lives were lower than low. Jeremy had stolen all of our money and pawned valuables, leaving me unable to pay rent and other expenses. Looking into the faces of my children, I decided to do whatever was necessary, to support my family. When facing eviction, without resources to feed my children, I'd probably sell my soul to save them.

I'll never forget what it felt like to walk into that interview, at the office on Main Street in Richmond, Virginia. Being transported into another world is aptly fitting, because the nondescript building with high security, housed a mini-museum. The decorations, obviously French, were beautiful, but the memory that strikes the hardest, is the smell of roses. They covered nearly every surface; colored to compliment the room's décor. Separate the roses and beautiful furnishings, is the powerhouse known as Ms. Martin. Sometimes you meet someone and you just know they are connected, and strong. She may be small in stature, but she's a sharp business woman and not someone you would want to cross. It was on my first assignment from Ms. Martin that I met the dashing Mark Chesney.

My assignments through the agency sent me to business dinners, lunches, and galas. The longer we spent time together, the deeper our friendship blossomed. Eventually, my assertiveness and opinions, caught his keen financial mind. Mark gave me access to his Endowment, and soon I was integral to the financial decision-making. Of course, this shocked some people, no one more than me. My escort role made a definite shift: business partner.

Now, every time I hear, or think about Mark, it reminds me of Jeremy. My decision to be an escort, once revealed, caused Jeremy to seek me out that fateful December night. My decision to accept material objects, like dresses and gifts, angered him and he died believing those things were important to me. My decision to attend the Christmas Gala, instead of spending time with my family, knowing Jeremy had begun to turn a positive corner. It caused him to go to the Jefferson Hotel to find me. My decision to engage in conversation with Mark, overheard by Jeremy—assumptions were made. I fear he had the worst image in his head of me: *paid whore*. My decisions led to everything, including his death. Every decision along the way included Mark. As close of a friendship as we once had, it's impossible not to see my failures every time I think of Mark

Chesney. Therefore, I avoid him completely. Problem is, he won't stop. Everything from grocery deliveries, paid rent, money magically appearing in my bank account. The kindest act had to be Christmas. Oh, how I cry every time I recall seeing Jenny at my house on Christmas Eve. She used her key and yelled at me saying "Christmas is about the children and they *would* have a Christmas." Next thing I knew, delivery men were filling my apartment, with more gifts than any of my friends could afford. I'll never know how he coordinated it with her, but I know it was Mark, who paid for everything.

It's so difficult managing and balancing my emotions for this kind-hearted man, with my guilt that Jeremy died *because* of the time I spent with him. I'm truly heartbroken and confused. Granted, Jeremy's alcoholism and lack of personal control, made him get into a car drunk. The reason he did it that particular night is completely my fault—and Mark's.

The restraints are binding my legs and arms. I cannot move and my breaths are waning. The shrill sounds of someone screaming, are incredibly annoying. "Stop! Please stop screaming!" I yell, but no one listens. I vaguely hear a man's voice begging me to calm down, but it causes me to become more afraid.

An accident on Interstate 95, horrifies me. Small car, versus tractor trailer: no survivors. The small car burst into flames, trapping the occupant inside. The jack-knifed tractor trailer, flipped and mangled, a tree impaling the driver. A series of unfortunate events: ice on the roads, speeding, but none more significant than driving while intoxicated. Mangled metal, fire, and the smell of gas… and death.

Someone is rocking me, trying to soothe my pain. "Get away! Don't touch me! You're the reason this happened!" Gentle shushing and light kisses on my cheek, try and calm me, but it only upsets me more. Suddenly, I'm moving. Carried like I'm an infant, presented across the bed with luxurious linens. The room is a flurry of activity suddenly. There are people all around me. Anxious male voices, sounding very concerned. I thrash in the bed—I must get away! I'm picked up from the bed, held again like an infant, in someone's arms. They're different—the smell of different cologne permeates my nostrils. For a brief moment, I curl into the comforting arms. Home, it feels like… home. Calming sounds, spoken to me, attempting to settle me. For a moment, I'm at peace—it feels, good. Then, an image flashes before me of an angry Jeremy. He's calling me dreadful names, judging me. The soothing voice tries to negotiate my renewed screams. I become more uncontrollable, unmanageable. To no avail, I'm held down on both sides. The sharp pinch in my arm is quickly followed by a burning pain in my veins. Then, there is nothing but blackness. I'm alone, except for my thoughts, and the terrifying screams that never end.

"Wake up, Mommy!" Hope yells. "Please, wake up!"

Feeling the cool small hands on my shoulders, I briskly awaken to darkness all around me. I try to focus my weary eyes on the digital clock radio. It's the middle of the night. Sitting up in bed, "I-I'm so sorry, Hope. I didn't mean to scare you." Reaching out to her, she accepts the hug I desperately need to feel. Trying to escape the remnants of my nightmare, I soak up her goodness and love.

"Mom, you're okay. It was just another bad dream… I'm here now."

Inhaling deeply, I truly know she has the power to chase my demons away. *But, should she?* As much as I need absolution, I need to find strength and independence more.

Chapter Two

Unannounced Visitors and Would-Be Angry Neighbors

Lizzie

After the kids head off to school, I go to the kitchen to make my ritual cup of coffee. It's necessary living to me, just like breathing. Suddenly, a knock on the door startles me. Considering the children just left, I assume they have forgotten something. Then, it occurs to me they would use their key—*no, probably not the children.* I gingerly walk to the door, peeking out the peephole. *Oh god, no. It's Mark.*

"Let me in, Lizzie."

I stand there staring at the door, remaining completely quiet. It occurs to me, as long as he doesn't hear me, he will eventually go away. I hope. Quietly, I take a small step back, then another, all the while staring at the door. *Please, just go away Mark.*

"Last chance, Lizzie. We're talking today. You're not avoiding me any longer."

Only focused on the door, and careful not to make any noise, I'm my own worst nightmare when I walk backward into a chair. Flipping over the top in a move probably fit for hidden camera, I scream when hot coffee pours all over me. Trying to recover from the scalding burns, I vaguely notice the front door opening and the tall, breathtakingly, well-suited, Mark Chesney in all his handsome glory barreling through.

"Lizzie! Lizzie are you okay?" He races towards me, accessing the situation and finding me in a state of pure dishevelment. Fuck. "Are you burned? How hot was this coffee? Talk to me, Lizzie!"

Trying to find some sense of pride, "I'm fine, Mark. What are you doing in my apartment?"

Looking at me as if I've lost my mind, "Dammit you screamed. What the hell did you think I was going to do? Ignore you, like you've been ignoring me? Fuck that shit."

Shaking my head in frustration, "I appreciate the concern, but I'm okay and you can leave now."

Staring at me with harsh, burning eyes, "No, we need to talk. It's long overdue."

Exasperated because the last thing I wanted to do today, was have a heart-to-heart with this man, I begin to feel pretty pissed off. "We have nothing to say. Seriously, I'm fine. I'd really appreciate it if you'd leave. I'm busy and have things to do today. So, thank you for coming to my rescue, but please leave."

Moving to my couch, full of toys and newspapers, he plants his fine ass and becomes very comfortable. It's hard to miss the smell of his fine cologne and the swagger in his walk. He has such a commanding presence, and I find it difficult to argue with him. Seemingly unaffected by the mess surrounding him, he simply settles in. *Oh boy, he's not leaving.*

"Have a seat, Birdie. You've ignored me long enough. As far as you having things to do, don't lie to me. You never leave this apartment. I've given you space and time to heal, but it ends. Today."

Very flustered, I shake my head furiously and stomp over to the adjacent chair. "There's nothing to discuss. I'm fine—*we're fine*. There are things I'm dealing with; end of story."

"I call bullshit. We are not the same. You are definitely, not the same person as you once were. You don't answer the phone or the door. I try to help—."

"I don't need your help!" I scream loudly. "Why are you trying to help me? I haven't asked you for anything. And, excuse me for not being the same person as I once was. My husband died! He *died*! He's *not* coming back! My children will *never* see their father again. *Never* again will he have a chance to straighten out his life. They have *no* reason to be hopeful any longer! I didn't realize there was a behavior manual for how I am expected to act. All I want… is to be left *alone*, just me and my children. Why can't you respect that?"

"You know why!"

"No, I don't! The calls, the notes, the daily groceries, why? I didn't ask for *any* of it."

"You didn't have to! I don't need permission to help *MY friend*."

"Uh-huh. Friend? You mean escort." I softly reply sarcastically.

With a murderous look that I've never seen cross his face, he jumps up from the sofa, grabbing me around my arms, pulling me up hard, tightly in a standing position. "Don't… fucking say that… *ever* again," he quietly states with finality. "I am dangerously close to stripping you, reddening that beautiful ass of yours across my knee, that I'm fucking dying to get my hands on. We've discussed this before and I will *not* repeat myself again on the subject. Do... not... press me, Elizabeth. Now... sit down, we will discuss what's going on. Rationally."

Swallowing fast, a feeling comes over me reminding me that this man has many layers. His power in the finance world is well known. Just as powerful, however, are the emotions always bubbling, just under the surface. Losing his wife and child, led to our emotional connection. Mark doesn't let many people see his personal side. He let me in, however. Spending time together, has taught me he is a highly sexualized creature, and our attraction is always present. My desire to honor my wedding vows and his desire, not to dishonor my wishes, always seemed to leave us in a constant state of influx. More important to anything, however, is our combined desire to support children's charities. Therefore, we decided it was more important to maintain a close friendship, rather than a quick roll-in-the-hay, potentially destroying our respect for one another.

"That night, changed a lot for me too. I hated seeing you in agony. Jeremy's death affected me as well. Granted, it wasn't on the same level as you obviously, but nevertheless, it did. Seeing you emotionally crushed, Birdie, it devastated me. Every night when I can't sleep, it's because I hear your wails of pain. I replay the Children's Hospital Christmas Gala, over and over in my head. I ask myself—*could I have done something different? Is his death my fault?* Don't you see Lizzie, I'm in this with you!"

Staring at him, listening to his words, I'm reminded of our conversation while walking through the beautiful Lewis Ginter Botanical Gardens. I knew he was struggling with something that day. As we walked through the exhibits, admiring the horticultural beauty, he disclosed his deepest pain to me.

His wife loved spending time at the gardens, and he obliged her as often as he could. Mark once had a son. His name was Joshua, but Mark called him Josh. As a family, they spent their weekends imparting culture early into their son's life. Unfortunately, their beautiful life met a tragic end. His wife suffered from post-partum depression and alcoholism. She met with a therapist for the depression, but she kept a big secret. Vodka. More specifically, her addiction, causing her to hide bottles around their home. Mark, however, didn't learn about her alcoholism until it was too late. Two lives were ended, when his wife drove their car into the scenic James River. Mark was forever altered after the loss of his son and wife. He established an Endowment Fund in their honor, benefitting children's charities throughout Richmond. It was through our combined interests, I began to work for his Endowment.

Taking a deep breath, I know I must try and explain my feelings to this amazing man. I'm incredibly conflicted, because even though he has helped me so much in the past, I cannot ignore it was my association with him that ultimately angered Jeremy enough to go out driving and cause an accident.

"First, let me say, I genuinely appreciate everything you have done to help me and my children—."

"I don't want, or expect appreciation, Birdie. That's not why I'm here."

"Well, regardless, whether you want it or not, I'm saying it." Standing up, I walk towards the window, pulling back the curtains. Staring out my window, into the slight ripple currents of the James River, I cannot help but think about Mark's wife. Wondering about her last moments of life. *Did she intentionally drive into the water that fateful day? If not, was she awake or passed out upon impact? Did she fight aggressively to get out of the car before drowning? And Joshua... my heart breaks for you sweet precious child.* I hope he was asleep in his car seat. *Please God, I pray he didn't suffer a painful death.* Jeremy… *was his death a painful one? Did he see his life pass before his eyes? Was he focused on our children? On me?* "I can't stop thinking about Jeremy's death. I'm consumed with guilt, Mark."

Suddenly, I feel the warmth of his hands traveling up and down my arms, comforting me. I was so engrossed in my thoughts, I never felt him move behind me. His chin lands on the crown of my head, pulling my back into him. He has always passed electricity through to my body whenever he touched me. Yet today, instead of sexual chemistry, I feel his powerful strength entering my body through his touch. So simple, yet so powerfully therapeutic. "I know, babe. If I tell you to stop thinking about it, you won't do it. My grief has taught me: everyone heals in a different way. Pretending I can take your pain away with a few words, is a fallacy. Time is the answer, I promise you. However, I will not allow you to hide away in this apartment, letting his death control your life."

Shaking my head slightly, "It does control me—and it *should*. It's our fault, Mark."

Turning me around in his arms, facing him, he has a look of total confusion. "How is Jeremy's death *our* fault?" Suddenly needing space, I walk out of his grip, only to find him restraining me again. "Don't walk away from me, Lizzie. This is important, and we're going to straighten this the fuck out. Now."

Sensing his increasing anger, I know we're about to really get into the crux of this problem. I know he will not understand my way of thinking, but that's okay because I know in my heart we're to blame. Jeremy's death will forever be on my conscience. "You and I are not responsible, for Jeremy willfully getting into his car, causing a collision with a tractor trailer." He regards me carefully, waiting for my agreement, but it will never happen. "Lizzie? Tell me you understand it was his decision. His fault, Lizzie!" Shaking my head slightly "no", he grips my arms tightly and shakes my body firmly. "Wake the fuck up, Lizzie! I'm not letting you spiral deeply down the hole. Over my dead body! I *know*... you know I do. You are my friend and I'm not letting this happen. You will *not* lose yourself to the paralyzing grief the way I did. If I have to move in this apartment and babysit you twenty-four hours a day, I'll fucking do it! You have to move on."

My brain hears his words, but my heart doesn't agree with them. Jeremy behaved differently December 14, 2014. My life was exposed to him on that day by the do-gooder, Cindy Hall. He died, believing I was a whore. He found my expensive designer dresses and discovered the clothing for the children, and decided I was selling sex. When he confronted me, at the Jefferson Hotel that night, he overheard an ill-timed joke between Mark and myself. I never had time to explain, before a fight ensued. After that, I was separated from him, and never spoke to him again. Our last words were angry ones. "Babe, your kids need you. Hope is helping out, but she needs you back. *We all do.*"

Wait... how does he know anything about Hope? "What does that supposed to mean?"

Looking at me with hand-caught-in-the-cookie-jar eyes, "I-I... have been keeping tabs on you and before you get righteous with me, that's what friends do. We look out for one another."

Feeling overly irritated and wanting to lash out, I sneer back at him. "You know, I'm an adult Mark. I've been taking care of my family for quite some time now."

Sighing, and not hiding his disgust, "I realize that Ms. Independent."

"Well, I should certainly hope you would respect my independence and my wishes. Look Mark, the fact is I was in a desperate way, financially speaking. Never, in a million years, did I believe I would end up being your escort—"

"You were never *truly* an escort Elizabeth. We've fucking covered that fact considering the tremendous number of times you sent me home with balls so blue all I had to do was barely touch my dick and it exploded. Several times, in fact!"

Shaking my head in frustration because I know I'll never get anywhere with this man, I decide to try for a more direct method. "I really need you to focus on my words, and please don't diminish their sincerity. Okay?"

"I'll try, but I know what I know, to be the truth. You're an amazing lady, and I'll never believe otherwise."

"Well, I appreciate that, but I take responsibility for Jeremy's death on the night it took place. Granted, with his history, he was living a dangerous lifestyle. I understand that, but he died because he was upset over *my* actions. This had never happened before in our marriage. He never asked about my abilities to cover our expenses, because he was in an alcoholic fog. In the last months of our marriage, he was responding better. There were a new set of counselors working with him, and he was doing better. When Cindy Hall came here and showed him pictures, he must have decided the worst. He came to the hotel in anger and fought with you. I never had a chance to explain. Now, I never will. It's hard to look at my children sometimes. The bottom line is, my actions caused his anger and need to get drunk. I am responsible for his death."

He pulls me into a deeply loving embrace whispering, "I'll let you have this argument for now, but it's not over. Time will heal your wounds, Birdie. I promise you, you're not alone."

Enjoying his comfortable, soothing touch, I lay my head on his shoulder thinking how lucky I am to have met this wonderful man. My eyes land near the front door at two separate key rings laying on the floor. "By the way, how does you keeping tabs on me relate to how you had a key to open my door?"

Pulling away from me, he smirks "I cannot tell you all my secrets."

"Oh, I think you should start talking Mr. Chesney!"

Appearing chastised, "I'll make you a deal. If I tell you a few secrets, you must promise to work on the self-imposed guilt trip you've taken on yourself."

Knowing this promise is pointless and sensing I will not like his answers, I agree to the terms anyway. "Sure."

"You have a collection of friends looking out for you. Of course, you know about your neighbors who watch out for the children. Also, your friend Jenny has been quite accommodating: helping us determine specific needs like weekly groceries... and Christmas presents."

"So Jenny is in on this too!"

"How do think we knew about the macaroni-n-cheese obsession? Or, the dill pickle obsession?"

"I guess, I just never thought too much about it. Thanks for the rental payments. I will pay you back, I promise. But, wait, what did you mean about 'we'?"

Sheepishly grinning, "Oh, didn't I tell you? That's the *best* part! The person that arranged all of this wasn't me." Now very confused about who he could possibly be referring to, "The person who organized everything, also took care of the rent. He owns your building, babe. That's how I got the key. Jack Loving has most *definitely* been looking out for you lately."

Chapter Three

At Every Turn, You're On My Path

Jack

"It's a good deal: six years. You'll be out after three."

"Fuck that! I don't want to serve three days, much less three years!"

"I realize that Mr. Lindy, but if we go to trial and you're found guilty, you could get twenty years. The offer from the Commonwealth Attorney is a good one. In my opinion, take the deal. It is, however, your decision. Think it over, but we only have twenty-four hours before the deal expires.

Before the sound of him disconnecting the call, he sarcastically answers, "Yeah, whatever." Great, another happy client. It constantly annoys me, clients expect me to be a miracle worker. They commit serious crimes, but they don't think they should have to pull any time.

"Patricia, I'm done for now with the Lindy file. He's considering his plea agreement."

"Yes sir, Jack. Oh, and Jack?"

"Yes?"

"There was a slight change to the delivery for Ms. Macintyre today."

"Oh, how so?"

"Mr. Chesney phoned very early to inform me to cancel the delivery from Relay Foods. He indicated he would take care of it personally.

Feeling oddly territorial, it irritates me Mark made a change to my arrangement, for her delivery of groceries. Immediately following Jeremy Macintyre's death, I began to insert myself into the beautiful brunette's life. It doesn't really matter to me she doesn't know who is taking care of her from afar. I know, and that is all that matters.

On the night of the Children's Museum's Christmas Gala, I never expected my life to be upended, even more than it already was. I had zero interest in attending but promised my beloved mother that I would MC the event. My family are huge benefactors of the Children's Museum, and therefore I fully support their initiatives. However, being an MC, was not high on my list of fun things to do. When I accepted the role, I didn't anticipate my life blowing up into tiny little pieces or recognizing the woman of my future.

My wife, Victoria, and I were happily married for over ten years. We had two beautiful children, twins Bryce and Grace. When I agreed to MC the event, I didn't know Victoria was keeping a huge secret. She embezzled over three million dollars from my family's Trust. The information was discovered while transitioning a new audit firm. It was difficult to accept that the embezzlement occurred over several years, and I was completely in the dark. Moreover, our Trust was established to do good works in our local community, so I was devastated. Her family was extremely controlling, and I believe mentally abused her throughout her childhood, well into adulthood. The night of the Gala, my friend Mark Chesney, discovered her father had a history of gambling debts. I will never understand why Victoria didn't come to me for help, instead turning to subterfuge to hide her actions.

Considering we were newly separated, her absence from the Gala, was noticeable. Luckily, details of our separation, were kept quiet from the press. When asked where Victoria was, when she ordinarily would have been front and center, I explained she had a conflicting event. The first public event as a separated couple was uncomfortable yet oddly freeing.

As the Gala partied away, I once again had the privilege of seeing many friends and colleagues. One, in particular, the beauty, Lizzie Macintyre. She had accompanied Mark several times to various events. Each time in her presence, I would turn into a fumbling schoolboy. Seeing her caused my mouth to dry, my hands to tremble, and my thoughts to scatter. Of course the ever wise, Mark, paid close attention and noticed my rare moments of nervousness. Fucker seemed to enjoy it. His little smirks from across the room, when he caught me, watching her. At the time, their relationship was quite undefined to me. There was an obvious closeness, and admiration for one another, yet they were oddly professional. It all seemed strange, and after seeing them on multiple occasions, I was no closer to figuring them out.

Clarity regarding their relationship came, when I overheard men shouting in the hallway. Then, I discovered Lizzie standing between two grown men. Mark and Lizzie's husband, who I eventually would discover his identity, were fighting over her. In an effort to diffuse a volatile situation, I physically restrained Mr. Macintyre, and Mark and I assisted Lizzie, who needed minor medical care from the in-house physician. It was during this chaos, I learned Lizzie was dealing with an alcoholic husband. My heart broke for her. She was mortified with embarrassment. Coincidentally, Victoria, who was living at the Jefferson Hotel, occupied a room across from the room we obtained for Lizzie. Needing to deal with important matters regarding Victoria's father, I returned to Lizzie's room to ask Mark a question when the sounds of a woman wailing permeated the hallways. Reentering Lizzie's room, Mark relayed that the very man I had restrained earlier, and relocated to a different room to sleep off his binge, had been tragically killed in an automobile accident.

The moment was surreal. It didn't make any sense, but the woman in front of me, crying uncontrollably, evidenced the fact something really bad, definitely occurred. It was a terribly sad scene, and my heart broke for her. My need to protect this beautiful woman kicked in, and before I knew what I was doing, I was cradling her in my arms, cooing her with my sympathies. Without even knowing how best to handle the situation, my heart took over, and I heard myself making promises to her. Offering to take care of her, seeing her through this nightmare. The pull that this beautiful creature had on my body and soul was incredibly palpable. Seemingly a thread, connected between her heart and mine... *Lizzie, will you remember us tomorrow?* Powerfully touching moments, as if we were the only ones in the room, she only would accept my touch. She reached for me, held on, and wouldn't let go. It truly felt like we were alone, and everyone around us faded in the background. No, on paper, it didn't make sense to feel this attached to her. Yes, we were technically married, or otherwise not truly free at that moment. Yes, it felt *right*.

"Patricia, can you get Mark Chesney on the line, please?"

"Yes sir, Jack."

"Were your ears burning?" He chuckled through the phone.

"Ex-cuse me?"

"I was just talking about you and wondered if your ears were burning?"

"Ah, no. Who were you talking about me to?"

Laughing loudly, I can tell he's going to make me work for this information. "A certain beauty that you and I have an affinity for." Pausing for dramatic effect, I just groan in frustration. The idea that Mark has an *affinity* for Lizzie… does not make me happy. "I finally came clean to Lizzie. She knows that we've been helping her out, these last few months."

"No… shit! Was she mad? What did she say? Has she been happy with the food I've been sending? I can get an entire new menu together if she doesn't like it. It's really not a problem. Maybe… we do need to change it up some. I'll get Patricia to call—" I fire off questions at him as quick as my mind can process new thoughts.

"Stop! Just listen, Jack. Wait a minute and let's talk. Let me explain where we're at. Okay?"

"I know, that's fine. I'm just saying if she doesn't like something, I can fix it. No problem."

"Jack! The fucking groceries are not the problem!"

"Alright, what does she need then?"

"Her head is screwed up right now. Look, I can't give you all the details without breaking confidence. The bottom line? She blames herself for Jeremy's death. Even though, he was an alcoholic, who got behind the wheel of a car. She thinks it's her fault."

Recalling Mark's personal tragedy, losing his wife and child, it was a grueling time because there was nothing we could do. He was angrier than I've ever seen any other person on this planet. He avoided his friends and only focused on his work. He became a financial powerhouse during that time. His reputation and his clientele built significantly, and everyone wanted to feel the successful touch, of Mark Chesney. "That's ridiculous and unfortunately it reminds me of someone else I know that took on a similar burden."

"Yeah well, only time will heal those wounds. I took a big step today with her. Until now, she's been allowed to sit in her apartment, wallowing in self-pity. Forcing my way into her space, literally I might add, let's her know that the status quo is changing. When I left, I made sure she knew I was coming back, and she's leaving that stuffy place."

Shaking my head in agreement, I ponder what it must be like to stay in a small apartment all day, never leaving, because of unbearable grief. "So, what's your plan?"

"Lizzie needs a diversion. She and I made a connection, over my philanthropic work with children's charities. St. Patrick's Day is coming up. I think it will be a good opportunity, to reel her back into the fray, organizing something to raise money for a good cause."

Listening intently, I strategize how I can insert myself into the equation. Over these last few months, I've developed an addiction for the beautiful, Lizzie. Some might say, an unhealthy addiction. There's this connection, I feel for her, and I want an opportunity to explore it. I think about her constantly, and invariably my mind drifts to her luscious body. *Imagining her touch, her taste, her smell.*

Mark previously explained to me, Lizzie and her husband, were no longer a couple in the true married sense of the word. Knowing her heart was so good, she allowed him to live in a separate bedroom, hoping to assist in his recovery. I'm sure the children appreciated having their father home, but I wonder if his presence was also negative for them. When her husband died, it became necessary to put my would-be plan to spend time with her, on hold. Even so, I have watched her from afar. Patiently waiting—always observing. I know she would disapprove of the twenty-four per day surveillance, I have watching her. It's for my piece of mind, really. Since I cannot be there, I just want to know she's protected, and safe. Besides, her children need that extra bit of security, watching out for them. Mark states she is a fabulous mother, and I'm sure she is a great mom. If she weren't grief-filled, I'm certain she would actively walk them to the bus stop, and not rely on neighbors. It must be terribly debilitating, blaming yourself for someone else's death. "Mark, I want to co-sponsor the event."

He takes his time, considering his response. "I know you have a thing for her, Jack. I've always known it, but we have to be careful here. Getting her to agree to leave the apartment will be a feat in and of itself. Making her feel pressure, is not the answer. She's important to me and I'm not going to let anyone, even you, do anything to risk her emotional well-being. Treading carefully is the answer, trust me."

"You're going to think I'm insane, but I have a gut feeling about Lizzie Macintyre," I admit, I don't really know anything about how she lives her life. She and I had our lives turned upside down— our timing is horrible. Yes, that's true. The time we have spent together, I can't explain it, or tell Mark anything about why I feel the way I do. We're just totally connectable. There's something there, and I just need to spend some time with her… make her feel me when I hold her. "If it's meant to be, it will happen naturally. I just know it."

With a lethal sound in his voice, I can almost imagine him gripping the phone. "What I know, is this: if *my Birdie*, gets fucking hurt because of you, no amount of money will help you hide from me. Friends or no friends—I'm not joking with you. We take this slow, very slowly. You'll let me make the arrangements, then I'll loop you in. Got it?"

"I got it. And Mark?"

"Yeah?"

"Do us both a favor and watch out for her?"

"Yep. Time will tell my man. She's a special one though. Even I wouldn't bang her because I respect her too much."

"Mark! Not helping."

Laughing because he loves to goad me at every turn. "Later."

Before his disconnects, I hope he hears, "Thanks, man. Keep me posted, please."

Standing up and moving to my window, I look out over the downtown, Richmond area. Our building, which my Trust owns, affords us a perfect view of the James River. My eyes move east in the direction of Rockett's Landing. In the direction, *of Lizzie. I wonder what she is doing right now. Is she gazing at the river too?* I find enormous comfort looking out towards the water. Never once did I imagine, investing in the renovation of an old warehouse into a mixed residential/commercial business site, would become personal for me. How fortuitous is was to learn she was living there. In the building, I now own. At every turn, we keep appearing on one another's path. It just feels right, we were destined to meet each other.

Chapter Four

Dangerous Tornadoes in Small Packages

Lizzie

Pounding on the door continues. It started about ten minutes ago. If history repeats itself, it will stop in another five. Ten more minutes, still pounding, sheesh, enough already! After thirty minutes, I'm royally pissed! I dress in something presentable, and barrel towards the door, ready to do harm to whomever never learned basic social etiquette, while calling on someone. I quickly unlock the door, pulling it open, finding a small-framed woman, with a scary look on her face. All of my intentions to give my visitor hell, escape me immediately. Now I'm the one scared.

"Well, it's about time!" She mutters as she barrels past me through the door, without waiting for an invitation.

Carefully closing the door, and almost afraid to turn around, I take a deep breath because I'm having one of those moments of premonition: *my life is about to change, again.* Suddenly, my mouth is dry, and I feel a rush of heat and nervousness fall over my body.

Even my legs, lock up and I have trouble getting them to move. This woman, there's something about her that scares the shit out of me. "H-hello, Ms. Martin. What brings you by today?"

"What brings me by? Seriously, Lizzie! Do you even know how annoyed I am? I've knocked on your door for half a day? When someone knocks, it's customary to answer the damn door."

Feeling completely scolded, "I am truly sorry. If I had known it was you, I would have opened the door sooner. Please accept my apology."

With frustrated, narrowed eyes, she pulls her designer, cotton gloves from each finger, ever so delicately. "That's fine. Next time, open the door!"

"Yes ma'am, Ms. Martin."

She takes a look around my apartment and I am immediately embarrassed with the appearance. School papers lying around. Toys left on every available surface. Newspapers stacked up on the end tables. The real problem: mail. It's everywhere! I hate junk mail and I haven't cared lately to manage it, at all. She's never been to my home before, and I am mortified. Compared to the museum-like surroundings in her office on Main Street, she must think I live in a pig sty. Moving to the couch to make a clear space for her, she finally sits. "May I offer you something to drink? I have coffee."

"No, thank you dear. I cannot stay long especially since I spent most of my day outside on the stoop. We have business to discuss, Lizzie."

"Oh?" I ask confused. Shortly after Jeremy's death, I sent a note to Ms. Martin indicating that even though I appreciated her offer to manage her escort business, I must decline. Considering the state of my life, I had trouble managing anything, much less a business.

"Yes, we do. Several matters to discuss. I know you have been suffering, sweetheart. We have all allowed you space, probably too much space. I've come to refocus your attentions."

Moving to the window, I stare out into the waters of the James River. *Allowed me space... we?* Recalling Mark's visit yesterday, this has him written all over it. "I'm sorry you wasted a trip here today, Ms. Martin. I'm fine, really I am."

A harrumph sounds behind me, and I can feel her moving next to me. We both look out through the picture window, just standing there, staring at the fishermen on the bank of the river. Hoping for a daily catch, for sport or food. Lost in our own thoughts, we watch the activities surrounding river life. Suddenly, very tentatively, she spoke, "My father was an alcoholic. I was the oldest of three children. I grew up watching him abuse my mother. If we tried to intervene, he hurt her more. As we got older, he began to hit us too. Every single day, I hated coming home from school, because I never knew if he was there or not. He was a daily worker, so if he didn't have a job, the drinking increased and he was meaner. My mother was so beaten down physically and emotionally, she was incapable of making good decisions.

"As the years went on, it became apparent to me, we needed to get out, or we wouldn't survive. I tried to convince Mama to leave, but she was too scared. He had her under his thumb so completely, she couldn't see the light of day. One day, he was acting out particularly nasty. He beat Mama so badly she needed medical attention. My sister, brother and I were trying to get her out of the house and Daddy wouldn't let us go. He said, 'Let the bitch die.' My baby brother had gotten stronger and knowing the situation was bad, stood up to him. Everything changed for us that night. Everything. He held a knife to—he held a knife, to my brother's throat. The tip of the blade had begun to slice and I could see blood trickle down. I was never more scared than I was at that moment. It was our turning point. Scared out of my mind, I grabbed his .22 pistol and pushed it into the back of his head. I told him, 'You're going to let us leave, all of us. Never again, will you contact us for anything. If you do, I will kill you myself.' He released all of us and Mama went to the hospital.

"Long story short, I started turning tricks to support my family. Before too long, I realized if you were smart enough and treated people with respect, you could earn real money at this business. Doing this has allowed me opportunities to help other families in crisis. I don't regret one single thing I did, to save all of us. I may have paid a big price with my body, but my soul was free. That asshole died knowing he was not loved and I'm fine with that." Turning to face me, she pressed her small hands to my cheek, "Lizzie, you do not need to carry this burden any longer. You saved your children. They know that heavy drinking comes with a price, and will hopefully remember it as adults. The bottom line, however, is it was not healthy for them to see a drunk every day. Trust me, I know. Your conscience should be at peace with it sweetheart. It's time to let *your* soul fly free now."

Feeling my body become full of emotion, I broke down. I cried more tears than I ever thought possible in Ms. Martin's arms. Cried, for the guilt I was releasing, but didn't truly feel I had a right to release. Cried, for all the times my children had to see Jeremy at his worst, drunk and uncaring of their preciousness. Cried, for the many good memories I would always cherish from our marriage before the alcohol took his life. Cried, for the benefit of having a father in the future they will never experience. Cried, for the horrific way his life ended, oh so tragically. Cried, for my failures along the way, for, not helping him in his sobriety. I just cried, and cried, and cried. I don't know how long I remained in her arms. She didn't move or rush me.

All I felt was pure human compassion and understanding. At some point, my tears… just… stopped.

"Are we done with the self-blame and doubt? Can we move on now, Lizzie?"

Shaking my head, I whimpered my reply, "I'll try."

"Good, that's what I wanted to hear." She squeezed me with motherly love and set me back, inspecting my face for doubt. Apparently happy with my response, "Your children need their mom back. The full-time, loving mom they know and love. Also, we have an event to plan, Lizzie."

"An event? What kind of event?"

"A St. Patrick's Day party. We'll have it at Siné Irish Pub, over on East Cary Street. Mark wants us to organize an event to benefit his Endowment."

Running the dates through my mind, I become immediately concerned about timing. "Ms. Martin, there's barely any time—St. Patrick's Day is next month. There's no way to pull off an event so soon."

"There is, and you will. Mark has full confidence in you. Here's the contact information for the manager at Siné and list of attendees he wants you to invite." Grabbing my hands, tightly in hers, "This will be good for you. I promise, dear."

Taking the information from her, I get the distinct feeling I've been ambushed. It occurs to me that she's still in Richmond. "Ms. Martin, I thought you were moving abroad to have a lifetime of beautiful roses delivered daily?"

She walks to the door, pulling her gloves back into place, opens it, and speaks over her shoulder with a smirk on her face. "Oh, my plans haven't changed, they're just delayed a bit. I have some… connections, which need my personal attention. After everything is set, I'll be jetting off."

She blows air kisses and is about to leave when I ask, "How did you know I would agree to organize the event?"

"You still haven't technically, but I know you will do it. We're the same, you and I. You're a sucker for raising money for kids. We all believe in you, Lizzie."

Then, the formidable presence leaves, and somehow she has emboldened me with renewed confidence. Ah, breathing deeply, I check the clock and notice the kids will be home soon. *Where have the hours gone?* I guess I first need to take the most important step: being a better mom. Grabbing my cell phone, tennis shoes and coat, I head out into the chilly afternoon to meet the school bus. Yes, the kids will certainly be surprised to see me.

Chapter Five

Ex-wives Who Need A Hobby

Jack

"Jack, Ms. Macintyre's private security, line one."

"Thanks, Patricia.

"This is Jack Loving."

"Yes sir, Mr. Loving. Seth, from Security Limited. We wanted to notify you that Ms. Macintyre has walked from her apartment, down to the front circle of the complex. She appears to be waiting for her children, Sir. Since this has never occurred before on our watch, we wanted to notify you immediately of her change in routine."

Hearing his words, causes the biggest smile to break out on my face. This is major progress. Up until now, Lizzie never left the apartment. "Thanks for the update, Seth. That's incredible news. Please continue to monitor her from afar. I don't want her to find out she's being watched. Only intervene if there is a safety issue."

"Sir, yes, Sir."

"Oh, Seth?"

"Sir?"

"Can you email me some current photos? Nothing invasive—only public locations.

"You should receive them in under ten minutes."

"Thank you."

Five minutes later, my email contains three images of Lizzie talking with other parents. She looks at ease, and comfortable. Her hair is pulled back in a ponytail. She is dressed in warm-up pants, jacket, and tennis shoes. Even casual, she's stunning. I enlarge the next photo of her smiling face. Unable to stop staring at her... wow, she's just beautiful. Adding the photo to my phone's screensaver, "You owe me a date, Lizzie Macintyre. I'm coming to collect."

"Jack, Mr. Lindy, line two."

"Thank you, Patricia."

"Mr. Lindy, have you reached a decision on the Commonwealth Attorney's offer?"

"Actually, no. I have an offer of my own. I'm not serving a single day in prison and you're going to help me."

Mr. Lindy proceeds to explain he has additional information about an unrelated crime, he wishes to offer in exchange for immunity. Fuck. It's days like today, I really hate my job. The information is good and in all likelihood, when I present the offer, he'll end up never serving a day in jail. I agree to approach opposing Counsel with the new information.

My cell phone rings, and I groan in frustration. Victoria. She calls several times a week, and normally I send the call to voicemail. Even though I fully intend to go through with the divorce, she keeps calling. There is no way I can forgive everything that has happened.

I've made the point clear to her, and her lawyer, multiple times. Yet, here we are again, she's calling me. "Hello?"

"Oh, yes. Jack?"

"Yes, Victoria. I'm busy. Did you need something?"

Hearing her long sigh followed by a lengthy silence. "Sorry to be a bother. I-I was just thinking about you, and hoped maybe we could meet for coffee?"

"Vickie, look, nothing has changed for me. There is too much that has happened. We need to focus on the children now. It's time we moved on."

"I don't want to move on! And, I certainly don't want you to move on either. Is that what's going on? Have you moved on, Jack? Are you seeing Erin again?" She questions quickly and fearfully.

"Stop! What I do is no longer any of your business. I don't want to fight with you anymore. It's time to accept the inevitable. Please, we can't keep doing this—"

"Doing what? What exactly are you doing because you're MY husband? You shouldn't be doing anyone!"

"Seriously, Victoria. I'm hanging up because I'm busy. I have clients, and I can't have you distracting me from my work. You've brought this on yourself. If you'd come to me when all this first starting happening, instead of keeping secrets, we wouldn't be in this situation."

Then the tears began. Loud, full-body, wrenching tears filled my phone. Fuck. "Victoria, please, I'm not trying to be rude but I can't keep having this conversation. I think it's probably best, we leave it up to the lawyers. I'm sorry, I really am, but I need to go now. Please be okay, Vickie. I don't mean you any harm, and I want you to think about the counseling we talked about last time. You never know, it may be very helpful."

"Sure, Jack. I'm sorry to bother you." Then, the line disconnects. Recent conversations have always been this way. I hate to hear the hurt in her voice, but I can't be her savior. She needs to look elsewhere for support now."

Lost in my thoughts, rubbing my forehead to relieve the tension, I failed to hear Patricia over the intercom. "Jack?"

"Oh, sorry, Patricia."

"That's okay. Mark Chesney is on line one." Hmm, finally some possible good news.

"Mark? Please give me some good news."

"Lizzie, is organizing the St. Patrick's Day event at Siné. Is that good enough news for you?"

Feeling a light, relieving, yet excited comfort, come over me, "Ah, yeah. It's perfect news. I don't know how you did it, but I'm glad you convinced her to come out of the apartment."

"Well, I had a secret weapon." He laughed.

"Care to share?"

"Let's just say that she may be wrapped in a small package, but she packs a powerful punch."

"Huh?"

He chuckles, "Nothing. Seriously, though, Lizzie is helping organize the event. That means she's coming, but she's fragile, Jack, and I know you have a thing for her, but I wouldn't push too hard. It might backfire. I don't want her to degenerate, spiraling into her hell of self-guilt. That wouldn't be good for her children.

"Yeah."

The rest of the afternoon, I have trouble focusing on work. I can't help but think about the last few months. The overwhelming anger I have with Victoria's deception. My frustration that she didn't come to me for help. The contempt I feel, for her manipulative parents, and the empathy I feel, Victoria now requires therapy for their control. My children, oh how my heart breaks for the upheaval, they face. They spend several days per week, with their mother, but their residence is clearly my home.

It's awkward for me sometimes. The bedroom I shared with Vickie for many years, the one where we enjoyed each other's bodies on every imaginable surface, is now where I fantasize about Lizzie. My mornings, begin nearly the same way. I awaken, my cock heavy, needing relief and getting no physical affection, other than my own hand. Generally, I begin in my home gym, working out for a solid hour. Followed, by an intended quick shower, but somehow is lengthy due to my fantasies of Lizzie stretched out on my weight bench. Oh, how I desperately want to see her tied down, helpless, spread out wide for my morning pleasure. I imagine the sweat dripping from our bodies after we've had a morning workout. Her skin tasting salty, yet sweet. How I long to run my tongue down her neck, down across her nipples until they harden. Will they be pink and small? Flesh-color and large? My hand invariably finds my hardness and strokes, first lightly so I don't become too excited. Then, firmer so I may enjoy the pleasurable feeling. My hands are so desperate to touch the curves of her body. Desperately seeking her reactions to my fingers. Will she sigh quietly, or moan loudly? Can I make her come from touching and licking her nipples alone? God, I'm desperate for this woman. I need her so badly. Stroking my cock, while showering, I imagine her skin glistening. My tongue is eager for her taste, the texture of her body. My fantasies bring me closer, my dick is hard and I'm close. So close. Then, I imagine the taste of her inner core and it sends me over the edge. Every fucking time. The rivulets of my pleasure, disappear in the warm spray of the shower. The refreshing feeling of starting anew and ready to face a new day. Although admittedly, I pray for the time when I won't need to fantasize about her body, but actually enjoy it. I'm dedicated to the mission… it *will* happen. She'll be in my arms, again.

Then, the fragments of my mind can't let go of the pain belonging to the woman who appears in my morning fantasies. Unknowingly, she gives me so much pleasure, and I feel guilty because of it. Her life is in total upheaval. Mine too, really. But, I still seek her in my dreams. I'm desperate for her touch, her mind, and just merely, her physical presence. I need her and she doesn't know it yet, but she needs me too.

Chapter Six

Co-Sponsors With Hidden Agendas

Lizzie

It was difficult to get back into the swing of things, but over the last few weeks, I pushed through anyway. Ms. Martin was actually quite inspiring. She called me frequently, always under the guise of asking about the event, but I know it was really to check up on my emotional well-being.

I still have my inevitable moments of clarity. Never will I release the guilt that I contributed to Jeremy's death. Granted, I understand he chose to drink—*it was his decision*. However, on December 14, he was overcome with overwhelming information about me. Knowing how I was supporting the family, even though he was misled on the exact details, had to be a shock. Too much at once, and he snapped. *Oh, Jeremy. I wish I could talk to you just once more.*

Tomorrow is the big event. The St. Patrick's Day Bash at Siné, in Shockoe Bottom, benefitting the Chesney Endowment. Richmonders love a chance to party, and St. Patrick's Day is a very big deal. There are several big events around town, but one place to party authentically, is Siné. The traditional Irish pub, draws a huge crowd and partnering with them, gives us generous exposure. I was concerned some may not appreciate the alcohol component, mixing with a child's charity. So far, everyone has been supportive and sees the opportunity to raise a bunch of cash for a good cause.

Working from home, has been a good transition for me. I can work freely, yet there's no one around to question my sanity, when I burst into tears unexpectedly. This morning, I received a delivery, for the promotional materials I ordered for the event. Opening the banner, I receive quite a shock when it's different from the proof image I approved. Instead of the Chesney Endowment exclusively, it now reads "To benefit the Chesney Financial Limited Endowment and Bowes Family Trust Foundation." *What the hell?*

I rip through all the boxes of materials, and every single proof I approved, has been modified to include the Bowes' Trust. Completely shocked, a million things run through my mind. *Did the printer screw this up? Was this on there, and I totally missed it? Oh shit! I'll never get this corrected in time.*

Knowing I need answers, I decide to call Mark. Our conversations have been brief since his bombardment into my apartment. Being a very intuitive man, I believe he senses my discomfort and gives me space.

"Well, hello Birdie. How are you feeling today?"

"I, I guess I'm well Mark, but we have a problem."

He begins to chuckle and somehow I get the feeling he's behind this "problem." "I wondered how long it would take for you to give me a call." Hearing the screeching sound of a chair, I can imagine him staring out his office window. Watching the activity of downtown Richmond below. "Look, I wasn't totally transparent with you about this event, but the purpose is good all the same. Jack and

I, have wanted to co-sponsor something, for quite a while. This idea came up, and we pulled it together. I'm sure it will be just fine."

"Whoa—wait! Who exactly spearheaded this idea? You or Jack Loving?"

With a quiet snort that he tries to muffle unsuccessfully, "Does it really matter, babe? Look, we need to generate interest for the charity. St. Patrick's Day is huge in Richmond. It's a win-win. Loving seems to be keen on raffles these days and has an idea to pay $100 for a chance to win a Florida vacation. So, his people are organizing that part of it. It should raise a lot of money."

Listening to him, I feel like I'm the last person to find out their little secret. I worry there's more to this whole event, but then again my emotions are on edge these days. "So, I guess the promo materials will be just fine then. Silly me, I should pay more attention next time."

"Hey, don't get in a snit over this, babe. You're going in the right direction. I need you—my charity is a mess without you. Please… let's get back on track. Okay?"

"So, what's wrong, Mr. Chesney? Your dance card too empty these days? No available women left in Richmond—no escorts on speed dial? I'll have to ask Ms. Martin about taking care of you."

"Hey, Ms. Martin has my back, always has. As far as my dance card… no one can ever replace you, Birdie. You still haunt my dreams, and it fucking sucks. I find the complete package and I'm smart, or possibly dumb enough, to be gentlemanly with you." He groans deeply and I can't help but laugh because I know he's being truthful. He has the carnal needs of a raw, kinky, passionate lover, mixed with refined, graceful power. It's head-spinning really. Moreover, he's my friend and that's an unbreakable connection which is unfavorable to random hook-ups. "Seriously, I've always got your back. No matter what happens. I'll always be here."

"Thank you. These last few months, you've proven it to me."

"Hey, I'm not the only one, but that's a different story for another day. See ya—! "

Hearing the line disconnect, I'm left wondering: *what the hell was that supposed to mean?*

Arriving at six o'clock in the morning, was not on my favorite list of things to do today. It is, however, where I am because people are crazy about St. Patrick's Day. It doesn't matter that it's barely time for the chickens to wake up, the lunch crowd will soon be here and that means our event will be in full swing. Luckily, Mark arranged for a staff to help me, so along with the Siné staff, the setup is easy.

Standing back, I look at the large banner hanging across the bar when I notice a loosened clip. Taking a deep breath, I contemplate whether or not this clip is going to irritate me all day or not. Deciding yes, I climb the barstool and stand up on the bar and reach as high as I can. Even in heels, it's just out of my finger's grasp. So, I extend as far as I can when suddenly... everything happens so fast. I slip and scream a most unladylike, "Shit!" Bracing for a certain fall from quite a ways up, I try to catch myself on anything I can grip. Then, I feel it. The warmth of pleasant arms wrapped around me, tightly. The sounds of breathing heavy in my ears. The pounding beat of another's heart against my arm. The impending fear and pain from a clumsy fall disappeared into the beautiful embrace of a sexy, debonair savior named Jack Loving.

"Dammit Lizzie! You scared the hell out of me!"

Looking into his eyes, my mind tries to catch up with the sequencing of events, going from gloomy doom to luscious boom, in all of one-point-five seconds. Quickly assessing myself for zero pain, my body begins to enjoy the comfortable arms stretched ever more tightly around me. Those eyes, incredibly beautiful with specks of yellow and green, seem to invade my soul. Moving in and around my body, selfishly exploring all my hidden secrets. Something very critical passes between us in those elapsed moments. He reaches inside me and almost captures my senses, forever demanding to be in control of me, making me his.

When social etiquette would dictate letting someone go after they have efficiently, and gallantly, saved a falling woman from a five-foot fall, Jack Loving does the opposite. As the seconds tick by, he just holds onto me tighter. I'm so engrossed by the visual hold he has on me, I can feel his grip dig in, refusing to let go. It is… awkward. Even more, it feels familiar—like it isn't the first time being in his arms. Which is strange, because I've barely spoken to the man.

Chapter Seven

Jack Loving-Official Lifesaver For Lizzie Macintyre

Jack

When I walked into Siné this morning, I was in a fabulous mood. For months, I have strategized about ways to spend time with Lizzie Macintyre. When there is something you really want and it's unobtainable, your mind obsesses about lost moments, lost opportunities, lost realities where the exchange is real and feels right, and good. Those moments don't exist when you can't even spend five minutes with the person. So, I've patiently—*been impatient.* Counting the days, receiving the security reports, hoping for some change in her pattern bringing her out of the obvious depression she was in. Actually, it's been good for me to focus on someone else, instead of my own problems.

Knowing that this event was an inked deal, gave me encouragement. It gave me a firm date that I could see Lizzie, be in her presence. Last night, I didn't sleep. I tried, I really did try.

Tossing and turning, met mindless television, followed by a middle-of-the-night workout, followed by a lengthy shower, whereby I invariably had an amazing orgasm thinking about seeing Lizzie in a few hours. Sleep finally found me and three hours later, I jog happily up to the doors of Siné, opening them just in time, to see the gorgeous brunette on the tips of her heels, on the fucking bar—reaching up—unsafely, and begin to fall. I ran so fast, and just as she was tumbling, I reach out and grab her before she hits her head on the bar rail. Now, I'm furious!

"What the hell were you doing up there? Do you realize how unsafe it was for you to be up there in four-inch heels?"

"Yeah, I kinda realize that now."

"Good!" Shaking my head, I tear my eyes away and look towards the rays of light beginning to come through the front picture window. Desperately trying to regain some composure, I lecture myself on everything I've probably said wrong since I opened my mouth. This is definitely not how I saw this morning's dialogue going between us.

"Um… you… can let me go now."

Then, it occurred to me, how I was holding her. Restraining her against my chest, tightly. Suddenly, I'm embarrassed. I was so lost in my thoughts—so comfortable, I didn't realize just how inappropriately, I was holding her. Knowing, I really needed to let her go, I squeezed her a little tighter, and looked deeply into her eyes. Her sight, scorches my defenses, leaving me split open and helpless. Breathing deeply, I decide to risk further inappropriateness, leaning in, gently inhaling her scent near her neckline. Her smell… it's so distinct… so unique, so calming to my thoughts, I become lost in her. Gently, I place a small kiss at the edge of her hairline. Forcing myself to pull away, I can't bear to look at her. Quite possibly, I've crossed a line, choosing to take advantage of a weak moment, in favor of my own selfishness. Immediately releasing her, I set her on her own feet. "Sorry, I-I am…," not able to pull together a cohesive thought, I take small steps away from the woman, who seems to boggle my brain. Realizing I need to gain some clarity, and fast, I nervously run my fingers through my hair. "Hey, try not to fall off anymore bars. Okay? Next time, I may not be around to save you." She laughs and I turn to walk away. Not able to get away fast enough.

"Jack?"

Turning back, with my hand firmly wrapped around the door, "Yeah?"

Fiddling nervously with her fingers, "I really appreciate you saving me." Then it happens… she smiles the sweetest, sexiest smile and I'm blinded in her light.

Not wanting her to see my vulnerability, I shake my head, looking down and away. Trying to hide the smile that brightens my face. "No problem."

Just as I'm about to leave, "Did you need something, Jack?"

Turning back to face her, "Huh?" I see a change on her face. Like she's anxious and almost wishes to extend our conversation. Or maybe, I just want to see that reaction, I don't know. "Oh, I ah… I was just…" Taking a breath, I shake my head in frustration, I must look like a schoolboy, not the normally confident man I am. "I wanted to stop by, check on things this morning. See how we're set up to hopefully bring in some donations today, for the Trust."

Narrowing her eyes at me in apparent confusion, "So… did you get what you needed? Do you approve? I think you spent most of your time saving me, not checking on things."

Shaking my head in agreement, "You're right. I guess seeing you fall, nearly breaking your neck, shook me up a little bit."

"A little? You sounded rather angry."

Fuck. She pegged me square on. Hell yeah, I'm not just angry, I'm livid. With all the staff, I arranged to be here and help for this event. *Why the fuck wasn't someone else hanging the damn banner?* She had no business in heels wearing a short skirt, on a damn bar top, putting on a show for everybody standing around. Yeah, I'm not happy. Not even a little bit.

In an effort to calm myself from the now growing irrational proprietary thoughts I'm having, I calmly walk back to where she is standing. Helplessly, I just… stare at her. Up until now, I've relied on my memories and the occasional photos from my security team. So beautiful, her waves of hair flowing around her shoulders. Standing there, the sexiest little thing I've likely laid eyes on, yet she strikes me as the type who is naïve to her beauty. Not showy, she doesn't flaunt herself. Wearing a tight, little black leather skirt, green hosiery which is oddly sexy as hell. Black, patent leather fuck-me pumps, which support legs that seem to travel to the dreams of my mind's deepest erotic places. I can't help but recall how it felt for those glorious moments holding her, when one of my hands held tightly against one of those legs. Wanting so desperately to inch, just a little… bit… higher.

"Jack? Where did you go?"

Hearing her snickers, I know I've spent too long staring. *Could this be any more embarrassing?* I've gone from raging lunatic to creepy stalker in five minutes. "Oh, sorry. I was just thinking about why you were fixing the banner in the first place. The staff should have been available for that, not you. Especially in heels."

"It wasn't their fault. Everyone has been working hard to setup for today, and I noticed the clip not properly attached. I should have called on someone. Instead of waiting, I was impatient. All is well now. You saved me, we're all good."

I unfortunately, pick that moment to get choked on my own saliva from her words. Coughing impossibly without control. *If you only knew.* "Saved you... yeah, you ah, definitely needed saving. Jack Loving-official lifesaver for Lizzie Macintyre. Sign me up." Then, probably firmer than I had a right, "Next time, Lizzie, no standing on bars. Especially in short skirts, and in heels. Okay?"

A slight head nod is the only response I received. I know as well as I'm standing here that these moments will haunt my morning showers for a long time to come. Separate out the fear of her cracking her skull open, and I'm left with the fact I got a great view of stretching up on the top of that bar top, looking totally fuckable. Then, I held her—tightly, much longer than socially appropriate for the situation. The feel of her body in my arms. The smell of her distinct scent filling my nostrils. The tautness in her leg muscles, as I fought incredibly hard not to move my hand higher up her leg. Finally, the delicate, and oh-so-fast taste, of her on my tongue, as I took advantage of a quick kiss. I should feel guilty, a heel, but I'm left feeling thankful for the opportunity to be in the right place, at the right fucking time.

"How about you running though the plans for the event with me?"

"Sure, no problem."

I quickly learned why Mark sings her organizational praises. She has everything arranged for today, quite impeccably. Outside, she has tents set up near the restaurant. Generally, this is an adult event, but many parents bring children. There are already stages set up around Shockoe Bottom, highlighting various musical acts. Lizzie has planned a large outdoor tent with activities specifically for kids. She has really thought things through to the smallest details. If you're in Shockoe Bottom, you're sure to have a great time on St. Patrick's Day.

My team has activities planned as well. Of course, my idea for the raffle was quite intentional. My hope is that the concept alone will bring memories back to her, of a certain raffle she still owes me a date for. Oh yes, Lizzie Macintyre, we will discuss our date before the night ends.

Chapter Eight

Various Shades of Green, With an Extra Shot of Jealousy on the Side

Lizzie

The lunch crowds were overwhelming, to say the least. There is a sea of green and gold, everywhere! Green hair, green clothes, green beads, green beer… just lots of green and gold. I've been busy running around making sure everyone was settled, and that things were running smoothly.

Mark popped in for a little while this morning. He said he was making an appearance, but knew I had everything under control. It was odd to see him dressed casually. I swear that man oozes sex appeal. Jack has hung around all day. He's been busy talking to lots of people. There always seems to be a line, waiting to see him. Especially women. For a brief moment, I take a second to sit down, and just watch everyone else. Trying to visualize through their eyes, the event's success or failure. The raffle has been hugely popular so far. Many people have handed over their credit cards. It kind of reminds me of the raffle at the Christmas Gala, except Jack isn't being auctioned off to the highest bidder. Oddly, I feel some relief over it, but it's not my place by any measure.

The sounds of cackling women gain my attention, and I turn to notice a group fawning, all over Jack. It's disgusting really. A buxom blonde with a deeply cut shirt, exposing her breasts for all to see, is competing with a red head with green tassels hanging from her shirt, where her nipples are surely located. One laughs, then the other, a little louder. One touches his arm, then the other, a little longer. If I didn't know better, they'd mount him right here in the middle of the street. Fucking bitches.

"If you're not careful, you're going to squeeze your cup of beer in two, spilling it all over yourself."

I nearly spill the beer anyway, when I'm startled from the voice speaking in my ear behind me. "Shit!" Turning to see Jenny beside me smirking, like the cat eating the canary. "You scared the hell out of me girl."

"That's because you were completely focused on the scene playing out in front of us. Little jealous are we?"

Feeling affronted, "What? Why would I be jealous?"

With a shrug of her shoulders, she stares in the direction of Jack and his bevy of beauties. "Oh, I don't know? Why don't you tell me? Are you holding something back from your good friend?"

A little insulted by her comments, she knows everything about me—good and bad. "There's nothing to tell. You just caught me watching the leeches hang on Jack. It's so obvious they're superficial, but he keeps giving them his time."

She nods her supporting comments. "I'm not surprised though. When the news broke Jack and his wife, Victoria, are divorcing, it was all over Richmond media. Television, social media, even Richmond Times Dispatch, had a huge article about the impact his family has made on the city. I had no idea they were behind so many businesses and charities. He apparently is a mega millionaire. He certainly is a nice man. You'd never know he was so wealthy, just by speaking to him. He's really down-to-earth." I turn to her—mouth wide open, not knowing what part of her comments to address first. "Close your mouth, Lizzie. Flies and all that."

Grabbing her arm firmly, I pull her down into the seat next to me. "Talk. Now."

"What do you mean?"

"First, what are you talking about with the media? Second, he's a nice man? How do you know *anything* about him? Speak, girl. I'm about to flip out!"

"Calm it, missy. Sheesh, you *are* jealous!"

"Am not! You're wasting time… and baiting me." I look at her with the most sincere begging eyes I can form. "Please, Jenny, what do you know?"

"Okay. While you were cooped up in your apartment, as beautiful as it may be, life for Jack Loving was a media firestorm. It was released to the press, he and his wife were divorcing. His statement said, "Irreconcilable differences," but some sources claimed there was cheating involved. More specifically, Jack was cheating on his wife. It's sad really because they have twins. Oh, how I'd love to have twins! Must be so nice to dress them alike, and take them—.""

"Jenny! Stop—did you say Jack cheated on his wife?"

"Yeah, that's what I heard on Facebook. Apparently, he has an old girlfriend and he got caught. At least that's what I heard anyway. I don't know if it's true. He seems like such a nice guy."

Feeling rather perturbed, a man, married for over ten years would cheat. With an ex-girlfriend no doubt. It really sucks. I kinda liked him, especially when I was in his arms. It felt—*so good*. So natural—*so right*. "That's what I thought too." Shaking my head in disgust, I'm very dismayed. He must really be a player. Standing there, not minding women were hanging all over him. Flirting with me this morning. Huh. Guess he's not a good guy, after all. "How do you know him, Jen?"

"Well! That's the interesting part. Originally I thought Mark Chesney was determined to look out for you, and he was, don't get me wrong. But, I quickly realized, Jack Loving was behind everything. And, before we get too far, what the hell is happening with you and Mark? Good gracious girl, you've got men raining all around you!"

"It's a very long story about me and Mark. Suffice it to say—he is *amazing*. We are however only friends and business associates. Sometimes, it gets a little warm between us, but how can any woman in her right mind not see a man like Mark Chesney, and not be affected by him? He's God's gift to women, but I need him in my life. So, platonic it must remain."

"Well, everything he does, he does it so sensually. I'd like just one night—one night, to fu—!"

"Jenny! Sex-on-the-brain much? When's the last time you got any? Back to Jack." I implore her with finality.

"Sorry. I *truly* am, but… no. I haven't had any, so Mark gets me stirred up. Guess I need that penis sleeve, after all. Jack took an immediate interest in you when Jeremy died. I didn't want to say anything at the time because you were so upset and so lost. You weren't thinking clearly and me, being your best friend, made a judgment call. His assistant called me out of the blue one day, to find out what your needs were. Christmas was about a week away, and I didn't know what you had planned. He paid for everything, Lizzie. His assistant came by with a check for $3,000. I took the money and bought everything for you, and the kids. Additionally, I bought groceries and household supplies. They asked me for a list of foods you and the children liked. He inquired about allergies, upcoming doctor appointments you or the children may need. The next thing I knew, he set you up with deliveries for groceries. Yes, it was very strange. Especially at first because I questioned his motives. Eventually, I learned he is a really nice man, wanting to do a good deed for my friend. And, I let him do it. Financially, I couldn't afford to, Lizzie. You know after my ex-shithead husband left me for the bimbo, my funds were very limited. It was a blessing. So, I hope you're not mad at me. If you are, tough shit, get over it."

Seriously contemplating the bomb, she just dropped in my lap over the last ten minutes, I'm left with more questions than answers. Why would he take an interest in *me*? It's as if he has immersed himself in my life, indirectly—yet *very* directly. Groceries? Christmas presents? Allergies? Doctor appointments? Rental payments? It's very strange. He doesn't even know me! And what about this cheating ordeal? I don't want anything to do with a man who cheats on his wife. He has kids the same age as one of mine! *No—not the man for me.* "I honestly do not know what to make of all this attention. This morning... there was a near accident, and it's okay because Jack saved me and I didn't get hurt."

"Accident? What the hell Liz?"

"Oh, it was fine. I stupidly stood on the bar... in heels. I fell, but Jack caught me, so it's okay. Crisis averted! Afterward though... it was odd, Jenny. He held onto me, very tightly. Like he didn't want to let me go. Then, there was this really deep visual thing that happened between us. It was as if he looked right through me, deep into my soul. We were just two people, sharing a very natural, honest and open moment. I've never experienced anything like it, in my life. It felt good—*too good*. I don't know what to make of it. Then, he kissed me on my cheek, and it was over. Another interesting thing is the *way* he held me. I don't believe I've ever been held so tightly against another person. It was as if he was cherishing every moment, and didn't want to let me go. Memorizing every second, begging me to feel the moments with him. It totally freaked me out. It felt *amazing*—really amazing! Then, he set me away from him and back on my feet. He looked really uncomfortable and bolted for the door. Weird. What do you think?"

"I-I think, I just had an orgasm. That's what I think."

"Jenny! Focus!"

"Oh, I am focused. Believe you me, I'm focused. Look, for whatever reason, the guy is seriously into you. You're a great girl. He's a very considerate man. Let it happen—*enjoy it*. Be open to experience it. You, my dear, deserve happiness."

"I don't know. It's so soon. Jeremy just died."

"Yes, he died. Face the facts, sweets. Your marriage was over long before he died. You moved into the 'friends' category. You don't owe him anything. Be at peace, sweetie."

"Yeah well, that has nothing to do with me accepting a cheating Jack Loving. That's a no-go area for me."

"Hey, this is me you're talking to! I know what it feels like to be in that position. I understand but talk to him about it. See if there's more to the story. Look at him, he's fucking gorgeous."

"I know. Hey… I know you have wanted to stay silent on the subject, but are you okay? Becoming single again, is a very big deal. You know I'm here if you want to talk."

"Thank you, but I'm good. It was a blessing in the form of heartache, but a blessing nonetheless."

Staring at Jack, laughing at something one of the bevies of beauties has said, just makes me question him more. If he can stand there and cackle with the fake titties, puffy lips, fake hair extensions, caked on makeup surrounding him, and that style of woman makes him happy? No, I'm definitely not his type. Just then, he must have sensed my assessing eyes on him. His face straightens, becomes more intense as he stares directly at me. The hands grabbing at his forearms, fall away when he pulls them to his sides, out of the way. The feeling of him looking through me returns, even as people walk between us down the sidewalk. The silicone-filled women, irritated by, not having his attention, turn in my direction. Curious to see what has pulled the decadent Jack Loving's attention away. He draws me in from afar. The hair that I'd give anything to run my fingers through, the eyes seeing everything, the jeans fitting him like a glove, outlining an ass I'd love to squeeze. His chest… oh that muscular chest. Not too bulky, but has no problem filling out a Henley shirt amazingly well. The electric connection that seems to flow between our bodies. I'm so entranced, I fail to notice he's coming closer until he's standing before me. Oh my, this man makes me lose time in such a delicious way.

Dawning the most delicious smile, he looks down over me. Directly at my eye level, his chest and suddenly I'm overcome with his smell. So masculine… so, hot. It pulls me in and I feel like a quirky teenager all over again. "Lizzie, how is everything going? Is there anything I can do to help?"

Just as I caught my wits about me, I open my mouth to respond and the buxom blonde appears behind him. "Jack, are you coming back? Misty and I have plans we want to discuss with you." If looks could kill, I'd be dead. Death by evil glare. She rolls her hand through his and links their fingers tightly. I can't help but focus my attention to their point of connection. It's so intentional, but he doesn't pull away. He just looks down at the joined hands, eyebrows raised. He says… nothing.

I turn to Jenny with a "what-the-fuck" look on my face, and she lets out a laugh, too improper for the moment for the witch not to know it's meant for her. I stand up, full dignity intact, "Everything is lovely, Mr. Loving. Running smoothly, as I expected." With that parting shot, I walk away to make rounds at the event. The *real* reason I'm here, not to play games with someone who prefers plastic, over real.

Chapter Nine

Just Hold On Babe, I Got You

Jack

I want to scream, "What the fuck just happened?" Literally want to scream it, from the top floors, across downtown Richmond. I've been standing near Lizzie, all day. Watching, and waiting. Keeping her in my sights, a protective eye in case anything should happen. Yes, the security team is working today. I do not have to worry about her physical safety, at least not once I called them back on shift. Originally, I called them off when she left home this morning because I knew I'd be close by all day. Then, I'm mortified and fucking pissed, when I discover she's a second away from breaking her neck. Left to her own devices, she'd be in the hospital by now. The crowds have been huge today, and considering there is alcohol involved, a good looking woman like Lizzie needs extra protection. Hence, they are back on duty.

So, I have kept her in my periphery all day. When she moved— I moved, always making excuses with whomever I'm speaking with at the moment. Then, I notice she is watching me. Not watching—

staring. It felt nice to be in the hook of her gaze. So, I took advantage and moved to her. I made a simple comment and wham—she gets formal with me and leaves me standing there feeling foolish.

I was in the middle of speaking with Misty and April about a business proposition they had when I noticed the beautiful Lizzie watching from afar. When I moved closer and April followed me, the visual bliss turned to a mortal kiss-off. She turned all formal with her "Mr. Loving" and walked away. Now, I'm left to figure out how to fix this problem. Again. It seems all I ever do is try and figure out ways to make this woman happy and just spend time with me.

Jenny looks to me, giving me a hard, disapproving once-over. Now I'm baffled by her behavior as well. Sometimes, I really don't understand women, at all. "Is there some problem I need to know about?"

With squinted eyes, she looks like she wants to castrate me. Then, she faces April, head on but speaks to me, "Absolutely not, Jack. Lizzie has everything under control. Please feel free to run along and play with Kitty… and Missy."

Oh shit, I can sense the onset of a cat fight, when April squeezes my hand really hard, and leans in toward her, "Our names… are Misty and April."

Jenny smiles a half smile, "Sorry, my mistake." Then, she up and walks away.

It may have been quite a while since I was in the dating game, and I may be slow on this, but I'm pleasantly surprised discovering my dear Lizzie, is jealous. It makes me quite happy because now I know—*I matter to her*. In some measure, it bothered her to see me with those women. Quite funny if you think about it.

The rest of the afternoon was packed with people. As the day went on, we pushed our designated driver program because green beer was flowing like the James River. Several times, I tried to carry on a conversation with Lizzie, and she was professional, but had no interest in personal exchanges. It really broke me, every time she would give me the cold shoulder. This is definitely not how I saw this day playing out. At minimum, I'd hoped we'd be friendly, chatting about mindless topics, getting to know a little about each other. Nah, that's not happening.

Deciding I had to do something drastic to change the tide, I called in a favor at Tobacco Company Restaurant, just up on Cary Street. It helps to plan last minute things, when your name is Jack Loving, although I'm not one to promote high-brow behavior. Being the impatient, and highly organized man that I am, I knew exactly where she was at. Plus, having your own three-man security team shadowing you at all time, makes keeping up with someone, much easier.

I arranged for a messenger to deliver a note, promising a large donation. Only catch, she had to appear at eight o'clock, in person, to pick up the check. When she opened the delivery, she seemed happy, then rather perturbed. Looking around at the event, I'm sure she was concerned about leaving… *that's the idea, darling.* Just before the scheduled time, she entered the famous Richmond landmark restaurant. It's an interesting setup: tobacco warehouse converted into a multi-level, atrium restaurant. The most beautiful antique elevator transporting you between the levels, all uniquely styled. My favorite table is a room within the larger room, enclosed by wood and glass. It's private, yet cozy. Comfortable, yet isolating. I don't want her to feel contained, yet that's exactly what I'd do, given the opportunity.

Once the hostess directed her to the correct floor, I watched from afar as she was seated. There's something about the way she occupies a space. So natural, far from the women she was obviously jealous of earlier today. As desperate as I am to occupy the space, I'm just as enamored with seeing her in her aloneness. She's absolutely striking.

She looks around the restaurant, and down at her watch. Obviously anxious about the time. Oh sweetheart, if I only had a night alone with you, time would be the last thing you'd be hoping to pass by. Deciding if I wait much longer, she may up and leave, I decide to make my move. As I approach the entry into the small room, she doesn't notice me because she's looking outside. I stand at the door, leaning against it, not wanting to startle her.

When she turns to see me, the genuine look of shock and confusion, is painted on her face. "Jack? What… what are *you* doing here?"

Unable to hide my sly smile, I don't give her a chance to up and leave, so I take the opportunity to sit down right away. "Well, I guess I have a confession to make." She continues to look around the restaurant, trying to decide if I've hijacked her meeting, or if I've lost my mind. "Your mystery donor, is me."

Instantly, her energy deflates right in front of me. Well shit, that didn't encourage my ego at all. With slumped shoulders, she looks at me like I've lost my mind. "I'm confused, Jack. Why am I here? Why did you go to all this trouble to bring me here, knowing we have a major fundraiser going on at this exact moment?"

"Lizzie, with your expertise, the fundraiser is taking care of itself. The staff knows what they're doing, and you deserve a break. You've been at it all day long and besides, I have my people watching over everything. Trust me, we're good."

"Trust you? No offense, I don't know you."

"No offense taken, but you know enough."

"I disagree."

"Lizzie, I think we need to clear the air. You'll learn I'm a very direct man. Guess that's why I'm a successful attorney. Somewhere along the way, we've had a minor misstep, and I don't like it. I'll be blunt, I brought you here tonight, to find out why you're suddenly showing me hostility? Plus, I wanted to have a nice meal with you, away from all the hoopla."

Looking very affronted, "I'm not hostile." It's obvious she's struggling with being cornered, quite literally, in this little room of this restaurant.

"Really? Why the formality earlier?"

"What do you mean?"

"Come on dear, calling me Mr. Loving in front of April earlier? I hardly think now that I've rescued you, from imminent brain injury, we should at least be on first name basis."

"Brain injury? That sounds a little much, don't you think? Besides, you were… *busy*, with… whatever her name was, and you should hardly concern yourself with what I think."

Hmm… should I drop my little bomb now on her that I fully intend to discover all of her inner most thoughts? Moving closer to her, I decide it's time to give her a clue. "Let's stop this banter, as much as I may enjoy it. I'll tell you what I *think*. You are quite intriguing, Lizzie Macintyre. When I first saw you with Mark, I was… well, I had many thoughts go through my mind, but captivated by you was high on the list. You're obviously quite beautiful, and I'm impressed with your abilities today." Looking bashful, she lowers her head. Ah, she has an issue receiving compliments. That is something, I'd like to change. She should know and feel confident about her assets. Reaching over, I lift her chin with my index finger. We stare at one another, no words spoken. I'm totally lost in her eyes, her beauty absorbs, and arrests me. All cognitive reasoning is lost, as I'm entranced in the spectacular state of her exquisiteness. Before I even realize what I'm doing, my finger is pulling her forward and I gently move in, touching my lips against hers. Her lips, so small and soft. At least I have the good manners not to take the kiss too far. A sweet peck, very warm and alluring. Not wanting to pull away, but knowing I need to go slow with her. She's been through so much— we both have recently. Our lips separate and I move my forehead against hers. I close my eyes, not wanting to lose this moment. I've built this woman up so much, in my mind's eye. Lately, I've questioned my sanity if she's even real. If our time together on *that* night was as meaningful to her, as it was to me. Seeing how she is distanced from me, I don't think she… remembers. Wondering if there is even a possibility for me—*for us*. Needing to find out, wanting to explore it, and her, I have to find out.

Pulling away, I grab her hand in mine. I smile, probably much larger than I should. I've wanted this moment for so long. Just… a simple moment without chaos, to experience and enjoy. Fuck, I'm getting too weepy. *What the hell is she doing to me?* "Lizzie, it shouldn't be a secret to you, I'm very interested in you. I'll be honest, I recognize you've been through a lot lately. I empathize because my life has been chaotic as well. On paper, it's probably bad for either one of us to get involved right now. Good thing I don't always pay attention to my analysts because I make decisions based on my gut feelings. I knew the *very first time* I saw you, I wanted to know more about you." Shaking my head, "I'll be blunt: I think there could be something there between us, Lizzie."

Watching her expression as I'm talking, I don't know what I should do… either stay or run like hell. She looks like a deer caught in the headlights. Normally my take charge attitude would push all the way, but knowing this woman has emotional issues she's dealing with, has turned me into a sentimental mess.

"I don't really know what to say, Jack. These last few months, actually, these last couple years, have been a disaster for me. Getting involved so soon after my husband's death, doesn't seem very smart."

"I hear you, I truly do. You've been through a lot, and I only know the short version of your story. Mark has shared very little, but he did state, your marriage was over a long time ago. The fact you cared more about your children and trying to help someone who in the end made his own choices anyway. I was there *that* night, Lizzie. You probably don't remember everything or me, but I remember every second. It killed me to see you go through that pain, and for whatever reason, I was drawn to you. There was this innate need to comfort you, hold you, to take care of you. I cannot explain it. It baffles my mind too. It always has."

"Earlier today, when you were holding me, it felt familiar. I didn't understand it at the time. We haven't spent any time together. How can it be... unless, you've held me before. Wait... *it was you*. Wasn't it? It *has* happened before. I'd forgotten completely about it because that night... it was crazy. Full of turmoil and grief. I didn't know losing someone could hurt so badly."

"Um, you're referring to the Christmas Gala? Yes, I was *there*. I left you in the hotel suite with Mark because I had urgent business to attend to. An unplanned return just moments after you learned about the accident, caused me to bear witness to your excruciating pain. I would have done anything to take the pain from you, Lizzie, it was agonizing to watch."

"But Mark was there... it was Mark, who cared for me." Tilting my head slightly in agreement. "I remember pieces from that night. Some memories are oddly mixed with my imagination from the accident scene, which I didn't go to. In my dreams, I remember Mark carrying me. It was Mark, right?"

"Does it really matter? Maybe you should focus on today and not the nights that haunt you, in the past. Just move on from today, one day at a time."

"Yes! Yes, it absolutely matters. I'm haunted in my dreams. When I lay in bed and cannot sleep, it drives me insane not knowing why I lost a block of time. It may have even been days. Days, Jack! Tell me, please. Why do I have this familiarity about you? Why can't I remember?"

My deepest hope would be for her to remember *that* night, all on her own. Yes, it was traumatic but as selfish as it may sound it was likely our beginning. If I fill in all the blanks, she may resent me. If our start began ironically in the midst of tragedy, she needs to recall it herself. However, the desperation in her eyes tells me I need to give her something. "Since it does seem to bother you so much, I'll give you a short recap. I returned just after you received the news of Jeremy's death. You were broken, and seeing you, it gutted me. Over and over, you kept repeating everything was your fault. Nothing we said to you, made a difference, and you became inconsolable. I arranged for the in-house hotel physician to treat you. He administered something to help you sleep. It worked—end of story."

"No, not an end to the story." She grows noticeably agitated, and my attempt to side skirt the question, has failed. "Why the familiarity Jack?"

Sheepishly, I bow my head, hoping to avoid having to recount our history and the entire evening. I can see she's persistent. "It is true. I did spend some time holding you in an effort to comfort you. That's probably what you're remembering."

"I knew it! So, when you held me this morning… it was similar… to before?"

"Yes."

"Okay, that's…good to know. Now I know I'm not completely losing my mind."

"No chance of that happening, babe."

"Listen, Jack. I really appreciate you going to all this trouble to get me alone, just to talk to me. I just think it's possible we're attracted to different things. You're a very handsome man, and you obviously have your choice of women hanging on your every word. I'm nothing like those women, and far less exciting."

Fuck, no. This shit stops…now. I quickly move my thumb up and lay it across her beautiful pink lips to silence her. Moving my thumb slowly across her lips, corner to corner, I take a moment to admire the small lines, just beginning to form around her eyes. Proof of her wisdom and life experiences. Lizzie stunningly ages well. Granting this earth with two children, her body is even more attractive, with her well-placed curves. If only she could understand, it is natural beauty that makes me hard and gets my blood circulating. Not buying improvements for oneself. That's where she and Victoria, are so markedly different. This version before me, is the one I'm fighting incredibly hard not to kiss, *again*.

"Don't assume you know what I am attracted to, because you are most likely, wrong. It's no secret sweetheart, you got very jealous today over Misty and April. I like that…*a lot*."

Moving her head to the side to recapture her own mouth, "I wasn't jealous!"

"You weren't?" I slowly place my hand gently over hers, laying on the table. I slowly begin working my hand up and down her forearm. I lean into her neck and pause not saying a word. Allowing the heat of my breath to cover her neck for several breaths, she sits frozen and silent. Just waiting for my next move, I can see her body physically relax. The expectation of her body's needs, so apparent, even though her brain would argue against it. "You were." Then, I entwine my hand through her fingers and squeeze firmly. I want her to feel my strength, passing through my hands into her body. She needs to know I'm serious about my convictions, once my mind is set. Little does she know, my mind was set long ago. I've been patiently waiting, but those days are done. Careful, not to touch, I speak quietly, with a determined edge, into her ear, "There is no reason to be jealous, babe. I know exactly what I want, and she's right…here." I quickly give her a firm kiss on her ear and back away from her completely, returning fully seated in my chair.

Lizzie is statuesque, almost to the point of, not breathing. Fully stunned by my strong approach. Good, I want her to know I'm serious about getting to know her. Picking up my menu, I motion to the server waiting nearby. After quickly ordering for the two of us, she looks at me in shock, apparently surprised I would know her food choices so well. "What if I'd wanted the asparagus instead?"

I shake my head firmly, and confidently answer, "You don't like asparagus."

Her mouth opens wide, "How do you know—?"

With shrugging shoulders and a smirking smile, "I just know." I want to burst out laughing, but know I need to quell my overconfidence. It's hard though because I want her to be as excited to spend time with me, as I am with her. In an effort to calm her fears, I bring her back around to her comfort zone: "Tell me your thoughts on today's event so far."

Homerun… ice broken. With a single question, she has calmed completely, and I'm allowed to just sit and listen to this intelligent, bright woman. She really excels at fundraisers and knows how to fit in with any occasion. Her previous occasions on Mark's arm, which I will kick his ass to prevent from happening in the future, have proven her versatility in any setting. It's hard not to keep my mind from imagining her on my arm, at the various functions I host, for the Bowes Trust.

Much too quickly, our meals are consumed, and it's time to return to the event down the street. Before leaving, I couldn't help but remind her of the raffle. "I understand today's raffle has been ultra-successful. Reminds me of another very successful raffle, wouldn't you say?"

For a slight moment, I could see her expression slip sadly and I'm not sure why. Then, she asked, "So, I guess you have satisfied your raffle responsibilities, I won. You are... in the clear, Mr. Loving."

With a determined laugh, "Oh no, no, no. This was my date. This in no way, counts towards the previously earned raffle date." I stare at her happily, and she just shakes her head not knowing how to take me. "In fact, I suggest we make a date for next Friday. I'll pick you up at 6:00?" She begins to act nervously, and I can tell that something is on her mind. "Okay, out with it. I've been straightforward with you, it's your turn."

"I don't know how to say this exactly. It's truly not my business, but I heard something today. Something about you, it wasn't very appealing."

Quite caught off guard, my interest is piqued. Deciding to minimize with a small dose of comedy, "Well I'm a lawyer, so I'm sure some people in Richmond don't care for me."

"It's not being a lawyer I'm concerned about, Jack. This is seriously damning."

Whoa, not expecting that statement. "Care to share your concerns, sweetheart?"

Noticeably stressed, she swallows hard and I feel for her because she's really uncomfortable. "I have an issue with spouses who have affairs. It's completely against my personal moral compass."

Leaning back in my chair, I feel completely deflated. Motherfuck, she thinks I cheated on Victoria. Even though press statements adamantly denied these rumors, people still think it's the real reason for our divorce. "Lizzie, first let me say, I'm glad you have a problem with infidelity. Second, these rumors of cheating are completely untrue. The only woman I had sex with, from the time I met my wife in college until our marriage ended, was Victoria. Period."

A look of understanding crosses her face, and I think she believes me. "I'm sorry for asking, it's just... I can't imagine ever being with someone, who would be unfaithful."

"Good, me either. Then we're on the same page. Look, I don't want to drag up all the nastiness of my divorce. The bottom line? It had absolutely nothing to do with cheating on either one of our parts. My marriage is irrevocably broken, and I'm moving on. Social media harbors persons who enjoy spreading gossip, and because of my position in the community, I'm a target. I apologize if you had negative thoughts about me, but please don't. Not about this anyway. Besides, we have to have a first date before you begin having some negative thoughts. Damn, so the chilly formalness was because you thought I was a cheater. We could have been over before we started because of lies and innuendo. Glad we could clear it up." I smile a cheesy smile, "So, Friday at six o'clock?"

Obviously caught off guard I would set a time for next weekend, she takes a moment to respond, "I-I have children, Jack."

"I'm firmly aware of your kids, Lizzie."

Looking surprised by my answer, "Um... I'll need to think about it. Finding a sitter, takes time."

Reaching over, I grab her hand again, looking firmly into her eyes, "Lizzie, no excuses. Not with me, I won't accept them. Not… going… to happen. I've waited a long time for this, we're going to get to know each other better, so that means spending time together. Most people call that *dating*." I look straight down at our entwined hands, "Just hold on, babe. I got you."

Chapter Ten

Our Fresh, New Beginning

Lizzie

Finally crawling into bed, I feel like I've been outside in a hurricane, desperately holding onto a fence post. Listening to total silence after a day filled with loud music showcasing several local bands including: Those Manic Seas, Snowy Owls, and Cosby & Against Grace, is comforting to my ears but I'm keyed up, unable to sleep. They put on an amazing outdoor concert and I just know they'll hit it big one day.

Totally and completely exhausted, it was nice I didn't have to drive home. Quite unexpectedly, Jack arranged for a car, to bring me home. I was unprepared when someone dressed in all black, looking like paramilitary-on-steroids, appeared before me. "Ms. Macintyre, my name is Seth. Mr. Loving has requested I personally escort you home this evening. Your vehicle will be delivered to you by morning." Ahh… ok? Wasn't prepared for the nice offer and didn't see it coming.

Staring at the window I have spent many hours perched in front of, I try to make sense of how quickly my life is changing. Obviously, the ending of a long-term marriage, living with an alcoholic, financial devastation, and ultimately Jeremy's death has been more than any person should have to endure. This last month has been just as chaotic. *How did I go from counting raindrops to being chauffeured by a multimillionaire who just basically told me… we're dating?*

Looking at the pieces, I'm beginning to see a pattern, I didn't see before. When Mark said Jack has been looking out for me over these last months, he wasn't joking. In my despair, I didn't pay attention to the fact it wasn't my girlfriends, neighbors and Mark doing these kind deeds for my family, it was Jack Loving of all people. The grocery deliveries, rental payments, Christmas presents… it was so much money and effort. *Why would someone go to so much trouble for someone they hardly know?* It's frustratingly baffling to my mind.

Our planned date is Friday and I am already nervous. It seems pretty apparent, this is a romantic date, not anything like the time I spent with Mark. *What should I wear?* He didn't mention where we are going, so is it dress up or dress down? I am so out of my league with this. I was practically a child when I met Jeremy. Considering he is the only man I have ever been with intimately, I'm nervous to take the leap with someone new. Problem is, my body doesn't think, it reacts. With one simple touch of his finger, he brings me into his space and my will concedes away. The way he moves his body, simply by walking, gesturing and especially when he's in deep thought, is spellbinding. He's every woman's sexy book boyfriend, come to real life. The most attractive part is his ability to relate to others, without an air of blue-blooded, high-society. You would never guess, just by talking to him, he is mega rich and lives a life most would only dream about. His stare draws you in, and he focuses on the words you're saying. Many times today, there was a line of people, waiting to speak with him. Every time I looked around, he seemed to be there, with his entourage of fans. He was approachable, friendly and I noticed he would pull his phone out occasionally, with a built-in stylus, apparently making notes of whatever conversations they were having, at the moment. Someone that rich might have assistants hanging around, but I only saw the discreet security guy that trailed him around, wherever he went. If fact, now that I think about it, he was oddly, similarly dressed to my paramilitary godlike-creature, Seth, who saw me safely home. Interesting.

Am I really at a place in my life, I should be dating? What will the children think about it? There are so many reasons why I shouldn't, but there's this comfortable feeling that overcomes me, and sends this warming electricity down my body. It's a very different experience for me. With Jeremy, there was love, and being so young, we grew up together. With Mark, it was lust-filled thoughts, whenever he touched me. I can't put my finger on how my body automatically gets caught, in Jack's web. Not only am I attracted to him because he's obviously handsome, there is this odd level of comfort I have with him, confusing the hell out of me. It's like I know him, on a more intimate level, and I shouldn't. Somehow good feelings stir in me, but then I also have the fringe specters in my mind. Then, the way my body just naturally wants to be controlled by him. With a simple glance, I have this urge to relinquish my control. It feels dangerous but turns me on at the same time. Maybe I'm just one of those people, who can't be alone. As needy as that sounds, it could be good for me he's pushing me to move on with my life.

A buzzing sound and the light of my cell phone startles me. Who could be texting me at three o'clock in the morning?

03:14 I hope you're safely tucked into your bed. Your work today was amazingly successful. Good job. Can't wait to see you again.

How did he get my cell phone number? Then again, why should I be surprised at the reach of Jack Loving? If he knows how I like my steak cooked, he surely knows my cell phone number.

03:18 Yes, safely in bed. It was a huge success. We can help a lot of kids, so I'm happy. Thanks for the ride.

03:20 My pleasure, babe. Now, go to sleep.

3:22 Yes, sir!

3:23 On second thought, maybe I should come over.

Ah, I'm caught off guard. Granted, I'm very interested, but spending time with him, in my apartment—with my kids asleep next door, is a little too forward for me. Luckily, before I think of something to say, the buzz takes me out of my worried thoughts.

3:27 I was only teasing you, Lizzie. Relax, and this time, GO TO SLEEP!

3:28 Goodnight, Jack

3:29 Goodnight, Lizzie

Tossing back and forth, my legs feel heavy and weighted down. My chest hurts, my breaths are labored. Bright flashes of light

appear, then disappear. Trying to focus on them, I see oranges and reds. It's fire! The smoke suddenly fills around me! Oh, God, PLEASE SAVE ME!

When all is surely lost, I focus my mind on saying goodbye, to those most important to me. I think of my babies: Hope and Ethan. My daughter, so strong willed and beautiful. One day, she will be an amazing mother, I'm sure. The giving and compassionate, Ethan, who no matter what, always has a smile on his face. Oh, how blessed I am to be honored with the privilege of loving them. Be good to one another, my dear babies! Always be friends—never allow senseless feuds to split you. I will watch over you from above. My love will always guide you. Goodbye...

Just as I close my eyes to accept my fate, I am pulled from the burning car moments before it explodes like a bomb. "I have you, Lizzie! You're safe! You're safe, sweetheart!" A man, with arms like small trees, carries me like a feather. He whispers warm, loving thoughts into my ears. I cannot understand what he's saying, but I feel his strength rocking my body back and forth. In a far off distance, I can hear my children yelling, "We need you! I love you, Mommy."

Overcome by the wealth of emotions, I feel so connected to my savior. This mysterious man, who knew nothing about me, but gave so much of himself... so selflessly. Pulling away from him, I lean back and try to see his face, but it's so dark and my eyes are filled with soot. The basic structure of his face appears, and for no reason, which I can explain, I place my hands on each of his cheeks. My thumb gently touches the center of his lips. He kisses the pad and I spread the wetness from one corner, back to the other corner, stopping in the middle. Leaning in, I gently lay my lips against his. He's caught off guard, but immediately pulls me into his chest. Heat fills my body, wanting to be closer, needing to feel more. He greedily attempts to deepen the kiss, and I let him. Hands circle the back of my head, pushing my mouth closer, his tongue enters me. The taste of cinnamon fills my taste buds, and I want more of it. I need all of it, all of him. Anything he wants, he takes. This is so different than what I'm used to and I really like it. My body craves the anticipation of this newness… please teach me, use me, help me heal. "I will take care of you, Lizzie. You'll see, you're stronger than you realize." He forcefully returns to kissing me, and the passion is dizzying. My body completely relaxes into him. The more he takes, the more I give.

"You slut! You're a fucking whore! People pay you money, and you wear fancy dresses trying to be someone you're not!" When it registers to me in my haze of erotic bliss, Jeremy is speaking to me, I'm mortified. He's filled with rage. Realizing he was watching me with my hands and legs like an octopus around this faceless man, causes me immediate guilt. Suddenly, the two men are fighting. Jeremy is obviously drunk and having difficulty landing a punch. His mouth, on the other hand, has no trouble continuing his vicious assault.

"Stop!" I scream. "Please stop it! Jeremy, I'm sorry, please stop!"

Then hands are touching all over me. My arms, my face, my legs—all in an effort to calm me. "Mommy! Please stop, Mommy!" Then, I hear the crying words of my sweet Ethan directly in my ear, "I love you, Mommy." Gasping for breath, I forcefully sit straight up in bed. Sweat has drenched my nightgown. My sheets are twisted into a knot, all around my legs. My eyes focus on the bright light pouring through the window. It's morning, and it was a dream. It wasn't real, or at least some of it was, I do not know. I'm haunted by the pieces of facts I do know to be true, and the odd items, I know nothing about. *What does all of this mean?*

Crying uncontrollably, I grab onto both of my children who are scared and hovered around me. My dreams are scarier for them, I'm sure. "I'm so sorry guys. Mommy is okay now. Thank you for waking me. *I love you so much.*"

"Are you sure you're okay, Mommy?" Ethan mumbles.

Wiping the sweat from my brow, trying to control the sniffles threatening to fall, and clearing away the twisted sheets from around me, "Much, much better. Thank you."

"Mama, I really think you need to go to the doctor. It's scary when I can't wake you up, when you're having one of these dreams. Why are you having them now?" Hope asks concerned for my welfare.

Reminding me she is wise beyond her years, I shake my head in agreement. "I don't know, but you're probably right, sweetheart." Squeezing her extra hard, "you're probably right."

After having a pretty traumatic start to the day, I pulled the kids into my bed and we laid there all morning watching mindless television. I think I've seen every show on Disney they've ever made. One day, Hope reminded me, she was supporting her interest in her corporation, by watching Disney. I looked at her in complete bewilderment. Then, with impatient disgust, she reminded me she is a shareholder. Recognition was made, when I recalled we purchased common shares in Disney, when each of the children were born. My daughter... *the executive.*

At ten o'clock, my phone received a text message:

10:00 a.m. From now on...answer the door

That's a strange message to send. No sooner than I managed to read the text, the doorbell rang. The children begin hollering about the door, so I make my way to the living room. Peering through the peephole, there is an older gentleman standing there with his arms full of bags. Opening the door, I greet him, "Hello?"

"Good morning, Ms. Macintyre. Glad to finally meet you. My name is Leonard, but you may call me Leo. I'm here to drop off your order for today. Looks like you have quite the variety, but there's an extra special item for you. I just need to run back to my delivery van to get it. My arms were full carrying these bags. Can I carry these in for you, or would you like to take them?"

Seeing the full bags, makes me wonder what in the world could be stuffed in there. "I'll take them from you. Gosh, this is a lot of food."

"Yes ma'am. Be right back."

Carrying the bags into the kitchen, I leave the door open, for the kind old man. I've never seen so much for three people. All fresh vegetables in one bag. Meats in another bag and cold dairy items in the third bag. Jack and I really need to discuss him sending so much, he really doesn't need to go to this trouble.

Returning to the door, I'm met at the same time, with an enormous floral display. It's designed more like a work of art, and not your grandmother's floral arrangement for sure. I love flowers, and this had to cost a small fortune. Considering I can't see my delivery man, on account of this enormous tablescape, I speak through the flowers, hoping he can hear me. "Wow! They're absolutely beautiful!"

"They truly are beautiful indeed, Ms. Macintyre. This is extremely heavy, and I was told to get it set up for you. Where shall I place it?" Pointing him towards the living room table, I'm totally overwhelmed.

"Thank you for carrying it in for me." He nods his acknowledgment and moves to exit and it occurs to me, I should tip him for his work. "Wait just a moment, I need to grab my purse."

He shakes his hands off at me, in a negative motion. "Oh, no ma'am. My services are well compensated. You do not need to pay me, thank you anyway though."

With a sigh, I understand it. I may not like it, but I understand it. "Thank you very much, Leo."

He tips his hat at me, "No problem, see you tomorrow Ms. Macintyre." I look at him with an inquiring eye. "Ten o'clock, ma'am. Food delivery, every day per exact instructions. And, if you want something specific, I'm happy to track it down for you. On Thursdays, the Farmer's Market is amazing. Have a good day!" Then he turns and trots away and I'm left wondering what rabbit hole I've fallen through.

Rushing to the beautiful display, I take time and smell every flower. Anxious to get an up-close look at what would most likely be, an award-winning design. Finding the card, creatively hidden, I'm excited to see what is written.

> *Dearest Birdie,*
> *Congrats on yesterday's event! I knew you'd do well, as always. Sorry I wasn't there much, but I had full confidence in you. See you soon.*
> *~Mark*

Flowers from Mark were quite unexpected. Then again, he seems to know me rather well, especially my affinity for flowers after our stroll through Lewis Ginter Botanical Gardens. As beautiful as they are, and as much as I appreciate them, I'm oddly disappointed they weren't from Jack. Immediately, I'm full of guilt for immediately assuming they would be from him.

Deciding I need to thank the men in my life… who have suddenly taken over, I send a quick text to Jack:

10:30 a.m. Thank you for my morning nourishment. It's really not necessary, but I appreciate it none the less. Between you and Mark, you're going to break Leo's back. Poor guy!

Seconds later, my phone buzzes an immediate reply:

10:30 a.m. What did you get from Mark?

10:31a.m. A massive floral display belonging in a magazine instead of filling my kitchen table. He wanted to say thanks for yesterday

10:33 a.m. Guess I'll have to up my game. ;)

10:34 a.m. No! You've done more than enough. Actually, we need to discuss all the attention. It's too much, really it is. I appreciate it, but I'm doing better now

10:36 a.m. Doing for you, makes me happy. I want to do these things for you, so this IS happening! Just learn to enjoy, sweetheart. Need to speak with a business associate, TTYL.

Wow, I see how it is with Jack. He's going to be relenting, I just know it. Deciding for a somewhat easier man to deal with this morning, I text Mark:

10:42 a.m. Thank you very much for the flowers. There are no words to describe their beauty. I'm overwhelmed and they're much appreciated.

11:00 a.m. I understand the feeling, babe. When I try and describe you, I'm left with the same loss of vocabulary. No thanks necessary. See you soon.

The rabbit hole I was thinking about before, yeah it just got a little deeper.

Chapter Eleven

Sarah Loving: Her Legacy... She Loves Baseball?

Jack

"G-o-o-d morning, sunshine." He roughly grumbles into the phone sounding like he just woke up.

"It was, at least for me until about five minutes ago." I quip into my phone.

"What's up? Something burning into you this early on a Sunday morning?"

"It's not early, man. It's 10:37 in the morning. I've already worked half a day while you've seemingly been sleeping, yet finding ways to undercut me at the same time. Let me guess, a piece of ass wore you out too much last night old man?"

"Ha! You only wish you had my skills and could keep up with me. I may be older than you, but it just means I've had more pussy than you, so choke on that asshat!"

"I concede the point, it may be true, but I guarantee you, I know fucking more than you do about making a woman scream."

He busts out laughing and maybe it's a draw between us, so friendly ribbing wins the day. "Don't know about that one, but I know you're not calling to compare sexual history so what's up?"

"I told you… what's up with you sending flowers to *my* girl?"

"*You're* girl? Since when is Lizzie, you're girl?"

"Just answer the damn question, why did you send them?"

With a quieter, stern voice, "I don't *need* your permission, Jack, but I wanted to say thanks for her hard work yesterday. I knew she'd have her morning delivery, so I coordinated them with Leonard, for the same time. She works for my Endowment, you know?"

"Yeah, I know, but an arrangement the size of Gibraltar? And, hijacking the delivery man too!"

"Yep, sure did! I thought she'd most likely open the door for her normal delivery. I didn't want them sitting outside her door. I would have ordered the size of fucking Mt. Everest if I could. Look, I'm sensing tension and we need to get something straight. Lizzie means a lot to me, Jack. I'm not giving up time with her because you're jealous. If you have a problem, deal with it. I'm not going away anytime soon, and you best be careful, Lizzie won't take kindly to you picking her friends."

"I know you're friends, and I didn't ask you to go away anytime soon. Problem is flowers: they're too personal. I'd prefer you not do it."

"Fuck off, Jack. You're overthinking this, but whatever. I won't hurt your tenderhearted feelings, by sending Lizzie flowers."

Believing I've made my point, "Thanks for being agreeable. Looking forward to seeing the final numbers from last night."

"Sure, me too."

This friendship between Mark and Lizzie is odd. I can't put my finger on it, but the feeling there's more to their story, nags at me. He has indicated numerous times, he respects her too much to ruin it with sex. At the same time, they've formed a rather tight bond. I'm sure watching her go through *that* night, marked him, as well. I don't want to come across like a jealous asshole, but I won't be anyone's fool either.

Today, I'm meeting my parents at the Country Club of Virginia, for brunch. Now that the children divide their time between Victoria and myself, my parents do not spend as much time with them. Our weekend tradition of catching up over brunch continues, however.

When news first broke of our separation, I avoided this place as much as possible. When you travel in wealthy circles, information spreads quickly. Being the subject of whispers, when I walked by, wasn't very enjoyable, and my patience was spread thin. Somehow the ridiculous rumor that our separation was caused by infidelity burned through me like an out-of-control wildfire. Mother kept telling me to avoid the fray, it would blow over. Father wanted a public statement denying the alleged affair. We somehow settled on a public statement, confirming our impending divorce, due to irreconcilable differences. Considering Lizzie brought it up just yesterday, I really think I should have denied it flatly to the press. The thought of her avoiding me, because she thinks I'm a cheater, pisses me the fuck off.

Generally, we have a reserved table overlooking the golf course. As I near it, I see Mother and Father, have already arrived. I cringe when I notice, they're not alone. Mother's personal financial advisor and strategist for the Trust is also seated. Bending down, I kiss my mother's cheek, shake my father's hand, and extend a hand to Mr. Rhodes. "Good day, everyone," I announce.

A round of "Jack" followed by "Hello, Jack," by my Mother, is heard. I allow them to finish their previous conversation and order in the meantime. It doesn't take a brain surgeon to miss the looks passed my way, by our server. Unfortunately, I've had an increase of overt friendliness since my marriage ended. As much as I may appreciate a kind look my way, the outward dramatic flirting, leaves a lot to be desired. The prolonged stares, the expanded forward-waist bend, conveniently showing a full rack. It's most unattractive. Granted, I love a tit shot, like any red-blooded American man, but not like this. They don't care anything about me, just my money. I always knew Victoria was attracted to me for my position and excessive wealth. The lesson came further into the relationship, and by then, I was obsessed with her for way different reasons.

"Jack, I wanted to have a chat over brunch about changes to my side of the Trust. Basically, I only want blood descendants, to have access to the accounts. We need to make sure provisions are in place, in case an early death should occur. I'm suggesting an administrator, to oversee the funds until any minor-aged child turns of age. Spouses should not have any access to the operation of the accounts." Fuck, and here I thought I was having a quiet lunch with my parents and now I have to discuss family business. "Oh, and there's a list of properties I'm considering purchasing, around the city. Some historical, some commercial, and I want to dip my toe into building a new baseball stadium."

"W-What? Since when did you have an interest in baseball, Mother?" Realizing I've practically shrieked my response across the restaurant, the gossip mongers will be texting my mother's plans before we even finish eating.

"I've always liked baseball, and even though we all love Richmond's Flying Squirrels, it's Single-A baseball. We need Triple-A, back in the city, and that's only going to happen with the right facilities. More importantly, I like making money for our portfolio." She looks at me and sees that I'm awestruck, unable to speak because my mother… *is interested in baseball?* I never saw that happening. "Richmond needs a new stadium. I'm probably among the very few who can finance it. There are many at-risk, youth programs, we can incorporate. And, by the way, I want it in Shockoe Bottom."

"Mother, do you even realize the controversy currently surrounding that plan? Many don't want it down there because of the site's association with the African slave trade and the burial grounds. It's sacred ground, Mother."

Looking at me, I see she's thought this through entirely. "I believe I can find a solution. The stadium's field will shift over from the previously proposed plan. Currently, there is nothing that honors the history and atrocities which occurred on the site. A parking lot, is not the way to honor those lost souls, which is what we now have. If we don't do something, there will be nothing. No one will ever build anything to honor them. If I do, it will be done with integrity and grace. Richmond, Virginia, was the Capitol of the Confederacy… *that is a fact.* History… is a breadcrumb trail of facts. It's not my job to rewrite it, just acknowledge it. I want this stadium to acknowledge, with a museum, our city's connection to the slave trade. When you visit the stadium, you visit a Museum honoring those lost souls. It will be the only baseball stadium in the country, whose focus will be on its city's history. If we don't keep educating, we stand to negatively impact a healthy moral compass. What better way to highlight and bring attention to something, than through the art of sport? We have a unique opportunity here, probably not available anywhere else in the country. I'm in my final act, and this will be my legacy, Jack."

Breathing deeply, I have major mixed feelings on this subject. If I understand what she's saying, the actual stadium won't be on the burial grounds. That's a relief at least. Well, if any man or woman can bring both sides to an agreement, and get approval for another team by the powers in the baseball world… it's Sarah Loving. Damn, Triple-A baseball returning to Richmond, major news and I'm stoked because there's no better game in the world than baseball.

Moving on to happier conversation, the time seems to fly-by when I suddenly hear from behind me… "Daddy!" Turning around instantly, I look for my children. No matter what is going on, parents always seem to have a six-sense about the voices of their kids. Coming towards me at a quick pace, Bryce, followed by Grace. Immediately, I'm confused about why they're here. It doesn't take long to wonder because as I scan the restaurant, she's en route. She knows we're always here at this time. Shaking my head, I prepare for the volcano to erupt because my parents haven't seen her since the big boardroom confrontation showdown. Holy shit, Victoria is here.

Hugging each of my children, I try to focus on how to avoid confrontation. As Victoria approaches, she's full of smiles and greets everyone as if nothing has changed between us. The gentlemen all stand upon her arrival, including myself. Years of my mother's impeccably engrained southern manners would dictate such a greeting. Knowing she has clear motivations, I react seemingly unaffected by her presence. When she walks up to me, her expression is bright, semi-flirtatious, and now I'm more convinced than ever, she wants something. Making an appearance here of all places, is calculating.

The server approaches and inquires whether or not to add more seating for the newly arrived guests. Before anyone can answer,

Mother replies, "We appreciate the offer, however, this is a private business meeting. We weren't aware they were planning to come. Otherwise, we would have saved Ms. Loving the trip. Moreover, I'm sure the children would be bored to tears?" Only my sweet mother can cut through the bullshit, insult someone and do it wearing a smile. God, I love her. "Children? I need some hugs and sugar, too. I've missed seeing you so much. Please, don't be sad that we're in a meeting." She receives the hugs she wishes for, and when Bryce hugs her, he notices the diagram for the baseball stadium. His eyes light up with curiosity and just as he is about to comment, she leans in close and whispers in his ear. Whatever she says satisfies his curiosity. He pulls away, with eyes as wide as saucers. Apparently, he supports his grandmother's efforts, to build a new stadium too.

Looking shocked by mom's response, not to include her, Victoria faces the server being fully chastised and requests a separate table. Before walking away, she quietly says to me, "Jack, I was hoping we could take the children to the Science Museum of Virginia, this afternoon. Bryce really wants to go to the planetarium. We promised him several times we would go as a family. Remember?" The Dome was recently renovated and is the most technologically advanced digital dome theater, in the world. He's been waiting, with baited breath, to visit since the renovations.

Ah, so this was her plan: use an outing with the kids as a way to trap my attention. Quite typical, I would say. Trying very hard not to let her bait me into a public altercation, I speak quietly in her ear. "Victoria, do *not* play games, especially here in front of the children." Pulling away, I focus on Bryce, "bud, I have other plans today, I'm very sorry. I'll tell you what, next weekend, you have the retreat Friday through Sunday morning. When you get home, if you're not too tired and up to it, I'll take you Sunday afternoon. Deal?"

It cuts me to the quick to see my son disappointed, but he accepts my answer with a nod. "Okay, Dad. You promise? And, is mom coming with us?"

"We'll talk about it later, buddy. For now, you and your sister, go with your mother. Enjoy brunch with her. We're discussing boring business stuff right now. I'd rather you enjoy the time with her instead." Kissing them on the cheek, I simply nod at Victoria, who is fuming as she walks away, without a word. She's pissed to put it lightly. Too bad, my dear. Don't use my kids to push your own agenda.

"I'm sorry about the interruption. Where were we?"

Chapter Twelve

Safety is Non-Negotiable

Lizzie

The alcohol was flowing, and my girlfriends and I were being silly as usual. Considering it was my first girls night out in months, it felt good to be out again. We met at our traditional meeting place, The Boathouse Restaurant. Being out amongst my friends, the crowd, and more importantly, just out of the comfort zone of my apartment. Slowly, but surely, I'm trying to get my life in order.

We had a lot to catch up on, and it was obvious they were handling me with kid's gloves. The conversation steered towards their shenanigans, and, of course, their love lives. These women do not hold back as far as that's concerned, and it's good for me to laugh. Marianne and Derek are still spicing up their bedroom, with every sexual aid known to man, and Janice and Robbie, have discovered that voyeurism, really turns them on. They've seemed to advance to whole new levels since I was away. Of course, Jenny is single now. So, it's odd to have one of us actively scouting for men.

"So, Lizzie, I'm glad your St. Patrick's Day event was so successful. I apologize for not coming." Marianne stated.

"That's understandable. If I had the chance to go to Wilmington, NC, and visit Wrightsville Beach, I would have been there too."

"Y'all *really* missed the real event," Jenny said under her breath.

"I don't get it. What event did we miss, Jenny?" Janice asked.

Jenny looked at me with a smile resembling the cat that ate the canary. "Can I tell them?"

Knowing exactly where she was going, but praying she'd stop, "There's nothing to tell," I firmly say.

Marianne's accessing eyes yo-yo between Jenny and me, "Spill it, now!"

"It's nothing! Jenny seems to think Jack Loving has a thing for me, that's all."

"I don't think... *I know.* And *you* know, I know. So, go ahead get them up to speed or I will," she chuckles. Really not wanting to talk about this, because it's just too soon. Especially due to the fact, that I don't really know what's going on myself. I apparently take too long deciding on a response, because Jenny beats me to it. "Jack Loving couldn't keep his eyes off her. She, on the other hand, got really pissy when these girls were literally hanging all over him. And... earlier in the day, Miss Lizzie here decides to take her life into her own hands, standing on the bar fixing a banner. Jack swooped in, at the exact moment she was falling and saved her from imminent brain damage. Yes... he's really into her... a lot. Plus, there are *other* reasons, which I won't mention. Bottom line is, Lizzie has an admirer."

The sighs and squeals surround the table. Her 'imminent brain damage' comment sounds an awful lot like something Jack would say. *Are they actually closer than I realize? Talking about me, when I'm not around?* "It's very new, there's nothing to report. He co-sponsored the event with Mark Chesney, and then we had dinner nearby at Tobacco Company. We were both there all day long, and it was a moment to get away from 'everything green and gold.' That's it, I promise."

The stares on the faces coming from around the table, tell me they aren't buying it. Not… at… all. No one is speaking, obviously waiting for me to continue. Finally, after feeling the pressure, I cave. Whispering, "We *might* be going on a date this Saturday."

"I knew it!"

"Seriously? Wow! He's so hot, Lizzie."

From Jenny, just a loud burst of laughter. I turn to look at her with raised eyebrows, begging her to just chill out. "Do you mind?"

"You do know, he has a major thing for you. Just relax and enjoy it, sweetie," Jenny replied.

"How can I relax when I have no idea what we're doing, much less how to dress?"

"This is good news, Liz. We'll help you figure something out. I can imagine how intimidating it must be. Jenny's right, just have fun." Marianne says eagerly.

Just then, this guy approaches our table. He's obviously been drinking and decides to drink-us-in with his rather flirtatious eye movements. Standing next to my chair, he places his hand on my shoulder, to steady himself. Leaning down, he is about to whisper something to me, when suddenly, this man dressed in all black, appears out of nowhere. He firmly tells my new visitor, "Sir, it's time to go." Grabbing him around the shoulders, the drunk man is just as shocked as we are. Before we can say a word, he is physically removed from the restaurant. It happened in probably, less than five seconds total. Jaw dropped, I don't even know what to say I'm so shocked and confused. Looking around the table, my friends are just as shocked.

Suddenly, Marianne says loudly, "What the fuck was that?"

"I don't have a damn clue, but I wonder if he wants to be my savior tonight? Jenny replies.

Having a moment to absorb what just happened, it suddenly dawns on me that this so-called "bouncer" was dressed in all black. He looked very similar to my chauffeur from the other night. The person arranged as my security, by Jack. Turning to Jenny, "that bouncer doesn't work here, Jenny. I've never seen him before tonight. Have you seen him in the last few months?"

"No, why? What are you getting at?"

Deep in thought, *how did he know I would be here?* "I'm not positive, but I'll bet he's working for Jack."

She gives a very unladylike snort. Shaking her head, "I wouldn't be surprised."

Suddenly feeling very irritated, and especially more so, since she thinks it's funny! "Stop laughing, Jenny. Why was he here? Was he following me?"

"Honey, you'll need to ask him those questions. I will say this: the man has totally been immersed in your life for quite a while now, and you didn't even know it. It wouldn't surprise me one bit if he had security watching you."

"Whoa, why would he have security on you, Lizzie? I thought you barely knew each other," Janice inquired.

"Yes, well, I'm getting a quick education lately, all is not what it seems. Jack Loving, is no stranger to my life apparently."

Just before midnight, I crawl into bed, totally wide awake unable to sleep. Even though I don't have proof, my gut feeling, is paramilitary man number two... works for Jack Loving. The longer I lay here and think about it, the more questions come to mind and the madder I seem to get.

Knowing it's really late, I decide to insert myself in Jack's life since he doesn't seem to mind inserting himself in mine. Figuring a text would be best at this hour, I go for it before I lose my nerve:

12:10 a.m. So, what happened to the drunk man?

12:12 a.m. The drunk man?

Oh, dear. What if I've jumped the gun? Maybe I shouldn't have texted. Sighing deeply, I decide to give it a chance and see if my gut feeling is right.

12:14 a.m. Yes, Jack. Don't deny it.

12:14 a.m. I won't deny anything if I did something deserving of a confession.

Well, shit. Now, I'm embarrassed. Before I type a response, he texts again:

12:16 a.m. He was drunk, Lizzie. This was a straightforward safety issue. I didn't want him hanging on, or touching you. He was removed, end of story.

Oh my god! He *was* behind it, and he has someone watching me. I really don't know how I feel about this because my first instinct, is to run the opposite way.

12:18 a.m. You're not responding, which tells me you're not happy. Trust me, I'm not exactly pleased, either. I don't want some drunk ass dude putting a finger on you. You're important to me, therefore I ordered him removed. My position was clear with you at dinner, we're dating. My job is to be concerned about your welfare.

We're dating? We're dating... thanks for the proclamation! All of this is too much. I don't know why, but this apparent obsession he has with me, is bullshit! I don't need another man with emotional problems. Hell no!

12:23 a.m. Lizzie, answer my texts.

12:28 a.m. I'm coming over.

No, no, no! He wouldn't, would he?

12:29 a.m. Absolutely, no!

12:30 a.m. Absolutely, oh yes. Besides, I want to see you in person. I won't stay long, I promise. On the way. Open the damn door, Liz.

Well, that exchange went well. He has lost his mind for sure. I'll just greet him at the door so he can see I'm perfectly safe. Then, he'll be on his way. Five minutes, done and over. Taking a look in the mirror, I realize I look like hell. My long hair is in a bun on top of my head. I have no makeup on, and I'm wearing the most unattractive set of pajamas I own. Oh dear god, he'll be frightened. Actually, that's good news. He'll take one look at the real me, be regretful of this craziness he's started and decide Missy, Misty, Mistletoe or whatever she calls herself, is more his speed. Great, plan made, ready to roll.

Minutes later, I hear a soft knock on my door. Of course, he owns the building therefore he knows where I live. *Damn the benefits of would-be millionaire boyfriends.* Taking a deep breath, I check the peephole. It's him, and I can already tell, he looks amazing. Dressed in blue jeans, a white button up dress shirt, rolled up to just below the elbow. His hair has that wind-blown swept back look. Lord, please help me, he looks scrumptious. This… may not go as easy as I had hoped. Dammit. "Stop ogling me from the peephole Lizzie, and open the door."

Friggin-A! Taking a long frustrated breath, I comply and open the door a few inches, and my face meets his hard chest. Without waiting for an invitation, he moves inward. Before I can say a word, he has the door open and closed behind him, then locked. Staring at the door knob, a frisson of fear falls over me. Not entirely clear why, I try to hide my discomfort with being locked into a space with Jack Loving. A man I barely know, yet a part of my mind, automatically trusts him.

"My children are asleep, Jack," I softly say to him.

"I should hope so. Especially at this hour," he teases. Standing there, I watch him as his eyes scan my body. From the knot of hair on my head, to my face, to the rounded neck of my homely pajama shirt, to the comfortable, yet more grandmotherly pajama bottoms, to my old, and very comfortable, slip-on slippers. A heated smile graces his face. He moves in closer to me and places his thumb on my lips. Rubbing the span from corner to corner, he pushes his thumb in slightly, wetting it and returning to moisten my lips completely. I'm caught in his spell already and he's barely touched me. I'm failing in my plan to resist him. Yes, failing miserably. Stroking my cheek, with the tips of his fingers, he whispers, "I have so much I want to say to you, babe. However, standing here at this moment, the most important thing I must get across to you is how amazingly beautiful and sexy, I find you at this moment." Sliding his fingers from my cheek to the side of my neck, he grasps me by the back of my neck, holding me firmly in place. "More importantly, the casual look you've got going on right now… major turn on, babe. I prefer au naturale any day of the week." *Well shit…plan busted.*

Slowly, the bends down, and my nostrils are filled with a familiar cologne, I find very invigorating. My body becomes weak-kneed, and somehow he's turned me into a weakling. He grabs at my body, holding me up tightly against him. Placing his lips on my neck, chill bumps immediately flash everywhere, and I release a loud sigh signifying my body's approval. Giving my neck three distinct kisses along the column, he pulls away, leaving me feeling unfulfilled and needy. Definitely not how I saw the first five minutes going between us. He sets me back, steadies me, "you could have worn a feed sack, and I would have wanted you just the same."

Shocked by his candidness, I realize my plan to scare him off, has failed miserably. "It's late, why did you come, Jack?"

Saying absolutely nothing, he turns toward the direction of the hall, and embraces my hand fully and pulls me behind him. Not comfortable with where this might be going, I pull my hand away from his. He stops and turns around, facing me fully. "Sweet, beautiful, sexy, Lizzie. You've misunderstood my intentions. I've come to tuck you into bed, totally innocently." Bending down and speaking only inches from my mouth, "I'm not here to take you to bed, sweetheart. Your children are here, and I wouldn't do that to you or them. Besides, *when* it happens, I need to make sure no one is around for miles because I intend to take you places you've only dreamed of going. Your screams, they'll happen many times over, all… night… long." Lost in the imagery of his words, I don't realize my legs are moving until we're half way to my bedroom. It's as if he knew exactly where to go because he efficiently pulled me along with ease.

Once there, he shuts the door and stands by the bed. Pulling back the covers, his arm motions me to sit and I comply. Leaning downward, he pulls my slippers off and leans forward near my face. "Good girl, I really like it when you do what I ask. Ordinarily, I might reward you, but you've been snippy."

"Snippy? No I have—"

Placing his index finger over my lips, I quiet immediately. He closes his eyes and shakes his head slightly, seemingly enjoying the moment. "Do you even see how crazy you drive me when you submit like that? You're incredible, babe. Problem is, earlier you got offended because I was looking out for your safety." I try to interrupt, but it comes out in sounds of garbling. "No, don't. It's late, and we can talk about this fully later. For now, what's important is you understand not to ignore me. No matter what happens, or how mad you may be, we don't ignore each other. Texts, phones, in-person or otherwise. Shake your head, 'yes.'" Knowing he's right, I do. "Good, time for bed." He motions me to lie down, and he pulls the linens tightly around me. Leaning forward, he seems to take his time memorizing my face. With a smile lifted on one side of his mouth, it takes everything I have, not to pull him forward over me in this bed.

"You really didn't need to drive all this way, and we really must talk more about everything, Jack." He grunts a sound of displeasure, "But... I'm happy to see you again. I'm glad you dropped by."

"No, *that*, makes it all the worthwhile to drive over here." He leans down and kisses me first with gentle light kisses, and my mouth automatically opens begging him to find my tongue. His sweeping motions are soft, then more demanding. He tastes like cinnamon and it makes me want more. All too soon, he pulls away. Standing up, "I'll lock up, and call you tomorrow. Goodnight, Liz." He winks at me, leans to turn the light off on the nightstand, and leaves quiet as a church mouse.

Laying there staring at the ceiling, I almost question my sanity if it really happened. If he really came? Although, I know he did because my lips still tingle from the amazing force with which he kissed me. Additionally, I have the faint taste of cinnamon, lingering in my mouth. *Cinnamon... why is that so familiar in the far specters of my brain?*

Chapter Thirteen

Asshole-Client Case, Finds Unexpected Conflict of Interest

Jack

Leaving Lizzie last night, took incredible will power. Realizing it was really forward of me to just show up uninvited, especially with her children there. I needed to see her, but I was desperate to touch her.

When Seth told me she met her friends at, The Boathouse, I had mixed feelings. Granted, if she was spending time out, it was progress. Problem is, I am very territorial about her. Some might say irrational, and they might be right. I was rather jealous in the beginning of my time with Victoria too. Now, I'm older, more experienced, wiser and more driven to get what I want. Every day that goes by, I want her more and more. Before, I was on the sidelines, now I'm not. So the idea of some guy flirting with her, drives me insane. She is a very striking woman. Her beautiful, long brunette hair, and body with amazingly huge, but well-proportioned tits, and ass with legs that go on for days. Her presence in a room is hardly missed especially from poachers out on a prowl. Throughout the night, security sent me texts updating me that she was perfectly fine. When the alcohol started flowing amongst her friends, I was a little concerned. The report was she had two glasses of wine, so that was good to know. However, when he called me to tell me a drunk guy was heading in her direction, I screamed rather loudly "intercept!" Thankfully, I heard the entire situation because Seth left the microphone on while he approached and removed, the drunk bastard. I laughed my ass off listening to Seth, scolding this dude about never approaching, much less touching, any of the ladies at that table, ever again. He's quite a scary guy when he needs to be.

When Lizzie texted, she caught me off guard. However, the fact that she put it all together on her own, just signifies how intelligent she really is. I truly hoped I could keep my security measures secret for a while longer. The problem is, she's smart and would have noticed them eventually. I'll need to make her understand security is not to check-up on her or control her movements. Someone is my financial position, is a target. Throw in the fact that I'm a criminal attorney, and we have a whole new set of concerns. I've grown up having full-time security around me, my entire life. Soon after we were married, Victoria had a driver. He was also her security guard in disguise. When you are among the mega-wealthy, kidnapping becomes an issue for concern. Since we don't live in seclusion, we need protection. If I intend to date Lizzie, she needs the same protection. Convincing her, she could be used against me, will not be an easy task. Therefore, I just made the arrangements, without consulting her. It will anger her, but I have faith she'll understand. Eventually.

Running my hands along her neck, kissing her, just felt... *so right*. The last thing I wanted to do was leave. Even though I shouldn't have been there, I needed to see her after the altercation with the drunk bastard. My time there went by so quickly, but while I was there, it felt good to be in her home. It smelled like her, and I would have enjoyed the good look around. The problem was, it felt *too* good and if I didn't leave soon, I would have broken my pledge nothing significant would happen between us. When I finally have the chance to be with Lizzie, I want all of her attention. For hours. How will she react to my touch, my taste? Something tells me, little Ms. Lizzie, is not one to sit idle in bed. I strongly believe she may test the limits of my control, and the idea of that, makes me very hard.

"Jack?" came through the speaker of my desktop phone.

"Yes, Patricia?"

"The Commonwealth Attorney from Richmond, is on line one. He wants to know if you have a minute to go over the Lindy case?"

Dammit, I am busy up to my neck, but I'm anxious to get this case behind me. Taking a deep breath to mentally prepare myself for dealing with this prick's case, I agree to take the call. "I'll take it. Thanks, Patricia. Oh! Patricia?"

"Yes, sir?"

"Schedule some time today for us to discuss your performance review. It's due and I want to get it taken care of."

"Absolutely! I wouldn't want to miss that!" She chuckles. My family and I owe a lot to her. She's been a faithful, loyal employee. When everything hit the fan with the investigation with Victoria, she proved her value ten times over.

"Okay, fine. Just let me know."

Opening my case file for Mr. Lindy, I accept the call from the prosecutor's office. "Hello there. This is Jack Loving."

"Hey there, Jack. It's Tom Bennett. Thanks for taking the call. I wanted to go over the email you sent, regarding additional information Mr. Lindy has, in exchange for reducing the sentence on his other case."

"That's correct. The information is quite compelling. He assures me, it's all true and accurate. He apparently has some video evidence as well."

"I'll be honest, this is one of those cases that can be a career maker or breaker. If it's true, the press will have a field day. What surprises me is you'd be willing to bring this information to us at all. Let's be frank... these are *your* people. Your family is most likely friendly with them. Have you thought about the social implications to your family? These are well-known people in the community. Several of them are State Representatives. If this is true, it will be a firestorm. If it's proven not true, all of us will go down with the ship, Jack."

"First, I take exception to being lumped into a class of *my* people. Yes, they have money and some have political influence. My family also has money, but that doesn't mean we associate or condone criminal activity. Furthermore, this is my *job*. I may not be comfortable where it takes me sometimes, but I'm good at it. If anyone in my social circle, has a problem with me doing my job, they are welcome to speak with me at any time."

"Well, alright then. I have the partial list of names you sent me. When will I receive the remaining names?"

"My client needs a written plea agreement on a lesser charge. Once received, we will forward the remaining names. He hasn't given it to me yet because he wants to be sure his deal is solid."

"Oh, if it pans out, we're solid. A political corruption and prostitution ring among well-known people is big news. I never imagined something like this was based here in Richmond. The fact that it even extends to D.C. will make this national news."

"I imagine it would be news worthy. Even though I know some of these people, it doesn't change the fact, a crime is a crime."

"Thanks, Jack. I'll be in touch with Mr. Lindy's agreement."

"Great, talk later then." When I disconnect, it occurs to me that I haven't clued my father in on this case. We have a general knowledge of all the open cases in the firm, but since this will hit home with people we know socially, he needs to know what's going on. Deciding no time like the present, I decide to walk to my father's office. First knocking, "Dad?"

"Yeah?"

Closing the door, "There's a case I need to bring you up to speed on."

He is busy at his computer, always multi-tasking. "Hmm... must be important if it couldn't wait until our manager's meeting?"

Shaking my head in agreement, "It is important. In fact, it's very delicate and you're not going to like it."

Immediately stopping all work, he looks up to me. "That certainly sounds ominous. What am I not going to like?"

Taking a seat in the chair in front of him, I explain the case against my client, Mr. Lindy. He's a real asshole and I can't stand the man, but it's not my job to like him... but defend him. Serving prison time will be his death sentence. Having too many enemies, has caught up with him. So, when the negotiations came to a standoff, he came to me with information on an unrelated case. The proposal: exchange the information to avoid serving time.

"So, this new information... why am I not going to like it?"

"We know some of the people involved."

"How? Who are they?" He asks growing more impatient.

"Many of them are benefactors for various charities. Several have political connections as well. And, of course, any good net that sweeps up wealthy, important people, has sex complicating the matter."

"How so?"

"Apparently, there is a prostitution ring here in Richmond, for wealthy and powerful people. Some of the favors were paid using women."

My father's eyebrows immediately shoot up, and he rises from his chair and faces the window. Deep in thought, I get the sense my father knows something. For that reason, I grow very concerned. "Did you know anything about these high-end call girls?" Not answering the question, I begin to think the worst. "Dad, I... *need...* an answer."

Turning back to face me, he has a look on his face of revulsion mixed with fear. "Not direct knowledge, in the physical way. Don't look at me that way, Jack! I love your mother more than my next breath. Nothing would cause me to use an escort!"

Trying to get my very erratic heart rate to calm, "Then what is it then? Why do you look so concerned?"

Closing his eyes and shaking his head, he gathers the strength to speak. He flops back into his chair and stares at his hands. I guess it's a coping mechanism so he won't have to lose his courage. "Over the years—several decades, in fact, I have been around and heard various conversations regarding a high-end escort service. Apparently, it's very hush-hush, and they have survived because the person that runs it, is extremely careful. I know quite a few people who still routinely use their services. It's a dirty little secret."

"Why didn't you say anything?"

"Why are you assuming I didn't?

"Did you? Did you report them?"

Turning his chair to face the window, "No. I never reported anything, but I've always cautioned against using them. Look, it's a complicated situation, and it's best I not try and explain it." Facing my direction, he looks me square in the eye. "Jack, considering what you've recently been through, you of all people should understand what it feels like to be used for your money. When you have money, you never know if people care for you legitimately as a person, or if their true allegiance, is to becoming rich and you're a side note. When you hire an escort, it takes all that nastiness out of the equation. You can take a lovely woman out to dinner, and she knows it's not going anywhere the next day. No expectations, no promises and more importantly—no hurt feelings. It may technically be against the law, but these ladies are *well* compensated. It's not like they're walking the streets, earning money for drugs. They receive healthcare and are paid very well, from what I was told."

Interrupting him, "I don't even *want* to know how you know so much about the lives of escorts!"

"No, you probably don't want to know, or should know. Suffice it to say, I can state to you with absolute honesty, I have *never* cheated on your mother."

"Well, that's something at least." Bending over, I lay my head in my hands, not sure how I'm ever going to deal with the situation. "We now have a *big* problem, Dad."

"I realize that, but you need to proceed. The chips will fall as they may."

"You had knowledge and didn't say anything! We have a conflict of interest. Problem is, if I remove myself, they're going to red-flag both of us because they will think we were part of this ring too. We both fit the profile!"

"Yes, they will, which is why you say nothing. We never had this conversation. Just defend your client, Jack. Do your job like you always have—win it for your client."

"Considering, recent developments, I'm going to keep the list of customers locked in my personal safe. I was going to show you, but now think it's best I don't. Besides, there's more people to add to the list. Mr. Lindy has only supplied a partial list so far. I will say, the much bigger government corruption is far more severe, but like always whenever sex is involved, it gets the focus."

"Yes, I think you're right."

Chapter Fourteen

You've Totally Blown My Mind

Lizzie

This morning, I received a call from Ms. Martin requesting I visit for lunch today. It's been quite a while since I was here. Standing outside the plain entrance on Main Street, it still baffles me that such a plain door hides such beauty behind it. Pushing the buzzer, I'm sure to smile at the cleverly hidden camera, most walkers-by never observe. "Oh, you've arrived at the perfect time. Come in dear!" After the buzzer sounds, I enter and immediately I'm hit with the aroma of sweet smelling roses and, of course, classical music. It will never get old, and my senses appreciate the treat.

Walking through, I'm careful to observe the museum quality of her artwork, adorning the rooms as I pass by. All presents from previous suitors, she once explained, she had to put them up somewhere, so why not the place she works. I'd love to have them inspiring my daily work. She must be incredibly special to the men she has known in her life because they sure have spent a mint courting her.

"Oh, Lizzie, it's so good to see you again dear." She greets me with a kiss.

"You, too, Ms. Martin." I kiss her back.

"I have our lunch set up in the back dining room. Let' go back there."

Moving to the back, I didn't even know she had a dining room. Seeing it, it's more like a grand dining room with flourishes of gold everywhere. The opulence in her space, never ceases to surprise me. "Wow, this is beautiful. Thank you for inviting me to lunch today."

Smiling at me, "Well, I have an ulterior motive, but first let's get caught up. Tell me about the event over the weekend."

So, I take the next few minutes explaining the success of the St. Patrick's Day event, she talked me into coordinating. Somehow, she already knew some of the details. "I didn't have a chance to say it before, but I really appreciate you pushing me to start living again. It has been a tough situation for my family. I don't know if I'll ever get over it, but I don't have as much guilt about it as I once did."

"That's progress, Lizzie. Day-by-day you'll make more progress. Just enjoy living, dear."

"Thank you, I'm trying."

"Good, well I brought you here because I want to start living too." I narrow my eyes in confusion, preparing to hear whatever she wants to say. "As you know, I made choices to save my family. I will never regret those choices because it meant my mother lived a long life. It also allowed me to educate my siblings. Today they are successful members of society, so I'm proud of them. I won't complain about my choice to be in the escort business, but it has limited the way I live my life. I'm facing the final stages of my time here on earth, and I selfishly want to enjoy it. This business serves a tremendous role to my clients. They rely on me, but also, my employees and their families rely on me, so I can't just close this business, Lizzie."

"I imagine not. How many employees do you have, Ms. Martin?"

She smiles at me, conniving as ever. "Officially…fifty or so?"

"And, unofficially?"

"If you repeat this Lizzie, this will not end well for us." Knowing that she means what she says, I know this is a woman who clawed her way to the top. She is a survivor…a fighter. Not a person to be crossed, *ever*. "Around two hundred."

My mouth drops open in shock. I cannot believe she is running a business with two hundred employees. "Seriously?"

"Yes ma'am. They come from all backgrounds, race, religions, and gender. You name it… I've got it. I have employees with PhD's, nurses, construction workers, other business owners, students, stay-at-home mothers and fathers, single parents, I could go on and on. I even have a doctor on staff. People do this for many different reasons. Bottom line, I have a lot of people who rely on me to keep this business confidential and protected. I have gone to great lengths to ensure anonymity. Nothing is written, so if the police should bust in here… they find nothing. Over the years, I've developed a system in my head. It works and will work."

"That's truly incredible. I'm in awe you have such a large business, with no written documentation."

"Well, I do have written documentation, but it's for my legitimate business. Very similar to your dates with Mark. It's a lucrative operation for me. You've seen your paychecks. They're from the legal side of the business. The government gets their share of taxes, and it makes things look acceptable from the outside. Some of the employees have both assignments: paycheck and cash."

"It seems almost impossible to keep straight, so I'm very impressed that you manage to do it so well."

"It works for me… I want it to work for you too." Grabbing my hand, she squeezes it firmly. "I want to start living my life with Henry, in France. He wants me there, and you're my hope for a normal life. I've never believed there was anyone trustworthy, and smart enough to do this, until I met you. Besides, Mark thinks you can do it too."

"I really don't understand why you have so much confidence in me. Running an escort business, is not something I've exactly aspired to be. Besides, it's illegal Ms. Martin. I have children to support, especially now, I'm the only parent they now have."

"That's exactly why you need to do it. Guaranteed substantial income, for you and your children. As far as anyone is concerned, I run a dating service. That part of the business is absolutely legal. They are not paid to have sex. If they have sex, it's consequential and I have nothing to do with it."

"Granted, I need an income but I'm not sure. This is risky for me."

"Let me share some numbers with you. Last year, my business brought in over forty million dollars."

"What!" I screamed and proceeded to have a choking fit. After several minutes resulting in smeared makeup down my face, I finally began breathing normally again. "Did you just tell me you made *forty… million… dollars,* last year?"

"Yes, I did. I'm practically ready to faint because I've never told anyone the true number before, but if you're going to run things, you will find out anyways."

"How is that even possible with only two hundred employees?"

"Simple really. The legitimate business' fifty employees, work on average, two assignments a week. Each assignment, is around two-hundred dollars, and the employee keeps forty percent... you know that part. The high-end business' one-hundred-fifty employees, bring in around five thousand dollars a week. Some people are valued higher, some less. Some work two assignments per week, some less. Bottom line is the revenue, is around five-thousand per week and with one-hundred fifty employees, that's seven-hundred-fifty thousand per week, times fifty-two weeks, comes to thirty-nine million per year. So, legitimate plus high-end, comes to over, forty million per year. After the escorts keep their percentage, I make around twenty-four million per year. See... simple."

"Ms. Martin, you just rattled off those numbers from memory like it was nothing at all. I'm so in awe, you just said all of that from the top of your head. How can you make so much money, and no one gets suspicious?" I ask completely interested.

"Trust me, there are bribes. However, no one knows my identity, except the escorts. I have mechanisms, and protocols in place, so I am kept in the clear. Some money for the high-end is kept in off-shore accounts. Clients pay in cash, and I pay out in cash. Other amounts... we'll discuss in a moment. No paper trail. Additionally, I'm careful with new clients. They are investigated very carefully. There are many more aspects you will need to learn, but this has worked for over thirty years, Lizzie. My clients are not just here in Richmond. There are many in District of Columbia, Maryland, some in New York and Chicago as well."

Listening to her, I truly feel like I'm about to faint. Actually, I must be in a movie. Somewhere along the way, I've fallen through the looking glass for sure. I always knew she was a complicated woman, now I know it for real. "I can't run this business on my own," I state with total certainty.

"I agree."

"What? I thought you told me all of this because you want me to run it for you?"

"Oh, I do, and I hope you will have it all, eventually. My goal is to give it to you in stages. You will take over the fifty employees right away, allowing me to move to France, and live in a perpetual state of sexual bliss. I will run the high-end business from overseas. However, I need you to handle the cash for me. You will pay out the employees, and stockpile the cash in the vault. Every three-four months, I will visit and take care of the transfers to my offshore accounts."

"Ms. Martin, if you've been doing this for over thirty years, you must have quite an enormous account. Sorry to be so bold, but… with everything we've discussed, what secrets could there be left to tell?"

She smirks and looks at me with the most peculiar look, almost as if she has a pretty massive set of secrets, hidden away in that little head of hers. "Very perceptive of you, Lizzie. Obviously, a girl cannot tell *all* of her secrets, but there is a pretty obvious one, I'm surprised you haven't picked up on. Until then, I'll leave you to it."

What in the hell is she talking about? I don't know whether to be insulted or choose to be protected, from this hysteria she wants to put me in the middle of? "That's a strange comment."

"Yes, nonetheless, back to your question about my assets. I give most of it away, Lizzie. I have more money than I will ever need in my lifetime. There are numerous non-profits, I support with anonymous donations. All over the world actually. It gives me purpose to know how many people are benefiting. You see, that's why I don't feel guilt about doing any of this. When I deliver a million dollar cashier's check to an orphanage, who won't receive that much in one-hundred years, *I celebrate*. When I pay for a homeless shelter, taking two hundred veterans off the street, *I celebrate*. When I build a home for one-hundred single women who only need job training and help with basic life lessons so they become productive members of society, *I celebrate*. When I built five facilities, around the U.S., for children who turned eighteen and aged out of foster care, becoming homeless with nowhere to go, *I celebrate*. I *enjoy* my victories, Lizzie. You've been helping Mark, with his Endowment, and that's wonderful. You two have made a difference. Working for me, you can make an even bigger impact. I don't want to stop what I'm doing, but I need to take a step back, slow down, and marry this man whom I've finally found. He makes me happy, but he's a world away. You're perfect for doing this job because you have a naturally giving heart. You can't train someone to have it… it's rare."

How can I not accept an offer like that? The way she tells the story, it's as if she's delivering the speech of her lifetime. Maybe, she is. Never in a million years, did I think she was this wealthy… probably more than Mark and Jack. That's incomprehensible to me because Jack Loving has more money than… well I don't know, but he's richy-rich! I suddenly find myself surrounded by the mega-wealthy, and I'm so out-of-touch, and out of my league dealing with these people. They don't live like me. *How can I ever measure up? Do I even want to?* The legal aspect scares the hell out of me, but if she's been doing it for thirty years, maybe she's got a solid system in place. I can see how bribery would become a necessary evil. *God, am I considering bribery now?* Ugh!

"Lizzie, I see the wheels in your brain spinning. Talk to me… tell me your thoughts," she pleads with genuine concern in her eyes.

"I'm scared of going to jail! That's my thoughts! I don't have a problem running the legitimate business. Knowing how desperate I was in that position as a struggling mother, I wouldn't want to take their income away. It's the other part, that's giving me a panic attack. Going to jail for bribery and prostitution, would be a problem for me," I quip back at her.

"You wouldn't go it alone, I promise you. Mark knows about everything, obviously. He's been quite helpful, considering his occupation. He actually helps me find worthwhile organizations, needing capital. I don't throw money at a problem, and hope for the best. My donations, solve problems. We offer concrete solutions, for generations to come."

"I don't doubt that, Ms. Martin. It's the illegal crimes, giving me pause."

"Okay, how's this. I will come up with another solution for the payoffs. I need you to collect the cash and do the payouts to the employees though. If I'm not here, it'll never work. I can't pay people from the other side of the world, when it's a cash-only business."

"Where would I store the cash?"

"Lizzie, do I have your vow of silence?"

"I guess so, besides you scare me. You're small but intimidating as hell!"

With a sly smile, "Good. Follow me." Walking out of the dining room, we walk to a smaller room, of course I never saw this room either. The walls are lined with books, and it's the most immaculate library I've ever seen in my life. Complete with a spiral staircase, it is quite possibly breathtaking. Walking over to an older book, she pulls the book forward and the entire wall of books moves forward around twelve inches and then slides completely to the left. Holy shit! I thought that only happened in movies. I'm faced with a solid wall and black panel around twelve inches square. She places her hand on the panel, and it lights up red. Suddenly, the solid wall moves and the lights inside automatically come on. Feeling very overwhelmed, my heart is racing, and I have a weird feeling and battle with myself on whether or not to walk inside. "Let's go. Come on, Lizzie." So… in I go.

This is not a movie, but it sure as shit could be. Lining the rooms are stainless steel shelving units, all covered with locked doors. She produces a key from somewhere and opens one of the doors. It's totally full, with stacks and stacks of bundled cash. Never in my life could I even begin to imagine being in the presence of this much money. The smell is very overwhelming. It has a dirty, musty odor, and it is disgusting. Whoever said they love the smell of money, obviously wasn't invited in this room. "So… this is the vault. The cash reserves are kept here until I process the donations. Over here, the counting table." A banquet length surface, containing an odd looking piece of machinery, sits in the center of the room. Next to it, are latex gloves. That's certainly odd. Pointing to the machine, "this is the counting machine. You can imagine how long it would take to count this much cash. I use gloves when handling cash, Lizzie. Call me paranoid, but I don't leave fingerprints on anything. The gloves are burned at the incinerator, at the back of the building."

Thinking back to the days when I picked up my checks, they were either laying on the table or she was wearing latex gloves. I thought it was because she was watering her plants. Stupid me. "Makes sense, I guess. So, I would need to hold the money in this room, and you will come every four months to retrieve it?"

"In the beginning, if that makes you happy?"

"Actually, every two months would be better. That way I'm only responsible for four million dollars instead of six. Excuse me while I faint by-the-way! This is so… there are no words for what this is, Ms. Martin. You do know that, right?"

"Oh Lizzie, your naiveté is so refreshing!" She outwardly laughs. "You will be responsible for the contents of this room. You do know that, right?"

Swallowing deeply, "this is exactly what scares the crap out of me. What happens if someone breaks in? Or, a fire? Or, heaven forbid, the police barge in. What do I do then?"

"Calm down child! Okay, let me bring you up to speed. First, this place is safer than Fort Knox. There is a sprinkler system, backup generator and a security system designed by a client who works for the U.S. Treasury. It's safe, trust me. You know about the outside camera and doors. What you don't know is, there is a system of panic switches located throughout the building for various reasons. Some, indicate Richmond police are needed. Others are specifically for people on my payroll for protection. The important ones, totally lock down the vault. If the police should 'barge in' as you stated, the first thing, you do, is hit that switch. The bookshelf will never move, the room will not be detectable. I will add your handprint to the panel so you can gain entry. Using the internet, I can access the cameras for every room here. They are time stamped, and date-coded. Easy."

Shaking my head, my ears hurt from so much information. Looking at my watch, I realize I've been here for two hours and soon the children will be home. "I need to get home to meet the school bus. Plus, I need time to process all of this."

"We'll start on Monday, nine a.m. Be prepared for lots of information. Remember, no notes of any kind. If it takes us three weeks for you to memorize everything, we'll practice four weeks instead." Shaking her head, she pats my hand, "we knew you were special, Lizzie. Granted, this is an unusual way to raise revenue for worthwhile organizations. Good samaritans come in many different forms, and I'm serving the community none the less. My work—

which shall be your work too, is just as important and relevant, to the good deeds performed by Mark and Jack. At the end of the day, we're all raising money to help others. Even if we are the most *unlikely samaritans*."

Considering her words carefully, I expect she probably has an even greater impact because she can raise vast amounts quickly. Compared to the physically draining work from this past weekend, this is a much easier way to raise money for sure. *Assuming I don't get thrown in jail.*

Chapter Fifteen

It Appears To Be a...Dating Service, Sir

Jack

"Jack, Ms. Macintyre's security is on line two."

"Thank you, Patricia."

"Jack Loving, speaking."

"Seth calling, Mr. Loving. I wanted to notify you of an event this afternoon. Ms. Macintyre entered a building on Main Street, just before noon. She stayed until approximately, two-thirty p.m. It took us quite a while to determine the location's purpose, but I can now confirm… it's, well… it appears to be a… dating service, Sir."

"What the FUCK did you just say?"

"She entered the building…."

"No! I got that part. What do they do there?"

"It *appears* to be a dating service, Sir. They match people up, is the best we got on our intel. It's not advertised openly. We had to really investigate to get this information. I will keep digging, but this is not your low-end, dating style company. It's exclusive and apparently expensive. Our initial inspection, determined they have extremely detailed security at this location, Sir."

"Where is she right now?" I ask angrily.

"Presently, she is at home. She just returned from the bus stop, picking up her children, Sir."

"Thanks, Seth. Stay on it."

"Sir, yes, Sir."

Jumping up from my chair, I stand in front of my window, and look down the river towards her apartment. I'm so pissed, I could fucking scream! What in the hell was she doing at a ridiculous dating service for so long—*or even, at all?* The woman is gorgeous. All she has to do is walk outside, and men would fall all over her. Using a service, to find a date… when we have a date planned, makes no damn sense to me. Apparently, I didn't make myself clear enough. She may not understand what being mine entails, but after this weekend, she fucking well, *will* know it. I only see red right now, to the point I want to pin her across my lap, and redden her ass good. Even though I haven't even seen it yet, I'd likely enjoy giving her a punishment our first time together.

Shit, this girl has me totally losing my mind. *Did I not make myself clear… multiple times now?* We are going to see if we have something between us. Call me a fool… I think we may have found the Holy Grail. Some may think it's a rebound situation, but I don't. Pacing back and forth in front of my window, I can't seem to release the nervous energy I have inside me. If her children weren't in the apartment, I'd storm over there now. Knowing I can't, I do the next best thing. Taking a deep breath to calm myself, I know I cannot appear angry, or agitated, or she'll know something is going on.

Dialing her number, she answers on the first ring. "Hello?"

Suddenly, all the anxiety I was feeling, begins to wash away. I can literally feel a warmness race across my shoulders, as I instantly begin to settle down. "Hey, babe. Am I calling at a bad time?"

"Um, no. Give me just a second, okay?" She speaks away from the receiver, but the sounds are muffled. "Sorry, I wanted to go to my bedroom for privacy."

"Ah, your bedroom. I'd like to have some privacy with you in your bedroom."

Sounding mockingly affronted, "Jack Loving! You shouldn't say such things!"

"Sorry… it's been quite a day. I just wanted to give you a call and hear your voice."

"Aww, that's really sweet of you. Too bad you're having a bad day, that's a shame."

"So… how was your day today? Do anything fun, or interesting?"

"No, not really."

Fuck. So she's not going to tell me, and I can't tell her I know. This is so screwed up. "Oh, okay. Well… I'm looking forward to our *date* tomorrow."

"Actually, I am too. I'm hoping you can give me a hint as to where we're going?"

"What's the fun in that? Just be prepared for anything."

"Jack, I'm a woman. Knowing what to wear is pretty important to us. Are we talking casual, semi-casual, formal?"

Yeah, pretty stupid on my part, of course, she'd want to know what to wear. "Let me ask you an honest question, okay?"

"Ah, sure… okay." She cautiously asks.

"Out of curiosity, would you be more comfortable doing something fun and casual or formal all the way? I'm happy with either."

"Well… I would say casual, but I don't want to make you change any plans you've made."

"Actually, that's the perfect answer. Casual it is then. I really can't wait to see you, Lizzie."

"You too, Jack."

"Alright, see you tomorrow at six o'clock… if not sooner." I groan into the phone because I know I have to let her go, and without answers on this ridiculous dating service visit she made. "I don't know if I can wait that long."

She chuckles at my impatience, "Sure you can. Bye, Jack."

When the line disconnects, I continue holding it against my ear like some sick schoolgirl. She has reduced me to a mushy mess. It's not like she's going to magically reappear on the phone line.

Staring down the river, I only see her face. Tomorrow has to be perfect. I'm glad she prefers casual because I know just the perfect place. In the meantime, I think I will ask a favor of my friend, Jenny.

Chapter Sixteen

Official First Date = Information Overload

Lizzie

A little before three o'clock, Jenny texts me that she's on the way, and I "better open the door." Well, I must have inconvenienced a lot of people because they all seem to know my history with ignoring the doorbell.

When, I hear her knock, I immediately open it. "See, I'm fully capable of opening the door without any problems."

"Yeah… bitch if you had not opened it this time, we would have had a major problem."

"Why? What's wrong?"

"Absolutely nothing. In fact, it's going perfectly great. So much so, I need you to pack a weekender for the kids. I'm taking them to Great Wolf Lodge!"

"Excuse me? What are you talking about?"

"I don't want you to worry about the kids this weekend, so I'm taking them away for a weekend of fun, in Williamsburg. I'm so excited! I've never been and always wanted to go. You know I'm a kid at heart."

"Whoa—wait… I asked you to watch them for a few hours, not the whole weekend. Look, if you're doing this because you think I'm having wild raunchy sex with Jack, you're wrong! That's not happening."

"Why not? If Jack Loving wanted to have wild, raunchy… or come to think about it, even slow and sultry sex with me… I'd do him in a New York minute! You'd better be smart and reconsider that decision."

"Jenny! I'm… I'm scared about having sex right now… with anyone. You know that Jeremy was my one and only. What if I'm not good enough anymore?"

"Honey, have you looked in the mirror lately? Your tits are massive. Your waist is teeny tiny, and you have an ass that men would die for. Seriously, Lizzie, your self-esteem needs to look at the whole package because you're HOT babe! Even if you'd just lay there in a coma, any guy with a working dick would get his jollies with you."

Taking in her compliments, are hard for me, but it's nice to hear all the same. "Well, it doesn't mean I'm having sex with him. It's the first date for goodness sake!"

"Hey, don't take the rules so seriously. This guy is not just looking for a piece of ass. He's been into you for a very long time. You should realize that by now. Just… go with what feels right in the moment. Whatever happens, don't feel guilty about it. Okay?"

Shaking my head in agreement, it just feels like my life is moving so fast. The last couple years has been one thing after another. I don't want to lead a perfectly good guy along. He really has gotten attached, and I don't know if I want to be tied down right now. Deciding to take it slow, I will just enjoy my date tonight. I'll keep an open mind, and see what happens.

Jenny surprises the kids with weekend passes to Great Wolf Lodge, and they practically scream the apartment down. They enjoy spending time with her anyway but going somewhere to swim at an indoor waterpark when it's still chilly at times, is pretty cool. Before leaving, she helps me pick out an outfit for tonight. Of course, the invasive girl had to see my undergarments. "Just making sure they're sexy enough." *Yeah… right.*

At just before six o'clock, there is knocking at my door. The butterflies have built up like crazy, and I'm nervous, almost to the point of being sick. I don't know why I feel this way, but I almost feel like Jack is totally consuming me. My hands are shaking, and my mouth feels really dry. Trying to shake off the vibes I'm having, I breathe deeply, and open the door.

Holy mother of god. The man is breathtaking. Leaning against the door frame, with one hand in his pocket and the other behind him. Just the way he dominates the space around him makes me incoherent and obviously rude because all I'm able to do is stare. With a simple half-smile, black denim jeans and casual red shirt pulled up to his elbows, I'm speechless. After awkwardness, because I've lost all language skills, "Hello, Lizzie. Will you invite me in?"

Embarrassed he caught me totally befuddled, I try to shake away the intense nervousness that I feel. Motioning him inward, "Ah sure, absolutely. Please come in, Jack."

As he stands upright, he produces a beautiful arrangement of mixed cut flowers, all in varying shades of red. They are truly stunning and creatively designed with varying types of flowers. "For you sweetheart." As I take them, he leans in and plants the gentlest kiss on my lips. Far too soon, he pulls away, and I'm left to enjoy the masculine scent that seems to incapacitate my social niceties. He moans softly, taking his time to open his eyes. "I've waited impatiently all day to do that." With a broad smile, he lets me go and shakes his head slightly, clearing his thoughts.

Feeling a little shy, I turn my head toward the kitchen. "These are incredibly beautiful. Thank you very much. I'd like to grab a vase and put them in some water. Would you like to sit down?"

Shaking his head "no," he doesn't help my case of the nerves by staring at me with that sexy smile, causing me to practically say "yes" to anything. Walking to the kitchen, I can feel his eyes, following me, watching me, as I move through my home. It's unnerving and invigorating at the same time. He is most definitely the predator, and I'm the prey. It's scary, but I like it. "You look very beautiful, Lizzie. I'm going to have a hard time keeping my eyes off of you all night."

With downcast eyes, I arrange the beautiful flowers, trying to hide the huge smile that wants to fill my face. "Thank you." Peeking up, I can't seem to control my eyes from wandering the length of him, shamelessly, up and down. "You are rather handsome yourself, Mr. Loving. The ladies will have a hard time controlling themselves, I'm sure." He catches my invasive perusal and laughs at me. Feeling once again embarrassed, I don't know how I will ever get through this night. He's just so... scrumptious. "Would you care for something to drink? I have beer, wine, soft drinks, sweet tea... you name it."

Without hesitation, "I name you... but that's a different matter entirely."

"Jack! Seriously. You're incorrigible."

"Maybe so, but I'm honest. No, Lizzie, I don't need anything to drink. I need you to come away from your hiding spot in the kitchen, and come here."

Shit, I guess my discomfort was too obvious. Moving the arrangement to my coffee table, I stand back and admire it once more. "I really do appreciate it. Flowers are sorta my thing, I guess you would say. They just make the world a beautiful place."

"Well, I think you fill that role pretty well." He walks up to me, with a swagger of confidence, hands in his pockets. When he reaches me, he looks down into my eyes, studying my face carefully. Suddenly, I feel his hands wrap either side of my hips. He pulls me in close to his body, and I wait patiently... and wait. Finally, "You're very nervous, Liz. I don't want you to be nervous or worried around me. I've waited a very long time for this date to happen. Please, relax and take a deep breath. I want us to go out, act like normal people who are out enjoying one another's company. Okay?"

I shake my head in agreement, and he leans down and kisses me. His lips are so soft and warm. He starts out gentle, with a prolonged simple kiss, then I feel his tongue attempting to breach through. A flush of warmth races through my body, and I open for him. Suddenly, I want to be closer, get closer. My body pushes into his, and he pulls me further in. Reaching my arms up, I place my hands around his neck, running my fingers through his slightly overgrown hair. He tastes like cinnamon, and I imagine exploring his mouth. Licking it all away from every deep crevice. Holding me, he controls the strength of our kiss and nearness of our bodies. My mind and my body are suddenly on fire from his touch. I want more, I need more. This man, who confounds and confuses me, also turns me into a whimpering, needy mess. Pulling his mouth away, I moan in frustration, and Jack smiles and returns a simple peck onto my lips. Placing his forehead on mine, I enjoy the tight embrace he affords me. "Baby, if we keep going like this, I'm *not* going to be able to stop. Trust me, it's *killing* me. Believe me. I just don't want you thinking this is only physical for me. We need to get to know one another. Deal?"

Pulling my forehead from his, I know this is way too soon to get physical. Damn... I got totally lost in the moment. *What the hell am I doing?*The way he holds me, touches me, kisses me... I lose all faculties. "Deal."

With a final sweep of his hands, tightly down my body, he releases me. "How do you feel about pizza?"

Now that caught me off guard. I really didn't know what to expect on our first "real" dinner date, but pizza... no, didn't see that one coming. However, I actually love the idea. "Pizza, is a great idea."

He grasps my hand firmly and pulls me towards the door. "Cool. I love it too."

Minutes later, we arrive at Bottom's Up Pizza. It's my absolute favorite place for pizza because it's that good! Where else can you get diversity like Chesapeake crabmeat, Mexican, Southwestern, Hawaiian, and, of course, all combinations of Italian. The slices are so thick, most people can only eat one slice. Needless to say, being at my favorite place, makes me happy.

Dinner was amazing. Most every topic imaginable was discussed... except our ex's. I explained how I have always enjoyed charity work, raising money for various charities. Granted, I left out the period of time I was too poor, and embarrassed about Jeremy's drinking, to energize myself to be active in any aspect of charity work. Our conversation flowed so freely, it was as if we'd known each other forever. Jack talked about being a lawyer, even though he wasn't happy as one. I found that very interesting. Why stay in a career, when it makes you miserable? His only answer was, "it's a long boring story." He asked me about my career plans, and I felt oddly uncomfortable. He sensed it too. Not pressing for answers, I just explained that I helped Mark with his Endowment on occasion, and I was considering other options as well. Yeah… he knew something was up and I wasn't exactly being open, but he didn't press for more answers.

Things turn a little solemn when he asks. "So, tell me about your childhood. Where did you grow up?" My breath catches when the words leave his mouth. It's a subject I don't especially enjoy talking about because it's very painful. Taking a deep breath, I prepare myself to speak on a subject I desperately avoid most of the time. "Lizzie?"

Shaking my head, "No, it's just not easy for me to speak about it. Honestly, I try not to, but I *want* to tell you."

Grabbing my hand tightly, "Honey, you don't need to if it's too painful."

"It's fine. My parents died in a car crash when I was almost seventeen. My younger brother, well, he died too. It was an unfortunate accident." Tears fill my eyes, even though I try really hard to calm down, not getting too upset. Doing my best to breathe through it, I find comfort in Jack. He tightly holds one hand, rubs my back and shoulders, with the other. Somehow, he passes on his strength to me, allowing me to finish my depressing story. "I didn't have any other family, so I was eventually emancipated. Jenny's family took me in right away. They treated me like I was one of their own children. Luckily, I avoided foster care because of them. She is my very best friend, and I can never repay her and her family. They saved me, Jack. Emotionally, and physically. Life was really bad during that time of my life. My parents and I, we were very close. We were not wealthy, just average middle class, and very involved in our church. They instilled certain values in me while they were alive. Instead of spending holidays like Christmas and Thanksgiving at home, we served the homeless meals at various shelters. You asked me what inspires my sense of helping others… it was taught to me from a very early age. Now that I'm talking it through, I know where my ethos on the subject comes from. Until now, I never really connected those dots. So, thank you."

"Oh, sweetheart." He leans in and delivers a very sweet chaste kiss, upon my lips. "You don't need to thank me. I'm just so sorry it happened to you. Now, I'm even more impressed with Jenny. I'll have to give her my thanks because she's proven herself in my eyes to be more than a good friend, but a critical, lifelong, member of your family. So, that ups her score in my book."

"Yes, she's pretty special. Her family, too. In fact, she even showed up today and offered to take the kids for the weekend to Great Wolf Lodge in Williamsburg." Watching for his reaction, a moment of recognition quickly flashes, then he resumes his previous position. *Yeah… gotcha.*

"Did she now? That's kind of her to want to spend her weekend with them."

"Um hmm…." Smiling at him very pointedly, "Did you have anything to do with it, Jack?"

He opens his mouth to say something, then closes it. He removes his napkin from his lap and wipes his mouth—all stall tactics, I'm sure. With an upturned eyebrow, I wait for his response. Knowing he's caught, he finally ventures his admission. "Will you be mad if I did?"

"I'll be mad if you're dishonest," I reply very directly.

"In that case, I did arrange it. Being a parent myself, I knew your mind would be focused on getting back to them. It's selfish of me, I admit it, but I wanted us to have some time without worrying over the clock." Not saying anything in response, I just sit and listen. He grows a little concerned over my non-answer, "How upset are you? I did tell the truth, so I hope that helps."

"Jack, I don't want to feel like I'm being manipulated. The last few years, I have felt that way, and I don't like it." His face suddenly falls, obviously concerned over my comments. "With that being said, I understand why you did it, but you should have discussed it with me."

"Would you have allowed me to coordinate this if I had offered straight out?"

Running that question through my mind, I must be honest, "No, probably not."

Quick to answer, "That's what I thought. Therefore, I arranged it. I won't apologize for wanting uninterrupted time with you, babe."

Knowing I need to finally bring this up, and it won't be easy, I prepare to address his interference in my life. It's a little much, surely he will understand it. "But, Jack, we need to talk about something. I am extremely appreciative of your help, especially over recent months. Granted, I'm just now putting the pieces together."

"No thanks, are necessary. I wanted to do certain things for you. Therefore, I did them. End of story."

"Aww, no… not end of story. I'm much stronger now, really I am. Therefore, I'm fully capable of making decisions, especially ones pertaining to my children."

"Look, Lizzie, you just admitted you wouldn't go along with my plan to send them on a fun-filled weekend. Trust me, they will have more fun there, than if they'd stayed here—."

"That's not the point,—" I interrupt.

"Maybe not, but it's true. I will concede that my methods were a bit presumptuous if you will admit we needed this alone time together. We've had a great time getting to know one another. I already knew everything I needed to know about you, this was more or less for you anyways."

"What! Talking about presumptuous." I quip. Suddenly, this conversation has taken an unfortunate turn sideways, and it doesn't feel so great.

With raised eyebrows, "Hey," he says softly. "Let's not do this. I keep telling you I see us exploring this," motioning between us. "You need to know something about me. First, my intuition about people is pretty spot on. Maybe it's the lawyer, or maybe it's because I've needed to access people's ethics since I was very young. Whatever it is, I've known you *are* the real deal Lizzie Macintyre. I see you and me, in the early stages of a very long-term relationship. You haven't gotten there yet, I understand that. Please know, I see enough for the both of us."

Leaning close to my ear, he kisses me on the neck, and I automatically fold into his touch. With one simple kiss, he calms me and silences all my fears and frustrations over his actions. I hear him moan softly. *"You're mine, Lizzie. You'll see very soon, exactly what I intend to do about that."* Suddenly, my nipples harden, and I feel myself begin to squirm, looking for any available friction I can find to relieve my need. Even the noise or the full capacity of the restaurant doesn't serve as a deterrent. He takes in my face closely, then his eyes scan downward toward my lap. *Damn—this man doesn't miss anything!* "We're leaving. Now." As if there was a fire or something, he motions to the server. Our bill is immediately produced and we're out of there. Instantly.

Grabbing my hand, he pulls me up and helps me put my jacket on. Then, we're out the door and walking down the sidewalk like there's a fire or something. At an alleyway, he pulls me through, pushing me up against the brick wall. His hands are everywhere like he has a visceral need to touch my body or his life will surely expire. Pinning my body, he kisses me with more passion than I've ever known. His knee finds its way between my legs, one of which he holds up on the back of my thigh. Grinding me, he kisses the column of my neck while his other hand firmly rubs over every available surface of my body. It's so much sensation at once, I cry out. His mouth covers mine, silencing me, allowing me to only moan how great his touch feels. He presses himself into me, deliberately waiting for this exact moment, because he watches with great interest, my reaction for when I first will feel him. Oh my… it's… damn, just damn. He pushes, and circles himself in the exact perfect spot. I breathe heavily, too sporadically, and he knows what it's doing to me. It doesn't matter, I'm in a darkened alleyway, and there are many people walking around just nearby in popular Shockoe Bottom. At this moment, we're totally connected and all I want is to have *more*, feel *more* and give *more*. "Jack…"

He kisses me, hard. I can't keep up. The sensations are too much and it's hard to breathe when we're in so deeply with this kiss. "I got you, babe. I'll always take care of you, but we have to stop. This is not where I'm going to enjoy you for the first time."

Shaking my head in agreement, I know he's right. Grunting loudly, he is in as much obvious frustration as I am. Straightening my clothes, he checks his own as well. It's only when we turn to exit the alleyway, I notice two men, dressed in all black, facing Dock Street with their backs to us. Jack offers a slight head nod to one of them, and we walk swiftly to his car parked in a different spot then when we first arrived. He opens my car door for me, and once inside, we speed off. Reaching over, he lays his hand on my thigh, driving through the city.

Sitting there, I'm preoccupied with the two men dressed in black. Obviously sensing something is off, he squeezes my thigh. "Hey, talk to me."

I look over at him, and he raises his eyebrows expectantly. I pause for a few moments and stare out the front window, deciding how best to bring this up. Deciding to look out the side window instead, "Who were the two men in the alley?"

Just then, he pulls over into an empty spot. He turns his body in my direction, and with his index finger, pulls my head to face him. "Please, don't fear speaking to me about something. You can ask me anything, and I'll do my best to tell you. Okay?" I nod in understanding, "They are part of my security team. Working to keep me safe—you too."

Oh, well doesn't that just clear everything up then. My inclinations are correct, he has a very well organized security system in place, and somehow he has decided to put me under that umbrella, without even asking me how I feel about it. Whether he likes it or not, we really need to discuss this.

This whole situation just smacks me in the face. He and I… we come from different worlds. I've never in my life needed security. We went to dinner, and he needed not one, but two security guards. I can't even imagine having to live my life that way. During dinner, we talked about so many things. His money, not so much. Yes, he's a lawyer and his family is philanthropic, but that didn't translate for me, he has security threats. "Lizzie, we agreed to talk. I need you to do that. Let me know what's going through that beautiful brain of yours."

"We're very different, Jack. I was raised in a middle-class family. Having security guards in order to go to dinner, is incomprehensible to me. Seeing them, actually guarding you on the street. It puts things into perspective."

"How so?"

"Come on, Jack. I'm not from your world,"

With a very serious tone, "Listen here Elizabeth. Get this straight, right now. I could care less about your bank account. What is important to me, is *you* as a person. Period. By the way, what I'm seeing… I want, very much. Yes, I need security. Yes, I'm wealthy—*very* fucking wealthy. No, it doesn't matter to you. Why? Because I know you really well. At times, I hate my security but it's part of a necessary evil I was delivered into, when I was born. I'm the recipient of an enormous family Trust. By inheritance, my children will face what I'm facing. At times, it's a noose around my neck because being the next in line, my security is paramount. Unfortunately, it makes me a target for potential asshole kidnappers. Since I don't plan on being kidnaped, I have security. While we're at it, anyone I care about, can be a target as a way to get to me. I'm sure you've put together… that means you too. So, please, *please*… don't fight me on this. Be understanding, be accepting, be cooperative, just… let me take care of you. You have security too. Even if you don't like it, or think you need it, you have it because it makes me feel more at ease. Since we're being honest… you've had security since the Christmas Gala. I decided that night, you were mine, and I wasn't going to let you go. They've been around for quite a while, without you really noticing them, so please don't get mad about you having them now."

Here I sit, parked in Jack Loving's BMW, on the side of the road in downtown Richmond, feeling like I've just been run over with a bulldozer. Mouth ajar, I cannot even formulate a sound, or move because I'm paralyzed with information overload. Truly, I don't know whether to slap him or lean over and give him a blow job. I'm that conflicted.

Chapter Seventeen

Shiny Hidden Treasures

Jack

Well, I'm fucked. Totally, perfectly fucked since Lizzie did not like our conversation regarding my security measures. Everything was going well... really well. I was taking her back to her place... things got really nicely heated between us. Then it all went to shit because I could tell she was bothered by something. Of course, it drove me crazy because I don't like it when I can't solve a problem. *I'm a problem solver, Lizzie!*

The last thing I expected to come out of her mouth, sitting on the side of the road, was "I need some time by myself, to think." Fuck. My perfectly laid out plans, where neither of us had kids, was a total bust. Granted, I know it was early for her. For me, this is all I've been thinking about for months. My dick is about to fall off, a case of "blue-dickitis," because I want this girl so badly.

I did what she asked, and took her home. Walking her to the door, I was very unsure what to say or do. Before I walked away, I grabbed her tightly and held on probably much too long. Kissing her on the cheek, and before I walked away, I whispered, "I'm not letting you go, you know, I'm respecting your painful request, for now. You'll see me soon." Then, I left before she could reply. A spear was settled in my gut, twisting more firmly with every step I took.

Today, I'm very exhausted from lack of sleep. Nevertheless, I'm not letting this fester because I have a plan. Sitting outside her apartment, I'm waiting until exactly eight-thirty. That's early enough, but not too early to be rude. Mother wouldn't agree, I'm sure. Watching the clock, I make my move. Running up the stairs, I get to her door and just as I'm about to knock, the door opens. Motherfuck! He's a dead man.

"Well, good morning, Jack!" He says a little too chipper.

Dressed in a comfortable hoodie and jeans, stands before me a man who I know is very conflicted about Lizzie. Knowing it probably wouldn't take much, it truly bothers me how deep their connection runs. "Mark," I reply very tightly.

The door opens wide, and there stands Lizzie also dressed casually, with her hand resting on his forearm. Obviously, they were getting ready to go out. Guess I shouldn't have waited for a certain time, after all. Feeling pretty stupid about showing up, I turn to leave, when I hear, "Jack! Where are you going?"

Throwing my hand up, I shake my head and head towards the stairs. Needing to escape, I just want to hurry to the comfort of my car. Walking rather fast, and focused on thoughts involving Lizzie and Mark, ones that literally make me want to hit my so-called friend, I fail to hear oncoming footsteps. Pulling my car door open, it's suddenly forced shut. Turning around to face the offender, "What the fu—?"

"Don't or I'll lay you out!"

"Lay *me* out?" I scream very insulted and put off by the notion of Mark being able to even get a shot off on me.

So focused and angry at the situation, my private security quickly arrives and forms a wall of protection. They know Mark very well, and they're firmly aware of our close friendship. The situation must be baffling to them, to see us arguing. "Back off!" Mark screams at them. "You're an idiot, Loving! Don't get pissed at me because you screwed up!"

Totally shocked with his assessment of the situation, "I screwed up? What are you even doing here Mark? Want to tell me that? Huh?"

Mark just shakes his head in reply. "Not what you think, obviously."

"Really? Explain it to me then. I come here to straighten things out with Lizzie and I find you here at eight-thirty in the morning. What would you think?"

His face already red with anger, splits into laughter. Full on, barrel full-of-fun, laughter. Watching him, it's like being in a comedy show and suddenly I'm the one being punked. Leaning against my car for support, I crisscross my feet at the ankles, watching while he composes himself. Asshole.

"You're a jealous son-of-a-bitch, you know that?" He continues to laugh.

"Thanks for the assessment. I appreciate it."

"Oh, it's too much. Really, too much. I walked away from the prettiest brunette, legs as long as sin, naked and waiting for me in my bed, because of your sorry ass. I was moments away from getting it after I tied her up and made her… and myself, mind you… wait for thirty fucking minutes! So, I get a call from a very upset Lizzie, and what do I do? Yeah, I leave my sure thing and come here. Not because she wants anything from*me*… dickhead. She was upset over *you*! I was on my way to bring her to *you*. See, if you recall, she doesn't even know where you live."

No way. Feeling like the dickhead he's made me sound like, I bend over and put my hands on my knees. Shaking my head in shame, I did jump to conclusions. The problem is, I just don't know where I stand with her. Between Mark's not-so-hidden interest, and the many hours at the dating place, I'm making myself look like a bitch. Unequivocal, dirt bag of the year. This is not how I saw this weekend playing out. Standing up, I walk over to Mark, extend my hand, "Sorry for jumping to conclusions."

With narrowed eyes, he rejects me, "I told you, do not hurt, Lizzie. I'm not your competition, Jack. You're your own worst competition. Get it straight." He reaches for my hand, shakes it, and immediately leaves in his shiny, red sports car.

"Sorry guys," I say to the security team. A chin lift, common in bro-code, is all that is necessary to clear the air.

Taking my time, I slowly return to Lizzie's apartment. Perfect, now she thinks I'm a raving lunatic on top of everything else. Knowing this could go either way, I prepare for round two of knocking on Lizzie's door. I knock three times and stand back waiting for her reply.

The door opens, and she stands there, an obvious hurt look on her face. Not really knowing what to do, I do the one thing I know I need to gain comfort. Grabbing her face with both my hands, I lower my face to hers, kissing her with as many feelings of sorrow I can muster. When she reaches her arms around me, squeezing me tight, I know. *We'll be fine.*

Walking her backward into the room, I refuse to let her go. I kick the door closed with my foot, reaching behind me, locking the deadbolt. Returning my hand, I grab her around her back, holding her small frame, against me. I whisper a mumble against her lips, "I'm sorry." She shakes her head no and simply replies with a grunt.

Yet again, I can't seem to help myself when I'm alone with this woman. I'm like an octopus, waiting to touch and discover everything about her. Never losing focus on her lips, I open my eyes, staring at her. She slightly hesitates and opens her eyes. *A silent question… a silent confirmation.* That's good enough for me. I pick her up, and she giggles while trying to hold on around my neck. I walk her to her bedroom, standing beside the bed, foreheads pressed together.

"Are you sure?" I ask even though I'm afraid of the answer.

She scans my face and takes her thumb, running it along the crease of my mouth. Such a simple touch, filled with memories of her giving me the exact motion, so long ago. Reaching her mouth to mine, she moans her response. "Yes."

Laying her on the center of the bed, I carefully remove her shoes, socks, and jacket. Looking down at her, I'm suddenly struck with the multitude of ways, I want her. Realizing it's probably best to go slow with her, I take my time. Removing her shirt, a lacy pink bra is revealed. Straddling her, I take my time, kissing every available speck of skin. My fingers, work slowly over her, touching lightly, feeling her shuddered response. While kissing deeply between the "V" of her breasts, my fingers work to remove her pants. Pulling them off, I stand above her, working my hands slowly up the outside of her thighs. Shamelessly moving my eyes up and down her body, "You are very beautiful, Lizzie," I say softly. Reaching down, I kiss her playfully. Sucking on her bottom lip, giving it a gentle nip between my teeth. "You have been on my mind so much, girl." Closing my eyes, I kiss her deeply, laying my body across hers, pushing my hips against hers. Enjoying the feeling of rubbing against her body, even clothed it's good…*too good*. With a moan, she runs her nails across my shoulders, lighting me up through the fabric. "Uh-unh." I piston backward, remove my shirt and lay against her once again. "Yeah, baby. With the nails, I love it." Holding her face between my hands, she presses her nails in my skin, and I moan my satisfaction. With a line that runs straight to my crotch, nails do it for me every time.

"Lizzie, I'm going to make you come so hard, baby. Are you ready, because I won't stop until you do? Multiple times, in fact."

She looks at me with a question in her eyes. I continue to kiss her everywhere: her mouth, her neck, the top of her chest. "I'll try."

I chuckle a rather wicked laugh, "Oh babe, with me, you will. I won't stop until you're exhausted with pleasure. One of us will grow tired, and I guarantee it won't be me." She still doesn't look convinced, but she doesn't know how obsessed I am with sex. She'll feel it, or I'll die trying.

Sitting up, I straddle her, pulling her up against me. She's so beautiful, it's easy to become distracted by her. Her hair, the way it flows down across her breasts, like a trail to all the happy places. Reaching behind her, my spread fingers press firmly up her back meeting at the nape of her neck. Staring at her with heated eyes, I kiss her deeply while my fingers grab fistfuls of her hair. Pulling her head back, my lips are forced to travel from her mouth down the column of her neck. Her sighs fill the room, reminding me to push her further.

Releasing her hair, my fingers return to gentle touches, reaching her bra strap quickly unclipping. Pulling back, I'm sure to gain her attention. "Lizzie, you're beautiful." With a hand on each shoulder, I remove her bra slowly. Taking my first look at her unclothed chest, my breath hitches. She's gorgeous… and oh so fine. Pulling her chest against mine, I take a few moments to appreciate the skin-to-skin contact. Kissing her, my heart rate increases, so excited just to finally feel her and see her. Pushing her backward, I reach down and grasp both of her hands in mine. Pulling them up beside her and above her head, I move them around the slats in her headboard. *Oh yeah, baby. We can do so much with that headboard.* "No matter what... don't move your hands. If you move your hands, I'll stop. Understand?"

"Yeah," she shakily replies.

With narrowed eyes, I know as well as I'm laying here, those hands will move. *Umm... I'm going to have so much fun punishing you, sweetheart.* "Okay, don't let go."

Standing up, I admire the beauty before me, taking my time... making her wait. I grab each ankle, gently squeezing, spreading my fingers wide as I run them up the outsides of her leg. At the apex, I take my time running my fingers over her panties, feeling the warmth therein. With a quick tug, I pull them down and away. "You're beautiful, Lizzie." I can tell she's still nervous although she's squirming her ass around the bed. Spreading her legs, I take a deep breath, anxious to see the presents therein. Holy mother... she's pierced! "Fuuucckkk!" Diving in, in a not so elegant manner, I feel like a kid having sex for the first time. "Oh, Lizzie. That is the hottest thing I've ever seen."

"So... you're okay with it? I only did it last year." She asks very timidly.

My head bolts upward, "O-okay, with it? Honey, you're going to soon find out just how 'okay,' I *really* am with it. I was not expecting it at all, but I'm fucking thrilled with it." Crawling upwards to hold her tightly, I kiss her... hard. "We're going to be quite a match, you and I. Can you trust me, baby?"

"I wouldn't be here with you right now if I didn't think you were trustworthy, Jack."

"Well, I would hope so, but I'm serious. Honey, I am rather obsessed with sex. I like control... more like, I need it. Can you give me your body, Lizzie? I promise to always take care of your needs. We'll go places together, you've never been. Enjoy the ride... together."

"Okay, Jack."

"Good." Finding it difficult to control the smile splitting my face, "For now, we'll keep it light. I need to love on you for a while."

Returning slowly down her chest, I reach her core. Placing each leg over my shoulders, I use my fingers, spreading her lips wide. I'm so overwhelmed, face-to-face with her piercing, straight through the clitoral hood. Sexy as fuck! Moving in, I give her a long and leisurely lick all the way through her sensitive tissues. She squirms as I focus on her clit, lightly but with speed. Her ass moves more, unable to remain still. Her legs squeeze tightly around my head, as I increase the pressure with my tongue.

Breathing heavily, she moans and her chest begins to rise quickly. Moving one leg to the side, I lay my body across it, forcing her down. "J-Jack. That feels so good." Reaching up, I stroke one breast, gently squeezing and massaging. Playing with her nipple, I pinch it gently, feeling it pebble beneath my palm. Moaning loudly, she squirms and her hips buck upward. Then, her hand begins to run around my scalp. Just as she starts to pull, and even though it feels good as shit... I stop everything. No touching, no pinching, no licking... nothing. My body is in just as much hell with no physical contact, but it must be this way. "What? Why did you stop?"

Shaking my head, because it was inevitable. With a firm voice, "Where's your hand, babe?"

"Oh shit! I'm sorry! I'm so, so sorry. I forgot. Really, I won't do it next time. I promise."

I cross my arms over my chest, and I need a minute to calm myself down. My cock strains fiercely against my jeans, begging as much as she is at this point. "Hands around the slats, Lizzie," I command with a very serious tone.

"Yes, Sir."

Oh, fuck. Did she say that intentionally or randomly? Either way, it gets her my attention. Crawling up her body, I lay a sweet, gentle kiss across her lips, followed by a quick nip on her bottom lip. "Good girl." Moving back, I resume my attention to the places I know she wants it. It's so hot to learn everywhere that turns her on. Like a treasure map, waiting to find my riches. Within moments, her hips are moving with the pace of my licks. I squeeze her nipple more firmly, and she screams. The best sound, I've ever heard, "I'm coming, Jack… It… feels… so… FUCKING… good!" Her heart is literally pounding, and her nipples are completely erect. The best… the best part of it all: the taste of her pussy. Good god. She tastes fucking sensational!"

Watching her ride the wave, was hot as hell. Best trip ever by far! Realizing I can't let her come all the way down, I return to focusing my attention to her clit. "No, no, no."

Garbled with a full mouth, "yea, yea, yea." I lick her with laser focus, bringing her clit back. She tries to push her hips away, and I refuse it. Entering two fingers inside her, she takes a loud intake of air. With my palm upwards and my mouth firmly working her clit, I do not stop. I do not waiver. Within just a few minutes, she is screaming the room down. "Shit! Shit! Ahh, that is soooo good! Ahh!"

Moving quickly, I remove my pants and grab a condom from my wallet. Not wanting her to get too far out, time wise, I pull her ass to the edge of the bed. Legs straight up, I push them back, from the back of her thighs. With one quick thrust, I enter her, remaining perfectly still. She shudders from the intrusion, but I knew she was ready. My fingers prepared her well. Pushing her legs all the way back, her ass lifts up slightly, giving me the perfect angle.

Pumping into her, I move slowly, then speed up, always changing the pace. "I want one more, babe,"

Shaking her head, "No, there's no way. You killed me."

Laughing at her, "Oh you're definitely alive. You feel good as shit wrapped around my cock. One more, babe."

"I can't." She said very convincingly.

"Good thing I think otherwise." Pulling out, I stand her up, turning her to lean across the bed. Spreading her legs to my perfect height, I impale her once again. Reaching around, I find her clit with my fingers. Using circular strokes, I rub against her while fucking her tight channel with increased speed. "I want it, Lizzie."

"I can't."

"I want it now, Lizzie."

"I can't!"

Pushing her face all the way forward against the bed, I circle my hips, rubbing at just the perfect angle to arouse her G-spot. With a demanding voice, "Your orgasms are mine now, Lizzie. I want it. Right. Fucking. Now!"

Pushing my fingers as firmly as I can, and in the perfect synch with my thrusts, Lizzie suddenly stiffens board straight, and I know. I know she found it. Fuck yes! With a screaming moan that all the neighbors surely heard, my girl becomes a quivering, satiated woman. Seeing her this way, is all the encouragement I need. Ass in the air, legs spread, hair spread all over her back and bed, I'm done. "Fuuccckkk! Damn, Liz-zie." Bending over, I pull her back tightly into my chest. Enjoying the last moments of connection with her.

"I can't move. You killed me... I'm officially dead."

Kissing the back of her neck and down across the edges of her shoulder blades. "Uh, unh… we've just begun babe. I can't have you dying on me yet."

"Too bad. I'm done." She snickers.

Pulling out, I turn her over. "Stay here. I'll be right back. Returning from the bathroom, I begin washing her reverently. Cleaning her, even though I wish I had truly marked her.

As I'm about to walk away, she grabs me by the arm. "No one has ever done that for me."

Confused, I'm almost afraid to ask. "Which part? Made you come three times or cleaned you up afterward?"

Squeezing me for support, "Both."

Recognizing this is new for her, it makes me happy. "Good." Reaching over and kissing her with a loud smooch, "There'll be more of that sweetheart, so much more. Emphasis on the much more." I state firmly. I roll her slightly and pop her on the bottom and she flinches.

"Hey! What was that for?"

"A warning to get your ass up, so we can shower. I'm taking you to brunch for nourishment. You passing out on me from too much sex and not enough food, doesn't bode well with my plans."

"Oh really?"

With raised eyebrows, I tilt my head and narrow my eyes at her. "I was going to wait on this, but I can certainly introduce your backside to my knee *and* my hand."

"No, no, no." She jumps up, smiling ear to ear.

"That's what I thought." Watching her naked ass prance to the shower, makes me think we may be a little late for brunch. Seeing her reaction to my spanking, and the way I pushed her body for more, just reaffirms my speculation, I may have found a great match in Lizzie Macintyre.

Chapter Eighteen

A Look Inside The Life of Jack Loving, Jr.

Lizzie

Brunch was almost an early dinner. A quick shower turned into a lengthy one, complete with another orgasm for each of us. One thing I've learned about Jack Loving, *he's relentless*! He made a call to nearby Millie's Diner, and, of course, they seated us. Quite a feat actually for the packed house of the best brunch spot in the city. Although, I guess with his name, doors magically open, even if it is nearing the end of brunch.

While enjoying our delicious food, Jack has been quite affectionate. Keeping his free hand, tucked on my lap throughout our entire meal. With a quiet and nervous tone, "We haven't discussed it, and I definitely don't want to argue, but I assume you are accepting of the security measures?"

Breathing deeply, I hesitate to say anything because today has been *so* good, and I don't really want to argue either. "I don't know if *accepting* is the right word?" Looking around, I hadn't really considered where security would be, but I'm sure they're nearby. "Mark and I spoke for quite a while about it. He was helpful in making me see, you live in a very different world than most people. It's not your fault—it's your reality. If I'm going to date you, I need to be understanding of your reality."

With a seriously determined look, "If? No babe, after this morning, you really think I'm letting you out of my sight? No— *not* happening." He laughs determinedly.

"Jack, just as you want me to be understanding of your reality, you need to learn to appreciate mine as well. This is… not how I expected to live my life. You've always had security around so it's second nature to you."

"I realize that, but they are respectful. They know not to intervene unless it's necessary."

"So, when a guy approaches my friends and me in a bar, it's necessary for security to intervene?"

"Oh yes, very necessary."

"Why? He was probably just going to say hello. We would have laughed it off and sent him on his way."

"Well, you didn't need to because the team took care of it."

"Jack, you have to trust me to take care of certain things myself."

"You are a beautiful, sexy woman, Lizzie. Do you have any idea how crazy it made me knowing he touched you? I've been miles away for a very long time, with no access, yet some jackass gets to touch you? Not happening, babe." He shakes his head determinedly.

"Judging by what you've told me, I think this distance has been hard on you. Without me knowing it, you've been really taking care of me. I appreciate it, truly. However, I cannot be swallowed up by you, Jack. I need to feel I'm in control of my life, which is something I haven't felt in a very long time."

Staring at me, his eyes scan my face in deep thought. Not saying a word, his rigid body language says everything. "So, what do you want?" He asks cautiously.

Leaning in close to his ear, "I want to take things slow, but I also want frequent repeats of this morning." My lips find his ear lobe, and gently suck for a brief moment. Just as he turns his head to me, I pull away.

"You're a tease, Lizzie. I have half-a-mind to pull you into the back office and fuck you across the desk." He says quietly and I don't think for a second he's joking.

"Could you really go again after the morning we've had?"

With raised eyebrows, "Is that a challenge, sweetheart?"

Oh, damn. I may have poked the bear. "No, no. I was just inquiring. We're getting to know one another and, well…."

"Well…?"

Feeling very embarrassed, although I'd really like to know. I lean back and whisper, "So… you've come several times already. Surely you need to rest a while. You're not exactly a machine. I wouldn't want you to give out or anything."

Inhaling loudly, he grabs my thigh very firmly. Moving towards the inside, he makes methodic, small circles, not concerned about any possible audience. Laser focused on me and only us, "Lizzie, you are going to get the full-on treatment tonight. Since you apparently think I'm too old to keep up, I intend to show you, in lengthy… tremendously frustrating, detail… just how controlled I can be." Then, just as he is about to move closer to the place I want the most, I hold my breath… waiting. Willing him… totally oblivious to our surroundings. "Spread your legs," he whispers. Taking a quick look around, I shake my head, "no." "Either you spread your legs or I do it for you. And, trust me, you'll have to figure out how to be quiet, because I sure as fuck will enjoy you drenching my hand, when I make you orgasm right here, in the middle of Millie's." Shocked by his proposal, I bite my bottom lip. Hoping if I need to, I can refocus myself with pain rather than pleasure. "Oh… do you know how sexy that lip is, and how much I want to bite you right now?"

"No," I answer breathlessly.

"No, but you will." With laser focus, he pushes my legs apart, grasps the small ring on my clitoral hood… and pulls gently, then twists and flicks. The feeling is so overwhelming. It feels good, but it's not quite enough. It sets me on fire, wanting more… needing just a little… lower. I helplessly squirm ever so gently, totally caught in his grasp. "Hmm… something feel good?"

"Y-yeah," swallowing hard.

"I want *all* your orgasms, Lizzie. Anytime—*any* place, of *my* choosing. Trust me, you will never need to be worried about my cock. You, on the other hand? You need to rest that sweet, sweet pussy. I wouldn't want your cunt hurt from overuse. By the way… I'm seriously not joking about this. Therefore, be a good girl… be nice, and wait patiently."

He kissed me hard on the mouth, pulled away, and just as quickly stood up from the table. Reaching his hand out to me, he winks, and motions towards the door. Feeling rather left on the hook, I sit there speechless. How can he get me so worked up… again? Then, just get up, ready for us to leave? Grabbing his hand in frustration, I walk out. Not surprisingly, I overhear his joy of my turmoil left unfilled in my panties.

After Millie's, Jack takes me to his office building. It's huge! Giving me the grand tour, he explains his mother wisely purchased the building, and currently they lease the space unused by his law firm. The view from his office is really something. He explains that on a clear day, he can see for miles and miles. Overlooking the James River, it's quite the scenery to have from an office window. When days are stressful, it must be nice to look out across the city.

"You're fortunate to have this view, you know?"

"Oh, I certainly know indeed." Pointing down the river, "You see what is down there?"

Squinting to see, I finally realize it's my apartment building. "That's my building, right?"

"Ah, yes. It's my building too." He chuckles.

I land a playful punch, "You know what I mean."

He feigns pain, "I do. I'll be totally honest with you, Lizzie. More time than I feel was wise, I've stood in this spot, staring at your building in recent months. Not being able to see you, it was the next best thing."

"Oh, Jack." Walking over to him, perched on the corner of his desk, I wrap my arms around his neck. Holding him tightly, he holds me too. Standing there, in each other's comfort, it's odd we've moved so fast. Something nagging in the far recesses of my mind, tells me, "slow down." While my heart, which is thundering in my chest at his nearness, tells me "this is comfort, safety, generosity and more." It's a scary feeling being near this man. The more I learn about him, the more attached I grow. *Even though, he seems to enjoy my company, what if he should crush me? Would there be anything left of my already fragile soul? Are our backgrounds so diverse that we might not have common ground? Or, the really gutting thought: would he get bored with me... a widow with two children?*

Squeezing his neck tighter, he pulls back, grasping my face between his hands. He watches me carefully, saying nothing. Moving his thumb to the center of my mouth, he rubs to each corner, and back to the center. "You're so beautiful," he whispers. Pulling my face to his, he kisses me softly with his generous mouth. Holding my head firmly, he controls our kiss, dancing his tongue through my mouth. Feelings of warmth rush through my body. Moving one hand to my back, he pulls me closer to him. Grinding his hips into me, I feel his hardness press into my abdomen. Reaching slowly downwards, I run my hand down his side, landing in the center of his crotch. Grasping him firmly, he moans into my mouth, encouraging me to run the length of him. Even though we played for hours today, he wouldn't let me touch him fully. Every time I tried, he told me "No, babe, this is all about you. I've waited forever to pleasure you." Then in the shower, he pushed me spread eagle, hard against the shower wall. He fucked me standing up. That was new, and so, so good.

As his hips begin to fully gyrate in my hands, he pulls away completely. Shaking his head, he blows air through his lips, calming himself. "First, I want to feel nothing more than your hands on me. But, I don't want to start it here. We need to be sure you're not too sore because I have very…," kissing my neck up and down, "very," kissing the opposite side of my neck, "kinky things I want to do to this amazing body later tonight." Returning to my lips, he kisses me deeply and squeezes me tightly to him. "Come on, I'll finish showing you around."

With intertwined fingers, unfortunately, he pulls me through his empty offices. Pointing out specific people, he said I should remember their names, "just in case." *Ok… what does that mean?* One, in particular, his assistant, Patricia. Apparently, she's very loyal to his family and excellent at her job and very discreet. He spoke very highly of her. A burn moves through me at the thought of him working so closely with someone. Until I looked around her office and saw many pictures of group family photos. Several were close-up shots of her, and her husband. The love was apparent. Whew, an immediate relief. He pointed out his father's offices and even an office that his mother uses on occasion when she's in the building. It must be nice to work closely with your family and have such a warm relationship with them. Every time Jack speaks of them, the love in his eyes is very obvious.

After we fully covered the dynamic building I've admired a million times, in the Richmond skyline, we leave hand-in-hand. "There's someplace I want to take you."

"Okay, Mr. Tour Guide operator. Show me what's next." He kisses me on the nose, and after opening my car door, we're off through the city yet again.

Driving on East Franklin Street, we pull into the private lot for the Pohlig Box Factory. Previously used as a paper box manufacturing business, the building was refurbished into loft apartments. Since it's not far from my apartment, I've noticed and admired the major renovations. Once we've parked, Jack rounds the car quickly, opening my door. Reaching a hand inside, "Come with me." He looks so happy. As if he's been waiting for this moment like a little kid.

Stepping out of the car, "There are apartments here. Why are we here?"

Biting his lip, I can tell he's excited… but nervous. "I want to show you something." Stepping inside, I can tell immediately this place is super cool. I love to see old buildings renovated for the next generations to enjoy. Exposed brick are met with granite and concrete. "Every apartment is uniquely different here. There are only sixty-five total." Pressing "three" the elevator zips us up, and we're faced with "P2" stamped on a beautiful old wooden door.

Opening the door, he stands back, allowing me to enter first. My mouth totally drops open. As I scan the space, it's beautifully decorated. Shades of brown, copper and cream, make everything look warm and inviting. Comfortable couches and an industrial-looking kitchen, confuse my mind on where to go first. "This is amazing, Jack! It's... just beautiful."

"I'm really pleased you like it, but you have so much more to see."

Turning to face him, "Who lives here exactly?"

Grabbing my hand, he pulls me to sit down with him on the couch. "Lizzie, we've been avoiding certain subjects up to this point. However, I think we need to cover a few topics."

My stomach fills with butterflies, and I'm really nervous. Yet again, I'm getting one of those feelings like my life is about to change. "Okay," I cautiously respond.

He turns to face me, then suddenly changes direction and pulls me into his lap. "Now, that's better. I can hold onto you so you can't run." Then he leans in, giving me a warm, sweet kiss. "We haven't discussed my children and we also haven't discussed my divorce." Closing my eyes, I don't know if I'm ready to hear about his marriage, but I guess it was sure to come up at some point. "Victoria and I were married over ten years, and when we had the twins, Bryce, and Grace, it was a surprise. Her birth control failed, but it turned out to be the best surprise ever. I love my kids so much, and it hurts me tremendously to see them go through our divorce. There is something, I want to tell you, but you need to keep it very confidential."

"Absolutely, no worries. I wouldn't betray your trust, Jack."

Holding me firmly around the side of my face, he pulls me in for a quick kiss, "I believe you, sweetheart. Not many people know the entire sordid story. It's not pretty, and honestly, it makes me mad as hell to discuss it because reliving it, just makes me angry. But, I want you to know what's going on.

"Victoria had a difficult childhood. Her parents were extremely controlling and honestly, we never saw eye-to-eye. It's hard for me to admit it, but I was nothing more than a checkbook to her. Straight from the start, I knew it but chose to ignore it. We met in college and when she realized I came from a wealthy family, she suddenly gave me her attention. Well, I guess you can imagine the rest. Eventually, we married and went on to have our children.

"I am the recipient of the Bowes Family Trust. It originated with Rudy Bowes who was a self-made man. He was a farmer who had a heart of gold. My mother inherited and after making very shrewd business decisions, she increased the value of the Trust, tremendously. We have made it our mission to serve the underprivileged, and fund charities we believe will have the greatest impact on our local region. Therefore, we continue to sponsor worthwhile events, raising additional capital.

"When Victoria and I married, I immediately decided to include her in all aspects of my financial affairs. I didn't want her to feel excluded from any part of my life. She attended all business meetings, and socially, she became an integral part of organizing our events. Additionally, she was… or still is, I'm not sure… on multiple boards of different charities. Last year, we changed auditing firms. It's not unusual to change every so often, and it was our time. The new firm found some… *irregularities*." Placing my hand over my mouth and hanging on his every syllable, I immediately think the worse… *no, no please no*. "After quite a bit of digging, they confirmed Victoria had embezzled over three million dollars."

"Oh, Jack, no!"

Shaking his head to confirm it, "It was a shitty time for sure. Honestly, without the strength of my parents, I don't know how I would have survived those dark days. Not only emotionally, but professionally, they intelligently navigated us all through the investigations. Then, afterward, my mother was a viper, squelching any possibility of the story being leaked. Not only did she steal from me, she stole from our children because this Trust is their legacy too."

"Can I ask what she used the money for in the first place?"

"Ah, well, that's the part that hurts the most. She was being pressured by her parents. Her father had gambling debts and a failing business. They had a sense of entitlement and convinced her to forge my name at the bank, withdrawing the money for their dark purposes. It kills me really because three million dollars would have been a tremendous help for quite a few charities."

Oh, damn, he is so right. That is a lot of money and would have been beneficial to so many people. I'm sure he feels guilt, but if she lied, it's on the bitch, not him. Reaching around, squirming in his lap, I hug him tightly around the neck. "It's not your fault, it's hers. You need to move on from this, Jack." Hugging me back tightly, he buries his head in my neck, giving me a slight confirmation. Damn, this is very upsetting to him. I cannot even imagine feeling that level of betrayal.

After a few minutes, quietly holding one another, he pulls away rubbing my back softly. "Anyways... now on to more positive thoughts. I just needed to explain my marriage failure because it was not about cheating." He pauses, looks around the room and grins. "I'm related to the original Pohlig family that owned this building."

"Of-cccooooourse, you are. So, let me guess, you own this building too?"

Throwing his head back to laugh, "Actually, no. I liked what they were doing to the place, and I wanted a piece of it still. So, I signed a short-term lease. Truthfully? When I have the kids, I stay at the house. It's the home they grew up in… it's where they feel comfortable. However, I see her everywhere, so I hate it. I leased this place for several reasons. One, if I don't have to be at home, I'm not. Second, it's close to work. Third… and this is most important… it's close to you. I want us to have someplace without memories of other people."

"Jack. I don't know what to say?"

"You don't have to say anything. I'm just being honest with you. I told you, I've been waiting for you for a very long time sweetheart. Previously, I was so caught up in our past, and there have been times I was fearful, not knowing if we would ever get the chance to have a real future together. This, this is a good day indeed."

"You do realize I have a home, right? And, kids?"

"Yes, I do realize it. I know we'll need to be creative. More importantly, we need to have a serious conversation about the children." *Oh god… what is he saying?*

"This is just moving really fast for me."

Pulling me into his chest, "Stop thinking… just go with it." Interlacing our fingers, "I told you before, just hold on to me, babe."

Chapter Nineteen

Resuscitating Orgasms

Lizzie

The rest of the afternoon, we lazed around watching movies. It was such a simple way to spend time, but in his arms it felt really good. Deciding to opt-in for dinner, we ordered Chinese. It was comical to learn our tastes were identical. General Tso chicken and also chicken with cashew nuts, was a quick decision. Made ordering very easy indeed. I keep having these moments where I ask myself: *is this how rich people enjoy spending their Saturday nights?* Jack seems perfectly content, spread out on his enormous, comfortable couch, me tucked in beside him. It just concerns me that he'd rather be at a fancy restaurant instead.

"What's going through that beautiful head of yours?" He asks obviously observant.

Twisting my head back to see him, "Nothing. Why would you ask?"

"Maybe because you're wringing your hands constantly, and you do that when you're in deep thought? Talk to me."

Releasing my hands immediately, I make a mental note to avoid drawing attention to myself. Rolling my eyes, "I think we need an understanding of sorts. Being able to ask the other questions, and receiving an honest answer in return, is very important."

"Agreed. What's the question?"

"If you weren't with me at this exact moment, where would you be tonight? I hardly think you'd be hanging out on your couch, watching movies, and eating Chinese food."

"O-okkkkay, I'll answer honestly, but let me ask you something first. Would you ask this question if I was a normal guy, making a middle-class salary?"

Thinking careful, he's probably right, I wouldn't. "No, but because we're different, I'm concerned you'd rather be out doing something more important instead of spending it this way."

"Total honesty... when I was married, Vickie had us out every Friday and Saturday night. Sometimes, it was an important event. Largely, it was about being seen and photographed. Except for the charity events close to my heart, I hated going out." Rolling me underneath him, he lays across, careful to support his weight. "Today has been by far, the best day I've had in a very, long time." Kissing me thoroughly, then moving down my neck, "Especially, because I can do this." Pulling my shirt up high around my neck, he kisses across my chest, "And, this..." he pulls my bra cup downward, pushing my breast upward revealing my nipple. "Now, this... this is particularly enjoyable." He licks soft licks across my nipple, then faster. Bringing it entirely between his lips, he sucks carefully, then harder, ending with a faint nip. Shocked at the slight pain it was incredibly enjoyable, sending a line of pleasure straight to my clit. Breathing erratically, I press my hips upwards, hoping for pressure to push against. He moves to the other breast, pulling it free, massaging them both. "Ummm, you like that don't you, baby?"

"Y-yes!"

Sitting up, he removes our shirts and my bra. "I love feeling my skin against yours, especially your hard nipples. Actually, I could suck on your breasts all day." The way he pays so much attention to them, kissing, sucking, lathing and nipping. I don't know how he knows the exact pressure to use, but every time, it sends a shock straight to my core. Burning me up from the inside out.

Removing my pants, he groans at my matching G-string. With three strips wrapping each hip, there's barely a patch to cover the crotch. "Fuck, babe, you have the sexiest panties." Moving the strip to the side, he moves his face close to me, inhaling deeply. "You smell so good. My cock is instantly hard from your scent alone." Removing the panties, he spreads my lips wide and gifts me with one long lick, end to end. Focusing on my ring, I can tell he's infatuated with it, flicking and sucking just enough to drive me crazy. Firm, quick attention paid to my swollen folds, enlarging my sensitive clit causing me to move and twist on the wide, comfortable haven where we have delighted all afternoon.

Standing above me, he inserts first one, then two fingers driving me closer to the edge, causing me to whimper. "Shh, babe. I've got what you need." Within moments, he finds the perfect spot inside me and rubs firmly. He licks up my body, stopping at my nipple, firm and erect. Giving teasing licks, I begin to feel his thumb rubbing my clit while his fingers still torture my channel. It's too much… too much sensation in all the places I crave. Breathing irregularly, I try to remain still, grabbing onto the couch forcing myself to enjoy the phenomenal ride. "Bare down, Lizzie. Squeeze baby." Doing as he says, his hands work at a furious rate, and squeezing as hard as I can, he gives a harder bite to my nipple and that's… *it*. I can't breathe, and my legs are locked, as my orgasm rolls through my body, overwhelming me completely. "Fuck that's hot! Watching you… it's incredible, just incredible." His lips attack mine, even the slight whisker-stubbled jaw further assisting my post orgasmic bliss. Once I come out of the fog, I open my eyes to him taking his time, licking my essence from his fingers. Oh, so dirty, but a turn on none the less. "Ummm, I need a bigger taste." He bends down, taking his time retrieving all of my juices. I try to push him away because I'm so sensitive, but he will have none of it. Taking my wrists, he holds my hands by my sides and licks me until he has his fill.

He crawls up my body, "Kiss me." He explores my mouth with a combination of deep and shallow licks. He whispers, "Do you taste yourself?" I shake my head, "Good, now you understand why it's every man's fantasy because you taste fucking *great*." Embracing him tightly, he really knows how to build a girl's confidence for sure. "Do you trust me, Lizzie?"

"Yes."

"Good. Lay on the rug." The "rug" as he calls it, is more like a cashmere sweater. I've never seen carpeting so soft. Laying down, I stare with great interest as he removes his pants and boxers. Heaven only knows how I will ever leave this man if for no other reason than to watch him walking around sans clothing. Obviously, he works out. Having a chest fit for a magazine, means he spends quite a bit of time in the gym. A thin, dark line of hair, trails down his chest, straight to the goodies below. Looking at him, causes me to behave crazily. I'm locked in to his body, tuning out everything going on around me. So, when he looks at me with a concerned face, I know I've totally checked out.

"Huh? Did you say something?"

Luckily, he judges the situation accurately and doesn't hold it against me. "Do you know what a turn on it is, to watch you staring at me? Like I'm your last meal?"

"Really? Because... I'm a little embarrassed. You really shouldn't be so lethal, you know. It's not fair to all of womankind."

"Well, as long as you're the one I'm sparring with, I'll kill you over and over, bringing you back to life with my resuscitating orgasms."

"In that case, kill me, *please.*"

Narrowing his eyes and trying unsuccessfully not to smirk at me, "Babe, you have no idea." Once I'm laid out on my "cashmerian" pillow, with a serious tone he asks, "Do you have a safe word, Lizzie?" *Oh, hell, here we go.*

"Yes. It's samaritan. Philanthropic is too long." I joke.

"Interesting choices, but very appropriate." He moves to lay down on his side facing me. You need to understand something about me. We need to be in total agreement, or I *will* stop. Or, you need to safe word if you're uncomfortable with some aspect of our play. I'm *very* serious about this, Lizzie. We're not kids, we're adults who have lived married lives. We need to be able to trust each other, to speak up if something's not quite right."

Listening to him, I'm met with a very serious side of his personality. One that is probably somewhat used in the battles of the courtroom. At times, I've sensed he was holding back with me, taking it slowly. Feeling very nervous, yet excited, I am really looking forward to fun times ahead, "I'm in complete agreement, Jack. Don't look at me like some fragile flower, because I'm not. Recent times may have caused me to spiral, but rest assured, at this moment, I'm really looking forward to all the different ways you're planning to have your way with me."

He inhales suddenly, not expecting my bold response. Sitting up, he reaches for my discarded panties. "Actually, I'm going to change my original plans I had intended for you. Lizzie, I'm a *creative* person sexually. You haven't had the chance to learn that yet, but you will. I'm not a DOM, in the true definition of the word. Because to me, a true DOM lives the lifestyle one hundred percent of the time. However, I'm more DOM-like, than not. There will be times we may use the DOM/sub-labels, but you should understand this is really about finding our comfort levels. You, whether you realize it or not, are absolutely submissive."

"No, I'm not!"

"You are babe. We're not going to get into a full-blown discussion about it, especially when I'm about to have my way with you—*but you are submissive.*" *How can he label me that way? I enjoy leading in the bedroom, so that's ridiculous.* "Stop thinking… listen." Trying to decide if I want to vent about this now, he places his thumb in the center of my mouth. "Look, I'm taking things slow with you, for a variety of reasons. We'll get to all the places I want to go with you, eventually. For now, I need to do something with this smart mouth you seem to have."

He calls it "smart mouth," I call it having wit. "What did you have in mind?"

"Oh, you're going to find out right now. Tell me again, what's your safe word, sweetheart?"

"It's good samaritan."

"Elizabeth, I'm not fucking around about this. Give me the safe word, and unless you want to be over my knee, you won't joke about it." *No, he wouldn't. Would he?*

"Fine, it's samaritan, SIR!"

With a surly groan, he places a pillow under my shoulders and neck, causing my chin to point upwards, unsupported. He grabs my hands and pulls them above my head. "Huh huh huh, a woman after my own heart. You want to know one of the best ways to curb your mouth?" I shake my head timidly, "Fuck it." In about two seconds flat, he ties my wrists to the leg of the coffee table, using my panties. Bending his face close to mine, "You good?"

"I'm great."

"Good. I cannot even tell you how many times, I jacked off imagining this little scene. You, at my mercy, just waiting for me. Real life is so much better, I must say." Giving me a quick, yet hard kiss, he pulls away. Positioning himself to straddle my body, I'm nearly face-to-face with a beautifully, impressive cock. This is the first time he's allowed me, an up close and personal view. Not even totally hard, he's very well endowed. Grabbing himself with one hand, he begins to slowly stroke right in front of me. Up and down, followed with an up with a twist on the end. He's so masterful the way he rubs himself. The entire time, he has a very controlled look on his face, staring into my eyes with total concentration. He lengthens and bends slightly forward, holding at the base, he pushes the head along my mouth slowly. From the center, moving to both sides… that seems to be our "thing" we do. "Stick your tongue out." With a slight movement of his hips, he runs the mushroomed cockhead all along my tongue. Seeing it glisten, is a major turn on. I move to enclose my lips over the head, and he pulls back immediately. "No… it's for me this time babe." God, I think I may convulse, right here on my cashmerian cloud of lust. He smacks his dick all over my mouth and tongue. "Yeah, I like this little smart mouth of yours. I think I'll fuck it. Open your mouth, and tilt your head backward." I comply, looking back behind me. He moves around in the opposite direction, straddling my arms above my head. He enters my mouth and scoots nearer to me. Pumping his hips, his cock easily slides in and I close my mouth around him. With my lips around him tightly, I can't see his expression and it's maddening. "There's a reason I love this position. It opens your throat more, and I get the benefit of having you deep throating, more easily." The moment I sense he's really enjoying it, he throws his head back and releases a gloriously loud moan. Yeah, I know he's enjoying it.

Using one hand on the floor to support his weight, the other hand sweetly caresses the side of my face, "Fuck, Lizzie. I've wanted this for so long. You just don't know how badly, I've wanted your mouth around my dick." Continuing to easily move in and out, I focus on relaxing my throat. Moving my head backward slightly more into the floor, I take in more, easily sliding his large cock down my throat. When I manage an exaggerated moan, it excites him to new levels. Suddenly, he spins around in the opposite direction, and I can see his face more clearly. He fills my mouth with his massive erection. Although there is no way I can take him fully, not having a gag reflex, is a *very* good thing.

Placing both hands on the floor beside my head, He holds his body above mine, except for our intimate connection at my mouth. His muscles are flexed, and I'd give anything to run my hands over them. We must really look a site. I'd give anything to have a view from above, seeing the muscles in his ass and legs as he pumps himself fully into my mouth.

"Your mouth is golden, babe." He watches my face carefully, probably to make sure I'm okay. "One day... I'm going to paint it white, but not to-day!!" He pulls out of my mouth, pivots on one knee, and lets out a riotous roar. Stroking himself until streams of cum, spray across my breasts. He shakes his head and looking at him, he reminds me of an Adonis with a sheen of sweat covering his now pumped, muscled chest. The guy is a pure masculine addiction to my brain.

He reaches up, untying my restraint. Pulling my arms down, he first rubs my shoulders, then working down to my wrists. He kisses all around them. Reaching for nearby tissues, he lovingly wipes everything away. Lying next to me on his side, he pulls my head into his and kisses me gently. Embracing me fully, "Thank you. That felt amazing!"

"I rather enjoyed it myself. You've been keeping that massive cock away from me, so it was about time."

"Ah, well, maybe so, but only because I've had this exact fantasy in my head for so long, I wanted it to happen like this. Actually, not exact because that felt *far* greater than I ever expected. Damn, girl! You almost had all of me in your mouth. It felt fantastic I must say."

Suddenly feeling shy, "Good, I'm glad you enjoyed it."

Running his hands all over me, I've noticed he's very affectionate after sex. He seems to need that connection. The centering and grounding feeling of post-coital bliss. "Talk to me: anything you weren't all that into?"

"No, I really enjoyed it." Turning my face into the crook of his neck, "I like being restrained."

He groans sexily, pushing me down to my back, he kisses me, "Don't hide from me. I want you to feel like you can tell me anything, and I'm a talker so be warned. Knowing how you feel about new things we try, is important to me."

Taking a deep breath, "Okay, several things, in fact. One, I like kinky sex so you won't have me complaining. In fact, bring it on Mr. J. Second, on a more serious note, I have a little bit of whiplash at how fast this is moving." I quietly confide.

"And yet… I feel like I've been waiting forever to spend time with you."

Somehow I feel this moment is as raw as any we could have at this point with one another. Me: reawakening from a terribly deficient marriage. And, Jack: finally enjoying the object of his obsession after anonymously controlling my life from afar—me.

"We really are at different places aren't we? Jeremy's death really sent my life spiraling because I blamed myself."

Rubbing my body with long comforting strokes, "Can I ask you something?"

"Sure."

"I was really caught off guard when I saw Mark at your apartment this morning. Now, I'm pissed at myself for walking off the way I did. It seems to be the elephant in the room for me, and I guess I'd like to clear it up some if I can. He has told me or alluded to, you two being friends. Good friends, in fact, which is surprising, because I have known him for a long time and never knew him to have close platonic female friends."

"We are very close friends. That's very true. If you're asking if I've slept with him, the answer is no." He visually relaxes before me. I didn't realize this bothered him as much as it apparently did.

"I've seen you two together at events. You looked *close*. It irritated the shit out of me, but at the same time, Mark would seemingly taunt you to me so I couldn't figure out his game."

"He is a charming 'ole fox isn't he?"

"Yeah, very charming." He quips sarcastically.

"Don't be jealous, Jack. Mark constantly sings your praises. Last night when I went home alone, I texted him about the whole silly ordeal. He talked me back from the cliff and he's your biggest advocate for sure."

Shaking his head, he evaluates my explanation. "One final question, then I'll leave it alone. "Why was Jeremy so upset the night of the Gala? He made some disgusting accusations about you, sweetheart. And, he was convinced Mark played a part. Why?"

Oh my god, if ever there were a time for my casmerian pillow cloud to swallow me up, please let it be now! "Jeremy was a very jealous man when he was drunk. I'm sure finding me at the Christmas Gala, at the

Jefferson Hotel, was a shock for him. Our lives had grown totally apart and seeing me there at the benefit, as Mark's business guest, was too much for him. He lashed out in the worst way possible."

"Obviously, in the worst way. I wanted to punch his lights out for the way he spoke to you. When I heard the venom he was spouting, it took me to new heights."

With him wrapped around my body, my mind is reeling. What if Jack finds out I was Mark's paid escort? Based on his firsthand account, he might believe Jeremy. He'll think I was a prostitute! My mind is spinning. Should I tell him everything, or let it go? I know Mark would never betray my trust, making it into something it wasn't.

"Actually, one final, really final question?"

Smiling at him, because he really does seem to want to know about me, "Sure."

"Why the clitoral ring?"

I bust out laughing, "I was wondering when you'd ask! Actually, it was my symbol of independence if you will. On a whim, a few weeks before the Christmas Gala, I did it. My friends were all discovering new areas of their sexuality, and I always heard it was amazingly stimulating for clitoral orgasms, so I did it. I was too afraid to pierce the clit because it's too much chance for error if you go to the wrong person."

"Well, I'm ecstatic about it. In fact, time for round two," he states definitively, slowly moving down my body. Pushing my legs up, he firmly holds my thighs against my chest. Soon overwhelmed with his ministrations, all thoughts and worries quickly waste away.

I can't breathe!" Too much smoke… I can't see either. My eyes are open but it's black everywhere and my eyes are beginning to hurt. Rubbing them, it feels like there's sand inside. A faint flash catches my attention, so I focus hard on it. Oh no! "FIRE! FIRE," I yell as loud as I can. No one can hear me or if they can, they aren't answering.

Trying to move, I feel something heavy laying across my legs. Pushing with all my might, I realize it's a… it's a person. A body, a heavy person. "HELP!! Someone, please help me!" Rolling out from under the weight, I climb through towards the fire, hoping to get a better look.

Our car, we're in my mom's minivan. Looking beside me, I see her slumped toward the window. Shaking her, "Mom, wake up! You have to wake up!" She cries out once in pain. "Elizabeth," she says weakly. "It's all up to you now. Be strong baby and save them. I-I can't." "We need you! I love you, Mommy," I beg her in reply. With a big breath in, she squeaks out, "Be good to one another, my dear babies! Always be friends—never allow senseless feuds to split you. I will watch over you from above. My love will always guide you. Goodbye…"

Then I hear screaming, high pitch screaming so loud it's piercing. "Shut up! Stopppp!" It doesn't stop… the screams prevail… they never stop, they live on. Watching the minivan from afar, I see a woman who has stopped to help, I yell to her… "THERE, OVER THERE!" Then… the piercing screams… just… stop.

"Lizzie! God, please, Lizzie!" I feel myself being shaken. I can't breathe. The tight restraints around me are holding on so viciously. "*Please*, Lizzie, wake up baby. Come to me sweetheart, I'll save you. I love you baby, come back, *please*."

I hear something in my ear, a whisper over and over. Feeling drenched with water, I push out of my restraints that bind me. My face is wet with tears, and I look up into the very concerned face of the most beautiful man ever. He whispers a silent prayer and picks me up, carrying me into the gigantic bathroom in the apartment, where we stayed last night. Setting me on the floor beside the tub, he turns the tub on with whirlpool jets. Without saying a word, he carefully removes the t-shirt I wore to bed, sans panties. Already naked, he lifts me into the warmth of the awaiting lavender-filled water. With a constant hand on me, he places me between his legs, constantly caressing every part of my body.

In his arms, I cry. Huge sad tears for a dream, I only remember pieces of. Everything seemed so real like it was happening right in front of me. Jack remains completely and totally silent. Never asking me to retell any part of it, just providing a constant source of attention and affection.

Oh, this man. Never in a million years, did I think I would be here, in the new apartment with a man I hardly know. *This man*, who has shown me incredible compassion, care, and concern. *This man*, who in my darkest hour, cared for my children and myself when I couldn't hardly do it myself. *This man*, who paid my rent, my food, hired security in case I really made a bad decision. *This man* ... whom I have come to depend on, and didn't even know it, much less know why. *This man*, who now has the power to hurt me, break me, leave me shattered. *This man*, whom society judges as a great humanitarian, but hardly know the great tremendous heart of his soul. *This man*, who has gotten very attached to me and because of my fucked-up life, stands to be publicly disgraced by my job as an escort. Never mind it, I never had sex on-the-job, only supported my kids—society won't care about it because sex is scandalous. *This man*, whom I vow to always protect, no matter how long we may be together. He shall never know about the real job with Ms. Martin. It's so easy to love this man. *Maybe… I already do.*

Chapter Twenty

The Rivers Are Flowing

Jack

After putting Lizzie in the bed last night following her night terror, I couldn't sleep. Staring at the walls, the ceiling, out the window. Nothing allowed my body to shut down, after an experience like she had. It killed me to see her so traumatized. Wanting to take it all away, I did the next best thing—provided love, comfort, and safety.

Finally, around five a.m., I messaged the security team to place an order with Leonard. Ordering a fully catered breakfast, I hope when she wakes up, she might be hungry. My brain knows my heart is wrong, she'll refuse it all.

As the hours pass, I watch her. Totally focused on her breaths, the little noises she makes in her sleep, even the way she scratches the itch on her nose. *This is what I wanted.* These are the simple things I wanted to see her do, on a daily basis. My heart is terribly hurt, knowing the reason she's sleeping so late, is because she's totally, mentally drained. Not wanting to wake her, but, unfortunately, aware of the hours quickly passing, I make the decision to rouse her from sleep.

Laying down beside her, I make gentle circular motions on her back. Kissing her shoulder with quick pecks, leading up her neck, she squirms releasing sexy little moans. Moving to her back, I gently climb on her, careful not to use all of my weight. Paying special attention to her chest, I kiss in the valley of her breasts, gently licking between each kiss.

She lifts slightly, grabbing either side of my face. Her eyes are barely open, as she begins kissing me everywhere. Chill bumps cover my body, as she runs her hands down my back, scraping me deeply, with nails making me instantly hard. Grinding my pelvis into her, I enjoy the contact my cock receives against her nearly bald pussy. The wet heat, is too much to bear, and I relax my contact against her.

"No, don't stop. Make love to me, Jack. Please."

Closing my eyes, I relish the sound of the words. So many times, I have masturbated, envisioning she would make this exact statement. Feeling so conflicted because she had such a bad night. She most assuredly needs time to process what happened, and heal from it. "Babe," I reply looking in her eyes. Noticing my hesitation, she reaches down, grabbing my cock and begins stroking it. Once the hardness meets her approval, she holds it firmly in her hands, placing it at the edge of her wet heat. Struck by her initiation, and anxious to see her working me, I lift up, watching for her next bold move.

She runs my cockhead through her swollen folds, circling around her enlarged clitoris. The cold metal of her ring, in stark contrast to her well-heated core, sends shivers down my spine. Fuck, this woman is a test for even the best man's control. With a firm hand, she raises her hips, pushing my cock into her tight channel.

"Oh, shit, babe. Wasn't expecting that." Lifting upwards, she pulls me back down on top of her. I look at her questioningly.

"Make love to me, Jack."

Kissing her with a quick hard peck, "Impatient much? Let me get a—"

"No. Bare. I want you so much. More importantly, after last night, I *need* you really badly."

"Lizzie, you're not thinking straight. We don't have to rush this, we have time."

"I am thinking straight. Actually, never more clearly in my entire life. I'm on the shot, Jack, and it's not like I have anything. You'd have to be doing something to catch it."

Trying hard not to laugh, and failing, I really look at her carefully. She's very determined. Not showing any signs of distress, or anything that would lead me to be cautious at the moment. "Are you absolutely positive about this, honey? Trust me, I really want you without a rubber. I won't even lie, but it's a big step. The *final* step, towards owning your body. You need to know what this means for us. "

She lifts her head and kisses me sweetly. Holding the back of my head, I feel her other hand grip me fully. Once again, she lifts her hips, pushing me inside. Reaching around, she grabs my ass, pulling me down on top of her. "Oh…Jack, J-Jack, it feels s-so good." As I begin to pump into her, the slick, wet heat overwhelms my senses.

"You have by far, the best…pussy. Damn Lizzie, I imagined this day, I hoped for this day, I even prayed for this day. Even still, it doesn't even compare to my dreams. This…is…*mine*." Between each hard stroke, "Mine, mine, mine." Moving my hips in a circle, I grind my fully engorged cock into the deep spot within, setting me on fire every time. "I don't give a damn what happens in the future,

I'm *never* giving this away. You need to sign-on babe because you're under contract."

Kneading her breasts in my hands, I sit up, resting on the back of my heels. Lifting her ass up on my thighs, I hold her hips firmly. Pulling her body into mine, as I piston my hips into her. Reaching down, I massage and firmly caress her generous breasts. Watching them bounce and sway, is the epitome of every young boy's wet dreams. Her nipples… *oh so sexy*, are the perfect size. Pretty pink and beautifully proportioned, they couldn't be more perfect. Licking my fingers, I tweak them between my thumb and index finger. "Oh, yes! I love it when you pinch my nipples."

"I bet you do. You'll especially love it one day, when I make you come by only nipple play." She gives me a small smile. "No, no… don't doubt it. You will get there. You and I will go ev-e-ry-where, together. Just you wait and see." Bending over, I stretch my legs back out to a full length, kissing her passionately. She moans in my mouth, encouraging me. Leaning back, I rewet my fingers and begin circular motions on her clit. Arching her back, she gets a strained look of concentration on her face. I know she's building. Her inner core is squeezing me painfully, but in an oh-so-great way. Pressing more firmly, her breaths become shallow, and her nipples stand fully erect. "Come, baby. Come all over my bare cock." With one hand, I move her legs closer together, bending them, pushing her ankles together. Enabling her pelvis to lift, she's at the perfect height, for me to move my hips, working her in the circular pattern she responds so well to. All at once, she explodes, a sudden gush of liquid, washes all around us, flowing down our legs leaving me… and her, totally saturated. She screams out, I don't know if from horror or from delight. *Personally, I'm fucking stoked!* Watching the wave ride out on her face, I'm anxious to see the lake effects. Pulling out, I spread her legs, "Oh fucking, YES!" Diving in, I bury my face in the saturated juices. Happy as a clam, I am so involved with clean-up, I suddenly notice she isn't saying anything, much less speaking. Forcing myself to stop, even though I *really* didn't want to, I lift up to find her hands covering her face. "Hey, what's wrong? Are you, okay?"

Refusing to remove her hands, I move up beside her. Pulling her hands away, "Stop, I'm embarrassed."

"For what? It was the hottest thing I've ever seen."

She looks at me, mouth totally dropped in horror. "How can you say that?"

"Ah, because you squirted, and it's really sexy… and for the record I want you to do it again."

Sitting up, "No, no, no. Not happening, and that wasn't… that wasn't… I don't know what that was, because it was a freaking river. And, by the way, that word is gross."

"I know! Great, right?" I chuckle, happy as hell recalling the moment it happened so unexpectedly.

"Jack! Be serious."

"I am serious. Wait… wait a minute. Is that the first time that you squirted? Excuse me, had a female ejaculation?"

Bowing her head, "Yeah."

Practically tackling her, I force her backward, "We're far from over, and, by the way, get used to the word because you'll hear it again." Re-entering her, I continue fucking her to sounds of a sloppy wet channel. Rolling my head back, I hold an ankle in each hand, driving inside of her. Totally enjoying myself, I lose track of time. When she grabs her titties between her palms, squeezing and playing with her nipples, I… totally… lose it. End of game… shot clock—zero. Dropping down on top of her, I'm completely drained. Being able to come inside of her, has to be the hardest time I've ever orgasmed in my adult life. It felt *that* good. Barely able to speak, sweat down my back and breathless, "You're amazing."

"If you say so." She says meekly.

Lifting my head, "Stop. You don't understand, but squirting is every man's dream. Baby, you soaked me and I loved every millisecond. It's about positioning, plus you're learning to control your body, it's a *good thing*."

"Control? That felt like a disaster."

"Honest question: did it feel different, but in a good way?"

"Truthfully… I was so overwhelmed by how good it felt, it was probably the best ever. But… I don't think that's what it was… and explains why I'm embarrassed."

Grabbing her and holding her tightly, I look at her intently. I want her to know, this is the best fucking thing ever! "Honey, listen to me, this is *not* what you fear it is. I promise you. Since it's the first time, it can be rather disconcerting. As long as I'm ecstatic, which, by the way… I'm over the fucking moon. Next time, I'll be more prepared. My girl needs three towels!" I laugh happily.

Feigning an insult, "You're a nut, you know that?"

"Maybe so, but I'm a happy one. Speaking of nuts, mine was stellar."

"Good."

Running my finger across her cheek, "Hey, I've enjoyed our fun this morning, but I need you to tell me you're at least okay from last night."

And… the shade comes down. "I'm fine, never better." Knowing she's not totally being honest, I let her have a pass for now. Bet your sweet ass though, Monday morning I'm contacting the specialist at VCU Medical Center about her night terrors. *Why is she having them now?* I'm almost convinced it's what they are, not simply a bad dream. However, I need more information before approaching her. That's a conversation which definitely will not be any fun—*for either of us.*

Chapter Twenty-One

Revelations of Dominance and Ex-Subs Who Won't Get a Clue

Jack

I had to explain to Lizzie, I promised to take Bryce to the Science Museum of Richmond today. It's technically my weekend with the children, but they had a planned overnight event so they're returning around lunch time. Victoria tried to pull a fast one, by inviting herself, thank goodness her scheme failed. It's still hard for them to adjust to our divorce, so telling them "no" to a family outing, bothers me quite a bit.

Driving Lizzie to her apartment, I held her hand the entire time. Even walking her to the door, I somehow had this need to feel her skin. Caressing, stroking, kissing her somehow centers me in a strange way. She has a very calming nature about her, and she's not a person who thrives on drama. Thank heavens, because I've lived the drama-filled life, for over ten years. Not going back, hell no.

Before walking away, I asked when I could see her again. It made my day to see hope in her eyes. She seemingly hated the separation, as much as I did. *Doubtful, really.* We agreed to meet for lunch this week, and of course ever faithful texting. Turning to walk away, I took about five steps, then ran back pushing her against the wall. Kissing her deeply, I explored all the deep recesses of her mouth and tongue. Ignoring the catcall from somewhere, I could really care less who sees us, I shamelessly groped her body. Pulling her leg up around my hip, I grinded my cock into her. Feeling just as excited, she held onto me, clawing and climbing up my body. Unable to breathe from feeling so full from her energy, I slowly pull away. "Umm… it kills me to leave you, but I have to. I'll call you later." Appearing just as distressed, I squeeze her tightly goodbye, give a hard kiss to her lips, and walk away briskly. I sat in the car for nearly ten minutes, debating how I could include all of us in one place. After this weekend, it's inevitable so why not start planning now?

"Dad, you're finally home!"

Caught off guard, because I wasn't expecting they would be home so soon, I follow the oncoming onslaught of feet running through the house. Turning the corner, I collide with Grace, dropping my overnight bag, who is barreling through to meet me. "Hey sweetheart," I bend over to hug her.

Quickly on her heels is Bryce, "Can we go now dad? You promised we'd go to the Science Museum today."

"Well, hello to you too son. Can you at least speak to me? How was your weekend?" I ask.

Shrugging his shoulders, which seems to be the pre-teen answer these days, he finally mumbles, "Fine. Seriously, can we go now?

Mom's been waiting for a long time, for you to get here, so we're ready to go *now*."

Fuck. There goes my incredible good mood. *What the hell is she doing here?* "Bry, let me talk to your mom privately, Okay? How about getting some lunch first, and we'll leave in thirty minutes. Good?"

"Yeah, I guess." Just like most pre-pubescent teenagers, he stomps off unhappy.

"Grace, you good with going this afternoon, too? If not, you can stay here with Ms. Phillips."

Rolling her eyes, "I'm not a baby dad. I can stay home without a nanny." Yeah, but the nanny knows how to shoot a gun to protect you against kidnappers.

"I'm sure you could, but you're still too young. Sorry. Decide what you want to do, because we're leaving soon."

Following in her twin's steps… literally, she stomps off too. Damn, I can't make anyone happy today. *Nah, take that back. I know a certain someone who I just left with a happy smile on her face.* Wanting to suddenly call her, I remember I have a situation to deal with… *oh fun.*

Going from room-to-room, I can't seem to locate her. The gnawing feeling inside, tells me exactly where I'll find her. Heading in the direction, I brace myself for the war of words. Opening the door to the bedroom suite, I find Victoria sitting in her favorite wingback chair, she commonly used for reading. Legs crossed, and hands collapsed in her lap, she has her eyes drilled on me from the beginning. It doesn't take a brain surgeon to see, she's irate as hell.

Pausing with my hand on the handle, "Victoria," I greet her formally.

Narrowing her eyes at me, she examines me head to foot. With a locked gaze on my weekender, this… will… be… *bad.* "Jack," she brusquely replies.

Deciding to close the door to insulate raised voices, "Can I help you with something?"

"Apparently," she snipes, "I needed to be here to parent our children in your absence."

"Don't Vickie, I don't want to fight with you today."

Looking at the perfectly pristine bed, she smarts off at it, "Sleep somewhere else, Jack?"

Walking over to my closet, I drop the bag, quietly debating how best to proceed with her. "What are you *really* doing here?"

"I came to see how the children liked their trip. Also, I was hoping you could rise above our differences, and be an adult. We were supposed to go to the planetarium, as a family. You're being unfair to the children to now exclude me, from a trip planned in advance."

Bull's-eye. She is correct, we promised them for years to take them back after the major renovations were complete. It was closed for quite a long time, and all of us missed it. Debating in my mind, whether or not this outing is really in the best interests of the children, is tough. The last thing I want to do is shut myself in a metal box, i.e. the car, riding to and from the museum. My biggest fear, she will say something in front of Grace and Bryce, confusing them into thinking this outing is a way to get us back together. Not going to happen—*ever*.

Apparently waiting too long to decide, she goes in for the jugular. "Is it Erin you're seeing, Jack?" She asks quietly.

"My personal life is just that… *my* personal life. I won't discuss it with you."

"How can you move on so easily, after so many years together?" Her eyes fill up with tears, and even though she ruined my trust in her, deep down I do care for her.

Moving to sit down on the bed, I lower my head contemplating how much to say to her. The lawyer in me is screaming, "Don't tell her anything!" While the man who made a family with this woman, just wants her to move on and find peace. "Vickie, we are divorcing," I quietly begin. "Even though that's the case, I want you to find happiness. With everything which has happened, I *need* some happiness. Please let's not make this any worse—*let me go.*"

Her face is stricken with pain, and a sword shreds my heart to bits for her. With tears streaming down her face, I have to alleviate part of her grief. "Vickie?" She raises her head up and vertical streams of black mascara line her face. Shaking my head, "It's not Erin."

She inhales and quickly covers her face with her hands. Moving her head side-to-side, she starts to cry harder. "Oh, thank god. I wouldn't survive you going back to her. I know you don't understand, but I've always felt inferior to her."

"Well, it's crazy. You shouldn't have felt that way."

She sits, quietly sobbing. Feeling like I need to do something, but knowing physical comfort is out of the question, I give her several tissues. "Thanks." Fuck, this is hard. "What's her name, Jack? Do I know her?"

Should've seen the question coming. Fuck me. Rolling my head around, trying to relieve the tension, I consider her question thoughtfully. Does she even know her—probably not? Victoria is pretty self-absorbed at events, and unless she saw me in awestruck mode, she never paid her any attention. Trying for diplomacy, "Honestly, I don't believe you do. Nevertheless, I don't see any benefit to you knowing her name. We're divorcing and the settlement is finalized. There's no need to create any awkward moments."

Her face crumbles in pain. "No need? Fuck you, Jack Loving! Bryce and Grace are *my* children, and you will *never* replace me in their eyes."

Holding my hands up in a calm-down motion, "Whoa, whoa, who said anything about replacing you? You're their mother. Always and forever, and she of all people would never try to interfere in your relationship."

"What's that supposed to mean? I have a right to know who my children are exposed to. Are you seriously going to tell me you wouldn't be mad as hell if I brought fuck-buddies home?"

"Lizzie is not my fuck-buddy! I care deeply for her!" Watching the exact moment of recognition in her eyes, I realize my mortal mistake. I allowed her to get me going and at first strike, I caved in, exposing her identity. "Dammit, Victoria! Can't you just leave well enough alone? She hasn't met the kids. Happy now? Nothing else should matter. Now, this subject is closed." Now, I'm the one stomping through my own damn house. "By the way, no more just dropping by. Understand?"

"Whatever you say, *husband*. Or should I say, *Sir*?" She sneers at me.

Turning around, I am filled with rage. How dare she mock my authority? Charging up to her, "You are *incredibly* lucky we're not married anymore. Stop your seething, it doesn't become you."

With a venomous smile, "What's the matter, *Sir*? New subbie, unwilling to let you be her DOM?" Staring at her, I quickly count, knowing she's baiting me. Encouraging her bratty behavior will not get her out of this house. She wants me to cave, hoping I'll throw her over my knee and give her torturous pleasure. Vickie loves to misbehave, hoping it will end with a belt and a good hard fuck.

"I'm no longer your DOM, and you sure as fuck are not my submissive. We're finished. Get out of my house."

"You're kidding yourself if you think you don't need a sub! I know better, and I especially know you *will* come back to me. I'd stake my life on it."

Listening to her, I try really hard, not to let her get to me, but she's hit something deep in my psyche. She's probably right about my innate need, and I'm sick about it. Lizzie may have submissive tendencies, but I'm more dominant than she is submissive. Victoria may be right... not me needing her, but me needing a sub. I thought I wouldn't, and I downplayed it to Lizzie, but I may have to face a cold hard fact. If only to myself. How it will effect Lizzie, I'm scared to think about it. Fuck!

"Just to show you how much I don't need you, much less any effect you have on me, I'll be the bigger person today. We'll take the children in separate vehicles. When it's over, you're going back to your suite at the Jefferson Hotel. Alone. I'm returning here with the children."

Walking downstairs, I find the kids patiently waiting. Victoria's clicking heels filling the stairwell, I decide to explain the plans for today, so no one has any false assumptions or expectations. We're doing this for the kids because it was promised for almost a year. Afterward, no more joint family outings. I'm not into playing charades.

Chapter Twenty-Two

Lessons Learned

Lizzie

Sitting in my apartment, alone, is rather miserable. What a strange twist of fate, because not long ago, I preferred to be here alone. Jack brought me back since he was needed at home to meet his children from camp. I was immediately disappointed but knew my kids were returning at five o'clock today anyway. Trying to seem unattached when he was leaving, I failed. He did too, we were practically a weeping mess. I was teary-eyed, he wasn't, but he was very quiet and very clingy. Touching me repeatedly with swipes of his hands, kissing me constantly, and promises of texts and phone calls. It was as if he was leaving for months, not just across town.

It's silly to have this twinge of regret, we had to return to our normal lives. Being with him, felt like a completely new world. One that includes an apartment at Pohlig's just nearby. When you really think about it, everything he does, is with me in mind. He wanted to be in a fresh place, clear of memories with his wife. Even though my apartment, was never a traditional marital residence, I can still sense Jeremy. Everywhere. I see the broken vodka bottles on the table. Or the gin bottle, thrown in the corner, left in broken pieces. Even in my bedroom, I'm haunted by the day I found he had stolen all of our money. Nothing was available to pay rent, much less groceries. It was a terrible day indeed. However, it was the turning point in our lives. I found the advertisement for Ms. Martin, interviewed, hired and sent on an assignment immediately. With my future close friend... Mark Chesney.

How is it even possible to have a story like mine? I'm more suited as a fictional television or movie character because I'm so screwed up. Now, I'm surrounded with millionaires... everywhere. I initially thought it was only Jack, but after I sunk my teeth in Mark's financials... he's in the seven-plus figure club as well. The part sending me over the edge is seeing the stacks and stacks of money in Ms. Martin's secret library room. *And, who has those, by the way?* I thought it was folklore, or maybe only seen in ancient, European castles. Nope... I'm here to tell you 111 East Main Street, the site of the famous Möesta Bakery-many moons ago, is the home of a millionaire Madame, who has more money in assets than probably Jack and Mark, *combined.* Yes ma'am, we have fallen down the rabbit hole.

Early Monday morning, I arrive at Ms. Martin's office. She sent me a text, indicating I was to park in the rear of the building, next to the red Jaguar. My eyes almost popped out of my head, seeing the sleek sports car. Waiting for me, was a geeky boy-man, who upon seeing me, almost tripped over his own feet. Obviously, his social skills are lacking, especially since he couldn't keep his eyes off my breasts.

Nevertheless, Ms. Martin apparently has full faith in him, because she gave him full access to the vault.

I was shocked this guy, who barely looked fifteen, had the run of the place. Almost nearly fainted, when she explained he works full-time for the U.S. Treasury, and had designed her entire security system. The saying you can't judge a book by the cover, is never truer, than with Mr. Treasury Guru. We spent several excruciating hours, going through the system in detail. Since she will not be stateside, I will be totally responsible in case there is a problem. The system was updated to register my handprint, and he gave me a set of the strangest keys I've ever seen in my life. It was difficult to focus on getting answers to my questions, when he practically drooled over my tits. Knowing we provide escorts to him, sorta freaks me out, but everybody needs somebody, I guess. Even if you have to pay for it.

Finally at around three o'clock, I gathered my purse to leave for the day. Since I was so busy in training, I didn't even think to check my cell phone. Bad mistake. If I didn't know it, the world had blown apart. Jack called me five times and left four text messages! The basic gist of the first text, "Lunch?" Text messages: two and three... "Where are you, Lizzie?" The fourth began the messages of real concern... "I'm worried CALL ME!" Deciding the phone messages would likely be more of the same, I elected to call him from the car, on the way home in private. Next in the line of really bad mistakes.

Cell phone in hand, I exit the rear of the building. Barely taking one step, I'm suddenly surrounded by three brutes in familiar paramilitary garb. One on each arm, and led by another who was speaking into his wrist about someone he referred to as, the "Queen." Whatever it meant, she had apparently exited and was "in route to the nest." Everything happened so fast, and before I could scream, Seth, my driver after the St. Patrick's Day event, magically appeared. Looking none too happy, I am really ready to explode on him. "What the hell are y'all doing?! You cannot just physically take me. I want some answers, right now!"

Sitting in the back of an all-black SUV, he stares at me motionless. However, the heat is rolling off of him. He is doing everything he can, not to scream at me. That part is obvious. "We're taking you to Mr. Loving at the Pohlig apartment. He's awaiting your arrival."

"That's it? No explanations as to why you just kidnaped me? I have to pick-up my children. You need to take me home, right now!" I scream at him.

Making no effort to offer any explanations, his only remaining comment was, "Your friend, Jenny, will meet the children at the bus stop."

Suddenly very relieved, I slump back in my seat. Before I can process anything, we arrive at Jack's apartment. Seth bolts out, grabbing me by the elbow. Within a minute flat, he speaks into his wrist and we're standing at an open door, with a seething, arms crossed over his chest, enraged Jack Loving, standing in the doorway. Not bothering to look at me, he tells Seth, "That's all for now. I'll be in touch, Seth." Grabbing me by the hand, he pulls me inside and slams the massive door hard.

"Jack! What's going on?"

With a quiet voice, far too controlled, "Don't talk, don't whisper, and especially, don't cry. The *only* thing I want you to do for the foreseeable future… is breathe." Pulling me through to his bedroom, I'm overwhelmed with glorious memories, we just shared. A sharp contrast to the impassioned, angry man who doesn't even want to hear my voice. Pointing to the bed, I carefully sit on the edge, curiously still gripping my cell phone.

Standing in the center of the room with his arms yet again crossed protectively over his chest, he resembles a balloon ready to pop. He shakes his head, running both hands through his overgrown hair. Pacing the floor, he refuses to say anything, and I know speaking at this point will be a huge mistake. I understand he was worried about me, but this is no way to communicate when you have problems.

With an authoritative voice, he says quietly, "Strip. All of it. Put the cell on the nightstand."

My warning bells are ringing, and my little hairs on the back of my neck are standing on end. Even still... deep in my core, I trust this man I barely know. "Now!" He barks at me. Releasing the phone, I begin to undress and he moves to sit in a nearby chair facing me. Carefully placing my blouse on the bed, "No. Floor: all of it." Tossing it on the floor, I quickly remove my skirt. The sharp inhalation of air causes me to look at him. He has the strangest look of pain across his face. Looking down at my bra and matching garters with nude stockings, *I'm so confused: is he enjoying the sight of me, or repulsed by it?* "Leave only the garter and stockings." If I didn't know better, he's even more incensed now that I'm half-naked.

Once I'm totally naked except for a garter belt and stockings, he flippantly points to the bed. I return to my seat on the edge, very cautiously. Even though I'm naked and this situation is highly unusual, knowing my cell phone is in reach, as well as a deeply rooted feeling he will not hurt me, convinces me to do as he asks. Looking extremely serious, he bends forward with his elbows on his knees. "Elizabeth, do you trust me?"

Shaking my head, I also respond, "Yes."

"Why?" He asks angrily.

"Because you won't hurt me." I respond immediately.

With a wickedly conniving laugh, "Hurt, sweetheart, is subjective."

"You won't hurt or give me more than I can bear."

Lifting his head, he seems suddenly motivated, determined even. Watching me with heated eyes, "No, I will never give you more than you can bear. The thought of truly hurting you sends bile to my mouth. Don't ever forget it." Standing up, he comes closer, and even though he's attempting to hide it, his body shows the evidence of his arousal, caused by staring at me naked. "What's your safe word, Lizzie?"

"Samaritan," I say with confidence.

"Use it if you must, otherwise, no talking. I mean it," he remarks with almost a cruel-sounding edge. Shaking my head, I confirm my understanding. "Close your eyes." After a moment, I hear a drawer opening. Feeling his physical presence, a blindfold is placed around my eyes, followed by headphones which totally block out all sound. Feeling a little scared, it's really weird not being able to *see* or *hear*.

He pulls me up by both hands, and after turning me, applies a wrist restraint holding them together. He lays me awkwardly across his legs, which appear to have one planted on the floor and the other bent on the edge of the bed. Feeling anxious, I have no idea what has caused him to be so furious. Granted, I missed his calls and texts. But, the fact he had his security… change that, my "babysitter" track me down and kidnap me, is insane! If anyone has a reason to be fuming and full of wrath, it's me!

Still focused on processing the last forty-five minutes, I'm distracted with a soft, trailing feeling that transverses my ass. *Oh shit… I know what it is.* Tightening my ass cheeks, I prepare for the sting… but everything stops. Relaxing, after a few moments, the soft fronds causing me to tighten up. *Smack! Damn, that was hard!* Definitely not soft, it was a hand coming down *hard* on my ass. Realizing my mistake, no further tightening my cheeks because he wants me to feel the sting. After another round of soft, tickling motions, I unexpectedly receive the sting of the fronds. I scream out in error and receive another hard swat with his hand. I need to figure out his play, or I'm going to have a very red ass! Laying perfectly still, he gets into a pattern of soft and caressing, followed by the sting of the fronds. After completing the rotations all around the surface of my ass, he moves closer to my pussy. Interestingly enough, the pattern becomes very arousing. So when he trails the soft fronds through my swollen tissues, my ass automatically rises up, ready and willing to receive the bite of pain. When it comes down across my clit, it's amazingly gratifying. Pushing my ass higher, I beg to receive just… a… little… more. *Smack!* He instead gives me another hard smack across my already reddened ass cheek. Disappointed, I lower back across his legs, and he pushes them apart. I jerk when I feel the strong vibration of something, nearing my entrance. Pushing back into the object, I desperately want to feel it near my clit. He begins toying with me. A cruel game of keep-away. He gives it to me where I need it most, but takes it away before I come. Then he smacks me hard across the ass for being greedy. It's overwhelming, it's mean, it's nerve-wracking and quite possibly the most anticipated orgasm I've ever had. If I show my need or willingness, he punishes me. It's a game I'll never win. About to give up, he adds a delicious new element of agony to the mix. He enters me with multiple fingers, and while rubbing my G-spot, he bounces the vibrator on my clit. So good… getting much closer, but still not quite enough. "Fuck me! Stop, I give up!" I scream out. Suddenly everything… stops. *Oh, shit what have I done? This was a test, and I just massively failed it. Dammit!!*

He immediately removes my earphones. "Do you need to use your safe word?"

I say nothing, and shake my head "no" vehemently. After a few seconds, he picks me up and lays me across the bed on my back. Returning, I can feel he is naked. However, he's different. *Gone*, are the loving touches. *Gone*, are the kisses. In fact, he hasn't come near my mouth. *Gone*, are the compliments he normally showers me with. He's distant and it's then I realize, this is something far greater. *He's hurt.* It comes to me suddenly. He couldn't hear my voice… or, see my face. For hours, he was powerless. *He was scared.* The headphones and the blindfold, were my price to pay. Denying my orgasm… my penalty. This man… who feels everything far deeper than I realized. *My Jack—my DOM.*

He only touches me for balance and grip, not because he wants to. Upon entering me, I'm stretched viciously, taking him in all at once. Mixed with pleasure and pain, he rides me… *hard.* I know I probably won't get mine, but it's okay. I'll make sure to check my phone next time. *I really scared him*, and point made, but I'm crushed. It's my penance, my cross to bear.

Ripping my blindfold off, I'm immediately assaulted with the bright lights. Holding my wrists down above my head, with one of his, he plows into me at a break-neck pace. It's hard to breathe because the place deep, very deep inside, is begging to explode. I aim to hold back, it's what he wants.

"You're MINE! Do you understand? I won't give you away. Never again!"

"Yes, Jack," I manage to whisper breathlessly.

"Your pleasure… is mine. I want it right fucking now!" Reaching down, he presses between my ring and the top of my clit. On the very next deep stroke… euphoria. Both of us come at the same time. Feeling his cock enlarge inside me, he hits every spot that sends me aflame. Collapsing down, we're absolutely exhausted.

After a few minutes, he gently moves his hips, reawakening all my nerve endings. I experience a profound sense of loss when he pulls out. Acquiring a washcloth, he lovingly cleans me up, inspecting me very closely. Removing the wrist restraints and massaging in the same spot, he then escapes to the confines of the chair. *What the hell?*

"We need to talk, Lizzie."

"O-kkkkay." Feeling very exposed, I pull my knees to my chest. Hugging myself for support.

Looking very uncomfortable, "Why did you go to a dating agency today?"

Shocked and concerned by his wording, "What?"

"If you need or want something physically, we have to communicate. Going to someone else, is not the answer."

Kicking my legs out in front of me, I'm on high-alert. "W-wait, you... you think I was with someone today. As in... *having sex?* Are you insane?"

Looking very affronted, he narrows his eyes at me, "Weren't you?"

"No! I can't believe you would think of me like that. Why would I need someone else when you're totally obsessed with controlling and taking over my life, and you happen to be the best lay in town?"

"At least that's progress I guess." He sarcastically mumbles.

"Jack, I'm serious!"

"I'm very fucking serious. I'm not giving you up to some other guy. We need to fix the problem."

"There is no problem! Unless you're accusing me of cheating, then we have a serious problem."

Looking totally confused, "We need to start over. Explain why you were at that place today... and, last week as a matter of fact."

"How did you know that? Whoa, wait… Seth? Your man-candy, armed militia fighters, assigned to babysit and otherwise protect me with lethal force, armed with great looks and blindingly muscle bound? Those guys were watching me?"

"Yes, but apparently, they're not the only ones utilizing invasive surveillance tactics."

Shrugging my shoulders, "I can't help it if they're good looking."

"Lizzie!" He warns me.

"Sorry. I got distracted," I sweetly tease him. "It's my job—I work there, Jack."

"Aww, oh HELL NO!" He sits forward and yells at me.

"Excuse me?"

As if I have three heads, his eyes look like they are about to explode from staring at me. He swallows deeply, looking off into the distance. "Let me get this straight, you're working at a dating service?"

"Yes, I just said it. What did you think I was doing?"

"You *really* don't want to know what I was thinking."

"Actually, I think I do, want to know." By the second, I get more irritated with this inquisition.

Peaking his hands over his nose, he rubs his eyes in frustration. "Let's just say, I thought you were… a customer."

"A customer!" I jump up from the bed. He nods his confirmation. Hoping to calm myself, I begin to pace in the room because it all makes sense now. He knew I visited there at least twice, and thought it was a dating service. As a side note—and concern for another day… *how did he know anything about the business in the first place?* If he believes it's really a dating service, it's probably a good thing. "You assumed the worst, Jack. I'm not a customer, I'm an employee and why I was there. I know the owner, she's moving to

France and asked me to run the business. Today was my first day officially working there."

"Liz, I have to be honest with you. I don't like this idea at all. In fact… I hate it. Men are going to come in there, and try to date you. Do you have any clue how insanely jealous it will make me? Granted, it's horrible to tell you how I feel, but at least I'm upfront and honest."

This will be our first real challenge if he expects to date me. I owe Ms. Martin a lot for helping me and for being my friend. It pains me to see the stress written across his face. Deciding not to wear out the floor, I walk to him, bending on my knees in front of his chair. Reaching up, I massage both his knees, "You have no reason to be jealous. I'm not going to sleep with them."

Grasping me tightly at the shoulders, "Do you have any fucking clue how it felt not reaching you today? It began as a simple idea: hey, let's have lunch. Then, it turned into me thinking you regretted this weekend. When you didn't answer *any* of my texts or calls, I was very concerned. There's no other way around it, then, to be honest. You have to understand something about how I see our relationship… yes, I said relationship. You're mine, babe. I've waited a very long time on the sidelines, and I'm not going backward. Not knowing if you're okay, is a huge fucking problem for me." Pointing to the bed, "I truly hope you got the symbolism of what we just shared, because you having a blindfold and headphones was only *fractionally* as hard on you, as me not being able to see or talk to you. The fucking building has high-security Lizzie. Why? It doesn't make sense. I couldn't get to you, and it fucking killed me. I'm here to tell you, we were thirty minutes away from breaking the door down because I knew you needed to get to the children. I didn't know what the hell was happening!"

Oh no, how am I going to explain any of this to him? "I'm new, so I'm training right now. I was extremely busy, and I didn't think to look at my phone. It was very irresponsible, especially if the kids needed me for something. Also, I'm very sorry you were worried about me. This is new for me, Jack. I'm not accustomed to having people following me around, much less reporting on my whereabouts. It makes me uncomfortable."

"We've covered this, Liz. I'll always be a target, which makes you vulnerable. I realize this is different, but you have to work with me. I need to know where you are. Otherwise, I'll never have any peace of mind."

"Aren't you really saying you need control, especially over me? That's... that's what DOM's generally need, right?" I asked cautiously.

Then, it happened. He sat up straighter. Held his shoulders back. The most striking was the satisfaction that visually came over him, upon my recognition. He recognized, I already knew. The air around us, more than electrified. With a raised eyebrow, he cocks his head at me, "I didn't think you were ready. It's my job to anticipate your needs, and I've had to do it from afar, often using others to accomplish it. Therefore, I was taking it slowly with you. Should have known you'd be too damn perceptive. If you're thinking of running, I will... follow you. I'm incapable of playing on the sidelines, third string. Don't ask me to do it, because I can-not... do it. Not anymore."

Reaching up, I gently kiss him, enjoying the first real affectionate contact we've had today. Just a simple, prolonged kiss, I imagine could last forever. Even then, it would be too short. Pulling away, I look in his eyes, seeking strength and courage. "I'm much stronger than you realize. Having you on the sidelines, is unimaginable to me too. I've come to rely on you, without knowing it and I'm strengthened because of it. I'm good with giving you what you need, too. Use me, make me your safe haven, Jack. *You're already mine.*

Chapter Twenty-Three

Asshole Clients And Screaming Banshees

Jack

"Mr. Lindy, I have the Plea Agreement. In exchange for your information, they will agree to five years, probation."

"Fuck that shit! I want to walk away clean. My info is huge, and you know it. My girl kept records of her clients. She wasn't stupid— she recognizes famous faces. The conversations she overheard, and the fucking pillow-talk those assholes bragged about, is worth far more than convicting me of my stupid charge."

"It's a felony, Mr. Lindy. Definitely *not* a stupid charge."

"Whatever! I want to walk away."

"Mr. Lindy, I have negotiated the best deal, I possibly could, for you. If you feel you would like to secure alternative counsel, you're free to do so."

Staring at me like he wants to take me out back and shoot me, he eventually becomes resigned and signs the agreement. Damn. I was hoping he'd take me up on the offer of getting a new lawyer.

"Whatever, I just want this behind me. I'm going to laugh my ass off watching these rich pricks get raked over the coals on television."

"Aren't you concerned at all about your sister? She will be dragged through hell because of this. You are aware, right? This agreement in no way protects her, from prosecution."

"Aw, that snooty-nose bitch. She always tries to judge my life, telling me what to do. Living in her fancy house, driving her Beemer, thinking she's better than everyone else. How do you go from working as an IT Manager by day and paid escort by night? She's a criminal, but she doesn't see it that way."

Listening to him, it saddens me, he has no earthly idea what a firestorm he's about to bring down on her, all out of jealousy. It's so screwed up. "How did you get this information, by the way?"

"She let me stay at her house when my girlfriend kicked me out. I used her computer for something, and I was snooping, I admit it. She had all these records of her tricks. At the time, I was so shocked, I didn't know what to think. What I remember most, was sitting there thinking this is good blackmail material in case I need it one day. Oh, I needed it all right. Just not how I intended to use it. I didn't think I'd ever turn it over to the cops, but glad I made that USB copy because it keeps me out of a jail cell."

"Yeah, but it might put her in it," I reply so incensed that he could be this cruel to someone who was trying to help him in the first place.

"Aw, fuck her. I don't care about her anymore. She thinks she's so perfect, we'll just see won't we?"

Asshole! "I'll be in touch, Mr. Lindy. We're all done for today." So enraged with this dickwad, I just want him out of my office. I don't even want to breathe the same air as him. This is exactly why I want out of criminal law. These people have zero loyalty to anyone, and I'm tired of helping them get back on the streets.

After he leaves, I put the USB in my computer. I need to verify that he has turned over the number of people he promised. I'm surprised to find she made very detailed records. This is excruciating for me because I know I'll never be able to look at these people in the same light again. The records include dates, locations, and even... sexual preferences. My eyes will require sandpaper, to forget about some people's kink. I'm damn sure open minded, but some of these people have serious perversions for sure.

I get to one name, and my heart begins to race. *Oh, no—please no!* Gripping my neck with both hands, I begin to furiously run my hands through my hair. Knowing this will be very public, these people's reputations will be smeared in the press. Even if untrue, their names in association with this scandal, will destroy them and their businesses, and, of course, their families. Racing to my perch at the window, I stare out towards the water, hoping for a sign that I've dreamed up all of this, but it's not to be. My mind begins to remember the day I learned something pretty shocking, about... *my friend.*

"Seriously, I know a lady who runs an escort business. Just fun times; no complications, no gold diggers!"

I stop playing and stand there, bent over and exhausted because I have played too fucking hard. Processing what he's telling me, I look at him questioningly, "So have you ever used this escort business?"

"Absolutely." He quickly responds, not looking a damn bit sorry about it.

"Really?" I stare at him like a deer caught in the headlights. "You? You can find dates anywhere. Why do you need that?"

"Like I said, it's easy—no relationships, no expectations, no gold diggers. There are some that just escort you to events and that's

it. Others are known to enjoy some between-the-sheets action. It depends on what you're looking for and what your tastes are." He smirks at me knowingly. He and I have enjoyed conversations in the past about our affinity for all things BDSM. "Besides, you'd be shocked if you knew the people that used escorts routinely. It's a dirty little secret around here."

Still not believing that something like this exists in little 'ole RVA, I just shake my head incredulously. "I think I have enough problems right now, I don't need anymore."

Mark leans over and pats me on the back, "Well, bud, let me know if you change your mind."

Oh, Mark. I wish I could protect you buddy. You've been a great friend to me. *This fucking SUCKS!!* I return to my chair and stare at my computer. *Can I do anything to save him?* There will be a complete investigation—"the cover-up is always worse than the crime," rings through my head. I've heard this said a million times, especially in my profession, but never have I faced a personal situation involving someone I knew. I cannot be implicated in this, at least I'm clear on that part. Dad knowing the escort business exists, is bad enough. If I attempt to change records, they will find it anyway because they will subpoena this woman's computer. Case closed. Shaking my head, I pinch my nose because I know this is going to get very bad. Feeling a severe headache coming on, this is horrible for Mark. Just then, I think about Lizzie. *Oh shit—they're friends!* She will be majorly pissed off at me, if she finds out I'm the attorney who assisted in this leak of information. *Now, what the fucking hell am I supposed to do?*

Feeling totally helpless, it occurs to me: *what's missing from this file?* All of the others have very lengthy comments, dates, and locations. Maybe I'm being presumptuous. Feeling slightly hopeful, I look at this from a defense attorney's perspective. First, it's just the name "Chesney." I immediately took that as, "Mark Chesney." Granted, he's the only high-profile Chesney I know, but it's something. Second, when I look at the dates, which are about a dozen over a three-year time period, the locations just say, "Richmond." They aren't specific addresses like the other clients. No hotels, no specific places. Interesting. *Why would she not keep complete records of the addresses like the other clients?* Then, there is the lack of comments. Based on what I know about Mark… surely his kinky ass would have pages of comments written about him. Something is very different about Mark, compared to the other clients. *But, what?*

Feeling totally wiped out from everything involving Lindy and his assholiness, I head home to spend some time with the kids. Honestly, I just want to hit my home gym, and work out the day's frustrations.

Realizing it's extremely quiet, I listen carefully—nope, no one's home. Checking the fridge, I see a note from the nanny. "At the library. Working on school projects." Huh, well alright then. Even though I would have surely benefitted from a hug or two, I'll accept a good burn in the gym instead. Heading into my bedroom suite, I head straight to the closet to change. Coming out, I get a major shock. I was so distracted coming in, I didn't even see her. There she sits—in her submissive position. Head bowed… naked. Well, fuck me running!

I'm so caught off guard, I'm paralyzed where I stand. Never in a million years, did I expect to come home and find her here. Especially, like that! It wasn't unusual for her to await my instructions when we were at play. She has an assigned spot and waited there patiently per my orders. Of course, it always worked to her favor, because she was rewarded... well... with multiple orgasms. That has ended, of course because we're getting a divorce. More importantly, I'm *not* her DOM.

Taking a deep breath, I consider how I'm going to deal with this situation. She, of course, hasn't muttered any sounds. Walking to her closet, I grab a full-length, red silk robe that I had made for her. "Victoria, look at me." She raises her head, glancing at the robe draped over my shoulder. "Please, get up and put this on."

Shaking her head, "no," she cracks a millisecond half-smile. It was quick, but I caught it. Thinking she will entice me with bratty behavior, will not work. I'm done with her. Somehow, she needs to accept it. We're divorcing and my heart is pulled in another direction.

"I am no longer your DOM, Victoria. Nothing you do will cause me to have sex with you. Stop humiliating yourself. Get up, or I'll force you up. Right now!" I yell at her.

"Oh, Jack, I love it when you get so forceful. Come on, you need this as much as I do. Your little slut can't satisfy you like I do. I have the advantage of a decade worth of marriage under my belt. She's a mouse compared to me. You know it... I saw it the other day. It's true."

Pulling her up by her arms, I wrap the robe around her shoulders. I didn't want to fight with anyone, especially not her vile comments. "Victoria, get out. Don't come back, because the locks will be changed. If you need something right now, you *know* where to find another DOM. Go there. Go there right now for all I care, just GO!!" I demand her, screaming at the top of my lungs.

"I saw you staring at my body just now, Jack. You can't help yourself. Too many years of memories, seeing me in this exact position, just like a good little submissive. Just waiting for her

Dominate husband to take care of her... you were aroused looking at me. Admit it!"

"What I will admit to, is noticing how rail thin you are. How much weight have you lost, Vickie? You're not just thin, but you look unhealthy. This is bad for you long-term. If you are having trouble, get some help. You have an impressionable daughter, for the love of god. Set a good example for her self-confidence, self-esteem, and self-awareness. You're so concerned about someone taking your place... then make sure you're still around to see it doesn't happen." Walking to the door, I turn around to face her. "You're not my sub, don't pull a stunt like this again or there will be consequences. Legal and severely embarrassing, Vickie. Please, go back to the Jefferson." I turn and head to my gym. Leaving behind, a screaming banshee, throwing objects against the door, making every prediction under the sun about my future failures with Lizzie. *Ah, babe. I need you so badly right now.*

Chapter Twenty-Four

Lizzie Macintyre, Madame

Lizzie

June, 2015 –

Over the last few months, Jack and I have been spending as much time together as possible. We have lunch frequently, at either his apartment or "the nest" as my security detail refers to it. I've learned to tune out Seth, and his band of merry, lip-smacking men. Every day, I go about my routine as normal and don't really look for them, as I did in the early stages of our relationship. Now that I've had time to process all of this, it makes total sense as to why I make Jack vulnerable. He cares deeply for me. Therefore, I'm a kidnapping risk.

I've truly never been happier than these last months. At times, I want to pinch myself, just to make sure it's actually happening. We spend a lot of time together, every other weekend. Of course, Skype has been known to heat up my sheets on occasion when we can't see each other. Jack is pushing for our children to meet—I'm still hesitant about it. Even though I'm moving on romantically, my children can't replace their father. I would never want them to think I'm trying to put Jack in his place. Also, I'm privately concerned about the disparity between similarly aged kids, from night and day financial backgrounds. Granted, I'm now in a completely different place financially and can provide much better than I used to, but I'll never be a millionaire. Not to mention, my children aren't set to inherit multi-million dollar trust funds. Huge difference.

One day while we were at a Richmond Flying Squirrels baseball game, sitting in box seats, that of course he owns, the dreaded topic of money came up. It always seems to be the third person in our relationship. While eating a hot dog, he just throws it out there like it's an average everyday conversation: "I had to give Victoria twenty-five million dollars to settle our marital assets." I choked. Literally. While turning blue, he panicked and began hitting my back. He yelled to the staff to call 911, all the while quickly jumping into position, performing the Heimlich maneuver. Yeah, lesson to take away, don't frivolously throw out a statement like that while eating a hot dog. Not a good time to shock with news of the sort. Eventually, after he saved my life, yet insisted I be fully evaluated by a medical physician, we returned to the matter-at-hand.

"We didn't have a prenuptial agreement. Therefore, she could have received almost three-hundred million, so I'm pretty happy with the outcome. She doesn't receive it all at once, but in stages throughout her life."

"Wow, it's a lot of money, Jack. I can't even imagine negotiating something like that. I'm sure it must have put a big dent in your portfolio. I'm really sorry you had to deal with it."

Shrugging it off, "I'm just mad because of all the people I can't help now. The money would have gone a long way. Moreover, I'm heartbroken it took my mother years of investing well, for me to have as much money, and to just give it away… it's gutting." Jack and I have discussed the situation of Victoria. He doesn't hide things from me. In fact, he's been an open book. She definitely wants him back, she has told him so several times. Returning to her, is so improbable in my mind, because visually he becomes disgusted and you can't fake that sort of offensiveness. Clue in Vic… your marriage is over, whether I'm in the picture or not.

I have come to learn, Jack and his parents have a special relationship. He's particularly close to his mother. Personally, I already knew she was a class act, long before I ever knew Jack, but hearing him speak about her, it's so endearing. "I'm sure you will work through it, you and your family are amazing philanthropists. Even though Victoria took such a big percentage, you'll earn it back because I have faith in you."

Holding my hands lovingly, he looks me square in the eye. "Every time the subject of money comes up, you shy away from it. I may have been burned by Victoria, but it in no way is a reflection of how I see myself being open financially, to someone else."

Very confused, I'm not clear what he's trying to say. "What are you saying?"

Looking at me very pointedly, "I still have close to half-a-billion in total assets. When I see my future, you're standing in the sun with me. Holding hands, helping others—you get it, Lizzie. Many don't… they imagine a garage full of sports cars, jewels, mansions around the world. In a lot of ways, my money has been a noose around my neck. Career-wise, I can't do what I'd love to do because I have to be safe. From a very early age, my decisions were limited, due to the terms of my Trust. Unsafe occupations, directly impact the fluidity of sponsoring worthwhile projects. If I'm dead, everything stops until my children are of age. I'll be honest and tell you, the first woman I ever truly loved, walked away from me because she was scared my life would swallow her whole. She was probably right. Nevertheless, I know… in my heart, I *know* you get my family's mission. We may enjoy finer things in life too, it's true. However, at our core is philanthropy. Lizzie, I want you on this journey with me. Sun up—till sundown, I want you there as my partner."

So after eating a near-fatal hot dog, there we sat, in the privacy of the ballpark, talking about the future. There were lots of balls called, even a successful numbers of strikes, as the innings rolled by that sunny afternoon at The Diamond. He didn't come right out and say, "Will you marry me," but it was pretty close. *God, why me?* How surreal to be in a situation where I go from being evicted, to being an escort, to running said escort business… and now, being asked to commit to this man forever. It's mind boggling! My answer to his vision of standing in the sun… a simple, "Okay." Besides, rain drops depress me anyway.

After that day, each day thereafter just meant more. Felt more intense, we felt more connected. Our close friends knew about our relationship, luckily—the press did not. Jack wasn't worried. He laughed about it, but I knew it would surely make the local news. More importantly, I was in constant fear he would know about my business. My *real* business.

I fear the day, someone would make the connection and I'd be exposed. Problem is, every day I work, I *see* the money coming in. Once I truly began running the business, I got involved in the illegal side. It surprised me how quickly my boundaries fell. Ms. Martin and I strategize on worthwhile charities, and we quickly disperse the money. I've never seen so much money, flow in and out of the library wall. I remember in one week, I funded ten charities, one-million dollars each, *anonymously all in cash*. When you follow up with news reports of "unknown angels prevent shelter from closing." Or, "housing for one-hundred female homeless veterans planned due to an anonymous donor," it's compelling and sucks you in quickly, driving you to raise more—help more people. After a while, you never think about where the money comes from, or on who's back it was raised. In the back of my mind, I just enjoy the good works I'm doing, not thinking about the consequences. To say it's an addiction, is an understatement.

Jack really doesn't like me working here. He says he doesn't get the attraction I feel, when I make others happy. Of course, I'm referring to our philanthropic work... he thinks I'm referring to making romantic connections. It bothers me so much, not to be honest with him, but I know ignorance is bliss. He has so much on the line: reputation as an attorney, and with his Trust. I won't put him in jeopardy like that. My brain tells me, I need to walk away, and my heart tells me to stay.

We're doing great work here. Ms. Martin is finally free to live her life in France, and by me taking this on, the employees here still have jobs. If I walk... everything will fold. It's a tremendous burden when it's all on your shoulders. Also, I've learned something about myself. I make a *damn*good Madame. Not only do the employees respect me, but I have found myself in the unusual situation of sex coach. I laugh when I think about all my girlfriend conversations, and them telling me I give the best advice. Apparently, the clients agree. I can't tell you how many phone calls I get from spouses where we end up chatting on the emotional aspects of marriage. Our escorts supply the physical, and I discuss the emotional. I try not to think about the cheating aspect because it's offensive to me, and in a few situations, I even tell them it's wrong. On several occasions, it turns into a threesome with the other spouse. Now, that's unexpected. So, now I'm in this vicious cycle. Come to work as the local Madame, give millions away as the anonymous "Angel for

Good," as some local newspapers label, then go home to an amazing man, where I'm showered with so much love, it makes me feel guilty for being a Madame in the first place. There's no easy answers here. Just one, I *must* protect Jack.

The other amazing aspect of my relationship with Jack, is totally hot, sex! As time has gone by, we've learned more about one another. Initially, Jack downplayed his dominant nature. Knowing everything I had been through, he was really afraid to move too fast with me. Ha! When the puzzle pieces fit, and we both learned I *need* to be led in the bedroom, he was only too happy to run with it. Never in all my imagination, could I have envisioned some of our sexual play. The guy is a sexual god. He has taught me things about my body, I never knew. We often laugh about the day when I squirted for the first time. I was so freaked out and embarrassed! Now, it's a frequent occurrence, and it just means my orgasms are the better for it.

I made the mistake of telling him about Janice's shoe store encounter. Bad idea! A week later, we drove to Virginia Beach for the weekend. While there, he "supposedly" remembered he forgot to pack his water shoes. He drags me out with him, and five minutes before *it* happened, he pushed me in a doorway. Kissing me deeply, he begins to grope me everywhere. Then he instructs me, "Give the salesperson a peepshow. I'll reward you later." Releasing me, he walks away and finds the perfect chair to watch from. It wasn't lost on me, he made my eye-candy-militia, stand behind me. He didn't think I saw that tidbit… but, oh yeah—I totally did. Picking a random shoe at first, then decided—nope, I'm going for the tallest, fuck-me shoe I can find. After choosing, I sit patiently waiting for the salesperson. A really, good-looking guy walks up, apologizes and says he'll be right back. Making eye contact with Jack, he smiles and winks at me for encouragement.

A moment later, a beautiful blonde girl approaches. *Oh hell yeah! You want a show, you'll get a show.* She returns with my shoes, and I flirt with her shamelessly. Luckily, she flirts back. Taking frequent peeks, he watches calmly, seemingly unaffected. If not for the heat he attempts to hide behind those eyelids, no one would ever know he's about to come unglued. Then, it noticeably drives him crazy, when I lean close to the girl, whispering something in her ear. Playing the scene out similarly to Janice's shoe store story, I occasionally glance at Jack, who is staring at me ready to pounce any second. Spreading my legs wider, the girl looks around, determining no one is in the vicinity. Had she looked directly behind her, she would have noticed a wolf on the prowl. Sometimes you just know, when someone is in the moment with you. This girl was on the hook. No doubt, whatsoever.

Slowly, I reach for the edge of my sundress, inching it closer to my waist. Fully engrossed, she sits back... watching–waiting. With two fingers, I pull the fabric of the crotch, to the side. Revealing my shaved lips, my sweet, new friend smiles and hums her appreciation. Apparently, the wolf becomes anxious when he suddenly leaps in my direction. Walking around, he plops in the chair beside me, "So how we doing here?" Scaring her to death, my fun ceases.

She looks at him in total frustration, cutting her eyes back to me. "If there is anything else you might *need*, please let me know." Rolling her eyes at him, she stands up and walks away.

Facing him, I narrow my eyes in confusion. Clicking my tongue against the roof of my mouth, "Can I help you with something?" I ask very straight faced.

He smirks at me, "You're going to pay for that you know."

"Will I?" I ask seriously.

Shaking his head slowly, "Oh, yeah. Let me warn you right now. My fun, included a panty shot, leaving a stiffy in the wake. You changed up the plan and decided to terrorize me. Giving the prey a memory of *my* pussy, now she'll take it home as a bedtime story. I'd say it's deserving of delicious punishment for you sweetheart. Let's go."

So, these days, my sex life is amazingly great, and I love my day job. Mark, still has me working on his Endowment, so oftentimes I do everything at the mysterious little shop on Main Street. Jack and my cast of eye-candy-militia always led by Seth, follow me around making sure I don't become a liability for Jack. If they only knew, chaperoning me to Main Street, is probably his biggest liability ever.

Chapter Twenty-Five

Escorts and Chicken Recipes

Jack

"Mr. Lindy, the agreement is fully executed and binding. The charges against you have been dropped based on the information you turned over."

He laughs loudly, "Yeah… that's what I thought. I knew they'd like what I had to say."

"I want to remind you, you must remain silent about all matters, or you will be in violation. Heed my warning Mr. Lindy. The prosecutor will not hesitate to reinstate the charges if you disclose this situation."

"Well, I know the deal, you don't gotta worry about me. It'll be funny to watch and see what happens to all those rich fuckers. They think they're above the law, looking down on everyone else. Ha! They'll get what's coming to 'em."

"What about your sister? Have you further considered the risk of exposing her?"

"Nah, the bitch will deal. She'll be fine. Maybe she needs a knock down from her judgmental tower she stands on. Besides, maybe if she comes groveling back, I'll give some more good info I have, in exchange for getting her charges reduced. My reach is pretty deep, and I keep ammunition on lots of people, just for rainy days."

Sitting in my desk chair, it takes every bit of power I have, not to throw this asshole out my window, tumbling down onto the sidewalk below. He represents the epitome of why I hate criminal practice. Scum, who will turn on family, just to save themselves. I loathe people like him and despise myself for setting him free. "I guess this concludes our business for today, Mr. Lindy." Now... get the hell out of my office, and if bad karma finds you, great.

After, Lindy left my office this morning, I couldn't seem to settle in at work. No matter the task, my mind kept going back to his case. Tom Bennett, with the prosecutor's office, has been rather open about parts of their investigation. Over the last few months, they've been gathering information on the people involved, and I would suspect they are attempting to obtain video evidence. Some of them are married, but many are single, or newly divorced. The names I recognize, all are considered respected community members. They sit on various Boards, and obviously, have political affiliations. Those are the individuals, I expect will take the biggest hit in the press. They will be skewered, and boiled by the time the media has their say. Since this includes people from the Washington, D.C. area, it will go national without a doubt in my mind.

The name I keep coming back to, is Mark Chesney. *Why were the records omitting key details?* There has to be a reason. It's hard to separate my duty as Officer of the Court, from longtime friend. I'm so afraid for him personally and professionally, and sitting here unfocused on my daily work, I make the decision.

Scrolling through my list of contacts, I dial his personal cell phone.

"Hey Jack! I'm in the middle of something. Can I call you back?"

"Ordinarily, I'd say yes, but no. I need you to meet me for lunch today. Come to my apartment at Pohlig's, one o'clock. It's urgent."

"Well, that sounds ominous. Okay, I need to switch some appointments, but I'll be there."

"Great, thanks." Hanging up, I can feel the butterflies in my stomach. *Shit, what did I just do?* If they're watching him, the police will know we met. Considering my options, I grab some promotional posters from my office. The mock-up signage from the St. Patrick's Day event, still happens to be in my office. Good, I'll walk in carrying it, and tell him to leave with the materials. With my plan made, I set out—to break my oath and multiple laws in the process.

Pacing the floor, he finally arrives at promptly one o'clock. Opening the door, "Hey! What's so urgent?"

Scratching my forehead in contemplation, "Would you like a beer or something else? I picked up some take-out before I came over."

"Beer is good." I'm completely silent, as I move around my apartment. Now that we're here, I have no idea how to say any of this. Motioning him to join me at the table, we both sit down.

"Jack, obviously something is bothering you, and my first instinct is it's about Lizzie. What's happened? Is she okay?"

Shaking off the notion this has anything to do with her, thank god for that at least. Although, my fear of her finding out I played any part in this, and how it will effect Mark, concerns me greatly. She is close to him, and if she hurts—I hurt.

"No, no—she's fine. Lizzie is great, we're enjoying getting to know one another immensely. Honestly, I knew all along we just needed one-on-one time together, and I was right. Never in my dreams, could I have imagined being this happy with someone. If I could convince her to take the next step of letting our kids meet, and meeting my parents, I'd be thrilled. She's dragging her feet for some reason or another. Every day I ask, and every day she says 'soon, I promise.'"

He watches me with narrowed eyes, considering my words, evaluating Lizzie's intentions I'm sure. Even though we're buddies, it's not lost on me, his loyalty may ultimately lay with her, not me if it was really a choice. As comical as it may sound, it's just a testament to the amazing person Lizzie truly is. "Alright, the suspense is killing me. What's so urgent?"

Sliding my food aside, I steeple my hands against my chin. With a quick prayer for courage, "There's something big about to happen. In fact, it's best for both of us if this conversation never took place."

Mark sits back in his chair, concern written all over his face. "Okay, we're not discussing anything important. Just two friends enjoying lunch."

"Yes… in fact, I brought some promotional materials home with me. You need to take them with you, clearly visible when you leave today."

"That's sounds a lot like a cover story, Jack. You need to fess up. Are you in some kind of trouble?"

Shaking my hands "no," I am bottled up with nervous energy. By telling him anything, I'm breaking the law, and it honestly repulses me. "I'm not in trouble, but I fear you may be."

"Me?" He asks, pointing to himself. "I'm lost, why am I in trouble?"

Taking a rigidly deep breath, I sip my beer because my mouth is totally dry from nerves. "We had a conversation last year, where you mentioned using escorts."

He pauses, and takes in my very uncomfortable body language. Staring at one another, a good minute in silence passes by. "Tell me, Jack. Do I need to worry about this?"

Without answering, I slowly close my eyes, a confirmation to his very concerned face. "I'm an Officer of the Court. As such, I took an oath to follow the law at all times."

Shaking his head, he seems to understand, I need him to read between the ambiguous lines of our very strange conversation. Leaning close to me, he quietly asks, "You mentioned, something big is about to happen. I interpret it to mean, the escort service is being watched, or potentially raided."

Again, I close my eyes, fully and decisively. In agreement with his question. Damn, I wish I could simply tell him everything, but I'm going too far now as it is. I need some way to convey what I know about the records concerning him. Standing up, I walk around the room, looking for some sense of symbolism I can use. Grabbing Lizzie's cookbook from a kitchen shelf, I skim the pages. "I find some foods interesting, Mark. For example, chicken can me made probably fifty different ways in this book, but it's still chicken. The back index by food type, lists every recipe that chicken is contained in. So, those recipes are very easy to understand. You know where the chicken will be. The confusing part would be if there were a recipe but no ingredients. It's missing key pieces of information. I have no idea how to cook the meal, if the data is missing. Therefore, the book is flawed in my mind because critical pieces are missing. Hopefully, people will just overlook it, but when the cookbook is published, the flaws will be noticed. Don't you agree, Mark?" For fuck's sake! I cannot believe I had to compare an escort to chicken. My University of Richmond law degree was surely not beneficial because I feel like a stupid ignoramus!

Mark watches me, with his jaw open like I've totally gone batty. Examining the cookbook, he carefully points to the references in the back index. Cutting his eyes to me occasionally, his finger taps and I can see the cogs of his brain clearing out. Sitting quietly, I let him attempt to work through my clues. There's no way I can tell him everything. I just won't compromise myself completely. Believe it or not, I see the moment when clarity hits him.

"Well, I'll be damned. As fucking crazy as I thought you were, I think I understand it. The escort has records of clients. I'm on her list, but details on me aren't as specific. Does that sum it up pretty well?"

Total relief falls over me. This by far is the most high-stakes game of charades I've ever played. Letting my head fall with a thump, on the table, I simply gesture a thumb's up sign. Looking up at him, "Thank goodness you understand, because this is killing me. Take it seriously, because it's coming. The rat came after the chicken."

He rubs his face with his hands, deeply concerned. "I ahh… I really need to deal with this, so I need to get going."

"Sure, but my hands are tied. You'll need to find help somewhere else." Looking incredibly disappointed, I hand him the promotional materials. "It's really important that you hold these carefully when you leave. Who knows who may be watching, so we could use all the PR we could get for our charity work."

"Shit! So, I'm being watched? That's bullshit!"

In agreement, but there's nothing I can do, so I shrug in agreement. "Keep in touch, Mark."

"Yeah, and thanks. You really are in a tough spot, so thanks for the heads up."

"No worries."

After Mark leaves, I have this huge sense of relief. Now, he at least knows something is up. He can find legal counsel, and they can plan his defense. Little does he know, this situation is going to blow up. I fear no one, will be left unscathed. I'm just glad it's not going to personally affect me in any way.

Chapter Twenty-Six

Infinity

Jack

After meeting with Mark, I desperately needed to feel Lizzie's calming spirit. Luckily, she agreed to meet at my apartment in a few hours. Things have been going so well for us, and I feel guilty when I know Mark's world is about to become public fodder. I've allowed us time to get to know each other, over these last few months, but it's time to speed things along. Just like when I watched her from afar and made good choices, I'm hoping she'll see this in the same vein.

In that effort, I decide to finally loop my parents in, on what has kept me busy lately. They've asked if I'm dating anyone, and I confirmed it. However, I kept the details private, out of respect for Lizzie. My parents are extremely supportive, understanding people. Once they meet her, they'll see why I'm enthralled and head over heels.

"Hello, sweetheart! How are you? It seems like ages since you've called me."

"Apologies, Mother. It has been too long. That's why I'm phoning actually. Do you have dinner plans this evening?" I ask very hopeful she is free.

"No, nothing too serious. What did you have in mind?"

"The Country Club is my suggestion. Is that agreeable?"

"Absolutely! Ah, Jack—are you bringing your mysterious lady friend?" She asks, of course predicting my surprise.

"You know me too well, Mother. That *is* my plan."

Releasing a rare squeal, "Excellent, Dad seems to think I will be pleased."

"Dad? How does he know—?"

"Seriously, Jack. There's nothing your father doesn't know about. You should have predicted it. However, he's been close-lipped to me. I can't wait to meet the woman who has you beaming."

Softly laughing, she's so right. Ever since we truly began our time together, I'm ecstatic. There's a permanent smile there now. I didn't realize how miserable I was with Victoria. "I'll see you at six o'clock, Mother."

"Ok, dear, see you then!"

Time seems to crawl by until finally, I hear a knock at the door. Knowing it will be the last time I hear her knock, I can't help but smile at myself. It's all worked out perfectly. No hitches to speak of—she's *mine*. Opening the door wide for her, she leans up on her tip toes to greet me with a kiss. It's moments like these that keep me dreaming for more… *so much more.*

"Hello, baby. You had no idea how much I needed that."

"Aww, I'm sorry. Did you have a rough day?" She puts her hands around my neck, squeezing her body against mine.

"Actually, I did, but seeing you is the best therapy for a rough day."

"Good, well you have me, so everything's perfect."

"Not exactly perfect, yet, but I'm getting there. Actually, you have the medicine to make me better."

"Ohhh… so sexy Mr. Loving. What can I give you?" As she runs her hand down my chest and blatantly grabs my crotch.

"So forward, Ms. Macintyre." I fake feeling affronted. Kicking the door closed, I grab both her hands, pull them above her head as I press my body into hers, against the door. "What you can give me… is you… agreeing to my demands."

"Um, that's sounds like a no-brainer to me. Let me guess, do you want me bent over the back of the couch, outside on the patio, strapped against the headboard? Where will make you happy?"

"Let's start with an idea, first."

"O-kkaay," she answers unsure of my motives.

"Give me your hand," as she immediately hands it to me. "Close your eyes." Leaning down, I gently kiss her closed eyelid. Reaching in my pocket, I pull out the shiny object attached to a red ribbon and place it in her hand. Giving her another kiss for luck on the other closed eyelid, "Open your eyes, baby."

Slowly, her eyes open, and she takes in the gold key laying in her palm. Narrowing her eyes, "A key?" Shaking my head, I confirm the obvious. "What does it open?"

"A good guess, may be the door your sweet ass is pressed against."

"Jack, don't you think it's a little soon?"

"No, not at all. I'm just evening the score."

Totally confused, "That doesn't really explain anything, it just makes me more curious."

Reaching in my pocket, I pull out my key ring. Fingering through them, I stop at the exact one I have mindlessly played with, for over six months. Holding it up, "Look familiar?"

Recognition crosses her face, "My apartment key? Why do you have—? Oh, never mind, that's right… you own the building, and you're overly presumptuous about meddling into my life. That's why you have it."

With a raised eyebrow, I give silent warning, "Lizzie, everything I do, is in our best interests. Have I been wrong at any time?"

"Well, that's not the point, but anyway, I don't truly feel comfortable accepting your key."

Running my hand across her cheek, I'm constantly reminded of how beautiful she is. "It's time, Lizzie. Plus, if you need to meet me here, you can let yourself in. When are you going to fully accept, we're happening—no excuses. Take the key, use it and make me happy."

With a look not full of conviction, she closes her hand around the key. "Yes, Jack."

Leaning in, I kiss her deeply, full of passion. Enough conviction in my decision for the two of us. Pulling back, I whisper "One more thing sweetheart, and I will be a man fully restored from a very crappy day."

"What's that? She asks with curiosity.

"We're meeting my parents for dinner at the Country Club of Virginia."

Suddenly, her eyes enlarge the size of golf balls. She reaches for her hair and glances down at her clothes. "No!" She argues. "I can't meet them. It's too soon, and besides I'm dressed terribly." Shaking her head furiously, I realize this will be a tough sell, but it's happening so she needs to get on board.

Grabbing her hand, I quickly pull her through the apartment to my bedroom. Shouting her complaints, I ignore her, placing her before a massive walk-in closet. Pulling the door aside, a full closet is revealed of every imaginable bit of clothing and accessories, a woman might need. Had she explored on her own, she would have found this treasure trove before. "Change your clothes, if it makes you happy. You look beautiful as you are, but I want you perfectly comfortable."

Other than a loud inhalation when I revealed her gifts, she is stunned in silence. She slowly walks inside and begins fingering the blouses, dresses, slacks and accessories. I can see a million thoughts going through her head, but I have no idea what she will say. After a few minutes, "When did you do this? I see sweaters here too. When did you buy these things?"

"It was fully stocked in January."

"Are you serious?" She asks in a near shocking panic. "You do know you suffer from a serious obsessive disorder, right? This isn't normal."

"Who's to say what's normal anymore? I just know, I want you with me, in my life. Whatever it takes, babe." Stating confidently.

She shakes her head in confusion, trying to take in everything. Finally, she looks at me with serious eyes, "So… your parents?"

"Yes, my mother is dying to meet the mystery woman in my life. Apparently, dad's investigative skills are too good, so he knows it's you, but he hasn't revealed our secret to her. The time is right; we need to go public. The best, most controlled place to announce ourselves, is the Country Club."

With a look of resignation, taking a deep breath, "Okay. Let's go." Feeling like I've won the biggest case of my career, I rush her in the closet. Picking her up, I wrap her legs around my waist. Carrying her out of the closet, I drop her in the center of my bed. Looking down at her, I slowly run my hands up and down her legs. Never will I imagine a day when the sight of her alone, doesn't rip my thoughts to shreds. She controls me, manipulates my thoughts and forces me to act compulsively. Some men would be offended by this level of calculation. I'm not most men. She makes me burn hot, shatters my defenses and when she grabs me—it's pure nirvana. I've had many women, had serious relationships, married and considering I'm in my mid-thirties, seen a lot in my time on earth. Never before have I known a feeling so complete, as receiving her attention—her affection—*her love.* These are new feelings for me. Calling me obsessive, should alarm me, or give me pause. It doesn't. For as long as I'm obsessive about Lizzie, it truly means she has a wicked hold on my heart and mind. To me... it calls for celebration, not reason for concern.

Reaching in my drawer, I pull out the padded leg restraints. Making no effort to hide them, she watches my movements, curious what I'll do next. Setting them aside, I set about removing her clothes. Taking my time, I fold each one lovingly, building her interest and making her wait. Once she is completely naked, I position her spread-eagle, in the center of the bed. After carefully selecting the perfect bed, I know I can easily attach her ankle cuffs, to the end posts. Ensuring there is at least a finger's gap, she lays comfortably, awaiting my instructions. No conversation is necessary between us, just the imminent knowledge her pleasure is guaranteed.

Placing several pillows behind her head, she lifts her arms in anticipation of them being restrained. "Oh no, sweet Lizzie. You need your hands for what I have planned," I softly mumble. She looks intrigued—good. "Your obedience and your willingness to obey is integral to your success as a submissive. There's nothing more annoying to a DOM than to be questioned when you're told to do something, or to be hesitant, or delay doing what is asked. This entire relationship relies on trust, and if it's broken even once, it can be irreparably harmed. This is why it's very important to utilize safe words, and establish hard limits. Since you've already told me you don't have a problem with restraints, it's my plan for today. But...

you need to know, part of me being your best DOM, is pushing your limits. Frequently. I won't cross the boundary, but I will kiss it. Submission allows you to learn about yourself. Your hard limits may change over time; it's okay. What's important, is discussing when those limits need to change. We'll look for new ways to keep things interesting. You agreeable?"

"Absolutely," she smiles.

Moving a chair so I have the perfect view, I sit comfortably waiting for a perfect show. Watching her face intently, "Take your time, and slowly touch yourself. I want you to verbalize everything you're doing, explain the images in your head, and especially detail how it feels. Work on bringing yourself, right to the edge, then stopping. When you've satisfied me, I'll let you come. By the way, you're a stunning feast for my eyes. I'm incredibly lucky to see you this way, babe."

She stares down her body, arching her pelvis, giving me a provocative view. Grabbing an overflow of her breasts, she kneads them, pulling at her nipples. "You're not talking, babe. I want action… and adjectives."

With a chuckle, "I'm just starting, be patient. When I'm alone, I normally begin with my breasts by cupping them in my hands, squeezing them, and pushing them close together. Circling around the nipple, the sensations quickly begin and either by me touching or from the sensation alone, my nipples get hard. Sometimes, I flick one, and gently touch the other. No matter what I do, it always feels good. Especially when I'm about to come. If I pinch them hard, it really prolongs my orgasm. Do you want to come lick them for me, Jack? Right here… on this right one, in particular. It's the side you end up laying near. You suck this one a lot, and I think you're rather partial, aren't you? Come here… just a little lick." Enticing me, she narrows her heated eyes, presses her lips together with emphasis, and taunts me.

Ah, no. "Not your game, this is my fun, don't try to top me sweetie, or you won't like the punishment," I warn her.

Winking at me, "Come on, I'm just playing with you."

"We both know, it's not what you're doing. So… stop it. Now."

Fully chastised, she continues the touching and twisting of her nipples. "It feels so good. If I run my nails down my sides, I get chill bumps. See?" I wink my response. "Then, I initially run my fingers through my wet folds, just to determine how ready I am."

"And, how wet are you?"

"Oh, right now, I'm soaked because I know you're sitting there, staring at my pussy. It's scary but at the same time, it's a huge turn on, for me to do this for you." She gently runs her finger back to front, stopping on her clit. Just as I'm about to scold her for, not explaining… "Oh, sorry, I got carried away. My fingers begin at the front, then move to the back a couple times. I wet my fingers and begin to rub my nub in a circular pattern. Oooohh, Jack, this is nice, too nice. I'm swelling here, and it's building far quicker than normal." She tries to close her legs, but the restraints prevent it. She attempts to gyrate her pelvis, needing friction and unable to find any.

"Talk it through, Lizzie."

"I'm trying to hold it off… it's just… there." Removing her hands completely, she pulls in desperation at the comforter, mad she needed to stop. "Gah! I want it so bad, I need it, Jack. *Please*, can I start again? My body is on fire. I need to come, dammit!"

"No. Start again… this time, lick yourself from your fingers. Then, back to your breasts."

"Ah! You're driving me crazy."

"I know, but you'll love me more for it in the end." A very strange look crosses her face. She's paralyzed with something. Fear? Anger?

Knowing it's my job to anticipate and care for her needs, I make the radical decision to stop my method of play. Ordinarily, I'd wait it out, but she's trying to hide the tears in her eyes and I don't like the idea of her crying. "Stop," and immediately she ceases all movement. "Talk to me. Do you need to safe word?" She shakes her head "no," and rolls it facing away from me. *Oh, fuck no!* "Elizabeth. *Look* at me," I say with a deeply firm voice. Immediately, our eyes lock, and she has tears beginning to stream down her face. "This play was about using your words and recognizing how they build towards an amazing orgasm. Not, about tears. I need you to tell me why you're upset. It's my responsibility to care and comfort you, but I need you to talk to me."

Fighting the sniffles, "You said, 'I will love you more at the end.' I don't want to think about our ending."

Oh, motherfuck! That was taken totally out of context. "Sweetheart, it's not what I meant at all." Suddenly knowing only one way to make my feelings truly heard, I quickly undress. Considering I seem to sport an erection anytime she's near, I climb above her, slowly and easily entering her. Taking each of her hands in mine, I clasp them tightly beside her face. Moving my hips, I begin to quickly pump inside her. Normally, I stave off an early orgasm, delaying the gratifying feelings intercourse brings to both of us. Today, I want her to see me cut open, full of reckless abandon. Unguarded and weak, as I rush headlong at full-force. Her breaths are heavy, as she chases her own pleasure. Totally vulnerable, no acts, no role-play—just a mindless race. Hot, sloppy, abruptly naked to all the sensations filling my mind's eye. It's too much… the feeling too powerfully great. Locking eyes with her, at the exact moment when I am on the cusp of filling her with my pleasure, I fight the natural sensation to keep my eyes closed. "I love you!" I bellow with everything I have left. "There is no end—*infinity*." I struggle to croak out, engrossed in her screams of delight as her channel clamps down hard on my shaft, almost painfully. My hips power through the remaining moments of what had to be the most emotional orgasm of my life. She makes me indefensible—helpless and laid bare. I have no shields to protect me, for if she leaves me, I won't survive it. The real power and control is *hers*, and deep in my soul, it frightens me.

The minutes creep along, encapsulated in the comfort of our bed, we hold each other. No words are spoken, our bodies communicate everything needing to be said. Sensing her movement, I say a quick prayer to the universe, she won't suggest we invite the outside world into our bubble. Time is not my friend, however, when she points to the alarm clock, signifying the end of the best intimate moments of my life. It doesn't matter she didn't say the words back, I know how she feels. The pain clearly written across her face, for an ending, I'll never allow, told me more than any letters could formulate. She's mine—she's heart and soul, hook line and sinker, wholly mine. Hang on Ms. Macintyre... next step... *my wife*.

Chapter Twenty-Seven

Quashing The Whispers

Lizzie

Full of nervous energy, we ride in the back seat of Seth's SUV, in route to dinner at the Country Club. This is the first time, we've had a driver. Jack explained even though he enjoys driving, the security detail prefer to escort him wherever he goes as a precaution. Tonight, I actually appreciated the opportunity to cuddle up in his arms. We talked about our day since our afternoon activities didn't really allow for it. Jack confided he is working on a case, which will effect some of his friends. He was visually upset about it, and it bothers me to see him distracted.

Arriving at the Country Club, Seth pulled up under the covered portico, where a uniformed attendant kindly opened my door. He greeted Jack by his last name, and a simple tip of the hat, and "Ma'am" for me. There was no hiding the huge beaming smile adorning Jack's face, as he gently placed my hand, in the crook of his elbow.

With a tilt of his head, "Shall we Ms. Macintyre?"

"Absolutely, Mr. Loving." Excited to be here with him, the nerves begin to recede.

He always has a way of making me feel good and relevant, clearly important to him. As we approach the hostess, we're greeted similarly as the valet, except this time, Jack makes a point to introduce me. "My guest is Ms. Lizzie Macintyre. She will be around quite a bit, so please add her to my account. No limit, anything she desires. By the way, see she receives a temporary guest membership before we leave this evening."

"No problem, Mr. Loving." The young hostess replies with a fake smile. Yeah, so apparently, some had hopes for Jack ending his bachelor days… with them on his arm. *Ah, no, not happening, sweetie.* Surprisingly, Jack leans down and kisses me softly, directly on my lips. Rather shocked by his boldness, I have no choice but to enjoy the deliciousness.

Pulling away, his eyes twinkle in delight, "What was that for?" I ask.

Cutting his eyes around the room, "Several reasons, in fact. Mainly, to announce to this room, you're taken. I don't want any lonely men left with illusions of your availability. However, it's rather fortuitous that the bitchy hostesses are clear on who you are to me. I will not tolerate them being rude to you. Just as I'm announcing, you're mine… I expect and encourage you to reciprocate. Show your claws, because there's only one woman in this room whom I love."

Hearing him use the word love, actually gives me butterflies. Knowing he enjoys me being territorial over him, is quite unexpected. Fighting unsuccessfully to hide a most unladylike snort, I boldly stand on my tippy toes, giving Jack a longing look of appreciation, followed by a quick peck. *Point made, bitches!* Mixed with great pride, I hold my head up high, ignoring the gasps and whispers coming from every angle in the room.

Making our way to the table, Jack Loving, Sr., immediately stands and calls me by name, giving me a warm greeting and kiss on the cheek. Moving around the table, Jack stops at his mother, bends down and kisses her as well. She hugs him tightly, the look of love written all over their faces.

"Mother, may I present Ms. Elizabeth Macintyre, my girlfriend."

She clasps her hands together tightly at her chest, biting her bottom lip. The seconds tick by and it's almost uncomfortable, and had it not been for her pearly white smile, I might get the wrong idea. Shaking her head, she reaches out, ignoring my outstretched hand. Grabbing me in a tight embrace, she apparently has no concerns about me dating Jack.

"I can't believe it! After all this time, I truly cannot believe it's you. Jack, Sr., wouldn't tell me who our son was dating. He said we needed to stay out of it, and let it happen organically!" Had I known, I would have been coaching him along the way, making sure he didn't take a wrong turn."

I can't help but chuckle at her enthusiasm, and thoughts of nervousness simply fall away. "Why didn't you tell your mom, Jack?" I ask incredulously.

Just as he opened his mouth to respond, she jumped in, "He knew I'd get involved that's why!"

Pointing in her direction, Jack quips, "Yep… what she said."

"Seriously, Jack, enough with the slang, please."

With an upturned eye, he shrugs slightly but of course like any good Southern boy… he shut his mouth and did what his momma told him to do. "So, Lizzie, I have so much I want to ask you about, and I don't know where to start. First, I guess Jack owes me a major apology for forcing the raffle on him at the Christmas Gala. It all worked out in the end because we raised a lot of money, and you got the winning ticket for a date. It's what got you two together, right?" She asked with a smile so bright it could light up the Richmond skyline at night.

Hearing someone refer to the Christmas Gala, was like sending a hot poker down my bare spine. Just cut me open, and left me raw. Trying hard not to let it define my night, I put on a smile, and managed a polite response." The warm sensation of Jack's hand resting on my knee, and squeezing it, gives me the boost of oxygen I need to answer. "Yes ma'am, our date was surely special."

Once we covered that hurdle, the rest of dinner included polite conversation and funny jabs. The senior Loving's, are hysterical! They tease each other, and of course someone always brings up the topic of business, and Mrs. Loving cuts it off in the quick. There's no doubt, she is the one in charge, and her men, fall in line happily.

Throughout the dinner service, we were interrupted so many times I lost count. Each time, everyone was polite, but they were there for two reasons: business opportunities with Mrs. Loving and Jack, or to find out what I was doing at their table. People were shameless about it too. I saw it firsthand at the St. Patrick's Day event, everyone wanted Jack's time. It was very similar throughout dinner, except he wasn't the only Trust member who had money to spare. At one point, I looked at Mr. Loving, who sat idle drinking his bourbon. Yes, he and I were less popular.

However, apparently, Mrs. Loving finally reached her fill. Completely shocked at her brazen methods, she simply stood up, with her long-handled teaspoon and water glass. Tapping the side to gather everyone's attention, I hear a "You-whooo." Spinning around to gather her audience, she smiles largely sweet and strikes like a viper. "I know all of you have more important things to do than talk business with me and my family. It's after office hours, and I'm enjoying my son's new girlfriend. So, please… quiet down the whispers and table talk. They're happy, and I'm over the moon. Her name is Ms. Lizzie Macintyre, *yes*…. she's a former member here, and we should embrace her return." Taking another spin around the room, she passes on hardened eyes to whomever she deems appropriate. "I look forward to witnessing everyone's warm welcome, extended to our sweet girl."

Sitting in total shock, I was totally afraid to breathe, much less move. Only a well-respected, powerfully connected woman, could make a statement like hers, and minions fall in line. Wow. Immediately, the vibe around us seemed to calm. Instead of long-winded conversations, each and every person stopped by eventually to say "Welcome back, Ms. Macintyre." Damn, remind me to never cross Sarah Loving. She's brutal.

Chapter Twenty-Eight

Puppet Master And Match-Maker

Sarah Loving

I've always had a good sense about people. It has served me well my entire life. From the first day I met Jack's soon-to-be ex-wife, I knew she was terrible for my son. He had to figure it out on his own, I'm just disappointed it took so long.

Seeing my son unhappy, and miserable for almost a decade, has almost crushed me. When I learned what Victoria did to our family, I wanted to put her out to pasture. She'll get her due. I'll be sure of it. This is a very long, and complicated situation, for the legal system to deal with. In fact, it may be another year before she even goes to trial. It just puts unnecessary pressure on the children, and I hate that so much.

Jack was so depressed. He tried to hide it, but I know my son. The fear of letting me down weighed on his mind heavily. When his ex-girlfriend returned to town, I had hoped he would be happy because I know he cared deeply for her in the past. Those hopes were quickly dashed. Fate intervened when I happened to be at the right place, at the right time. From a distance, I saw him staring at Lizzie Macintyre. Not a glance, but a very heated stare. Paying close attention, like I always do, I watched them. Lizzie was very interested in my son too. I began to contemplate the implications of a potential liaison between them, and any negative resulting effects. Confusing to me, was Mark Chesney. For the life of me, I couldn't figure out what their relationship was. Until… I overheard it all.

Mark hired Lizzie as an escort for the events. Initially, I was furious and repulsed until I heard it wasn't a physical relationship. Shocking and confusing, to say the least. They had a deeply genuine friendship. Knowing about the difficulties Lizzie was facing with her alcoholic husband, I was despondent. Almost destitute, Mark changed everything in Lizzie's world. Initially, I wanted to run in and put her under my wing and save her from herself. Needing to be more careful, I watched those around me moving at a snail's pace, and it was driving me crazy. I'm a business woman, time is money. However, in my case, it's more personal. I needed to save my depressed son, and I owed Lizzie.

The raffle was pure happenstance. I needled Mark to buy tickets on Lizzie's behalf. He thought I was joking… I don't joke when I formulate a plan. Carefully spreading Mark's many tickets on the top, it was easy to grab one of his. Excellent, now Lizzie has a date with my son. When she came on the stage, she was a scared little mouse. It hurt me to not grab her and hug her to pieces. She's had a tough life. I know a lot about Lizzie's situation. Far more than anyone realizes. In recent years, there was an embarrassing situation at the Club, and I intervened on her behalf. I'm sure we'll discuss it at some point because she needs to know, I've always kept tabs on her. That, won't *ever* change.

It was terrible what she had to go through with her husband's loss. Asshole that he was. Personally, I thought she was destined for great things. Good career, excellent education. Having babies at a young age, changed my dreams for her. It was her decision to make in the end.

After the revealing information regarding being an escort for Mark, I had to get involved. And involved… I got. There's only one person in Richmond, serving up beauties to rich men. She's an enigma to most… a ghost because they don't even know the simple building on Main Street is home to a powerful Madame. Built from the ground up, she runs the business with the precision of a nuclear weapon. Doing so, has made her among the richest people I know. Since she's incredibly secretive, she trusts few, and allows almost no one in her inner circle. Except me.

Considering how much she earns, I have no idea how much money she truly has. Suffice it to say, she's smart. It's shouldn't be shocking, I would know her. Of course, I do, because when millions of dollars are passed in my beloved City, I make it my business to know such things. Moreover, many years ago, when I heard rumors of an escort service servicing rich men… yeah, I laid the law down with Charlene. My husband is off limits. After a while, we realized, we're more helpful to one another, rather than against each other. Yes, our relationship has served our combined interests well. Whereas, my donations are public, she's the private angel funding projects the world over. Two women, making significant progress. The most unlikely samaritans, working together.

Late one evening after dark, I phoned Charlene and informed her to have my drink ready. Knocking on the rear entrance, she opened the door, ushering me inside. Judging by our small stature, you'd think we're meek, mild and harmless. You would think wrong. We've had quite a long history. In secret, of course.

Greeting me with double kisses, "What brings you by Sarah?"

"I have a delicate matter, I need to ask you about?"

Nodding her head, "Okay. How can I help?"

"Lizzie Macintyre. Is she one of yours?"

Charlene busts out laughing, slamming her hand on the desk. "What is it about this girl that sends everyone's panties in a twist?"

Running her question over and over in my head, "She's special. So I take it—yes, she works for you?"

"Well… yes… and no. Mark has taken a shine to her and just so happens he had her first, trying her out for me. Normal protocol. Something about this girl has made him a weepy puppy. No sex… but he wants her exclusively. It's the craziest shit, I've ever seen."

"So, no sex with clients?"

"Nada—Mark has insisted she stay clean."

Taking and releasing a huge breath, I'm completely thankful. I don't completely get the relationship, but maybe it is an honest friendship. Good for them, if it's true. "Thank God! Look, I don't want her taking clients. I have big plans for her."

"Oh, that's intriguing!"

"Yeah, but I'm keeping quiet about it for now. I really need your help. Anything she needs, do it. She doesn't have a family, Char. Be that for her, please."

"Yeah, I know her asshole prick husband is a waste. He's just a drunk and doesn't deserve her."

"That's what I hear as well. I owe you for this."

"Sarah, you don't owe me nothing. It's what we do… we help those in need. Always have, always will.

In full agreement, I shake my head, "Always have, always will."

"Lizzie, how about we powder our nose?" As I stand from our table, heading towards the ladies room, without giving her time to respond.

"Sure."

Standing at the sink, I wash my hands, waiting for Lizzie. The ladies lounge is very plush. There are comfortable chairs and sofas, adorned with luxurious fabrics. Not knowing when I'll have her alone again, it's perfect for a private conversation. Taking a quick scan, I make sure we won't be overheard. As Lizzie approaches the sink, I move to sit in the wingback chair. "Come sit for a moment dear."

"Yes ma'am."

"I'm aware that you've had a difficult time recently. My heart breaks for you actually, especially your children. Full disclosure? I'm sorry your husband died, but I'd be lying if I wasn't thrilled you're dating my son." A look of pain crosses her face. "When someone dies, and they're close to you, it's impossible to get over it right away. I've suffered my own loss throughout the years, so I'm fully aware how difficult it can be to go on with life."

She lowers her head, clenching her hands together. Eventually, she nods slowly, "There are times, I feel guilty for being happy with Jack. Jeremy and I had a troubled marriage, but I never wanted him to die. I especially didn't want pain brought onto my children. My full disclosure? I should have worked harder to get him help. Part of me feels like I don't deserve any modicum of happiness and should stay alone for the rest of my life."

"Oh, no! Don't you dare feel that way, sweetheart." Standing up, I move next to her on the couch. Embracing her tightly, "Alcoholics are responsible for their own choices. Not us, it's their fault. You put up with him for a long time, and you deserve happiness." Holding her, she sobs on my chest, and I soothe her, running my fingers through her long beautiful hair.

"I apologize, I didn't mean to be so emotional."

"Lizzie, you are a mother who's hurting for her children. They lost their father and as such, lost out on many future opportunities. Memories will never be made. You have a right to be sad, to be angry, and feel the loss of a man you once loved. There is no timeframe for mourning a lost soul. You take it day-by-day. Additionally, you make new memories with a good man. Focus on new love, Lizzie."

"Thank you. I really appreciate it. You seem to understand what losing someone feels like."

Closing my eyes solemnly, I take a deep breath, "I do."

"I never got the chance to tell you how much it meant to me, what you did, long ago, here at the Club."

Shaking the notion away with my hand, "No thanks necessary. They treated you disrespectfully and very unprofessionally. I love it here, but that manager needed some redirection, so I was happy to give it to him." I said with a smirk and a wink.

Recalling the day I was having lunch, after my tennis lesson, there was quite a commotion at the lobby desk. What caught my attention was the snide remark I overheard the manager make to Lizzie, about her overdue bill not being paid by her drunk husband. Lizzie was there, attempting to gain access to her personal locker. She explained, due to her husband's job loss, she couldn't pay her dues. The manager refused to allow her access to her locker, or gain entrance to the Club grounds.

Understanding the Club has financial obligations to meet as well, I wasn't so much upset about discontinuing her membership. The part angering me, was the public way he chided her in the process. He could have quite simply had the conversation in the conference room, but he was being an ass and making an example out of her.

I walked directly into the conversation. "May I be of assistance, Mrs. Loving?" He asked too sweetly.

"Oh, I think you've done quite enough today. I plan to speak to the General Manager about the way you've spoken to this young woman."

A look of total fear entered his face, holding his hands up to halt my conversation, "Mrs. Loving. Please, there are extenuating circumstances. I apologize if I have upset you."

"Me—upset me? Are you serious? You shouldn't apologize to me, it's this beautiful lady you should apologize to." Positively chastised, he shut his mouth completely. "This is a bad economy, Sir. Be more understanding to those having difficult times. Furthermore, learn some manners and decorum while you're at it. Never speak to a lady that way and do not ever conduct financial conversations in this lobby. Are we clear?"

Cowering like a little boy, "Yes, Mrs. Loving."

"Now, we're going to settle this situation respectfully and amicably for everyone. First, you're going to put the balance of the Macintyre's account, on my bill. That way, should she wish to rejoin us, she will be in good standing. Next, she and I are going to the women's locker room where she will gather her remaining items. After, I will personally return the key. We're done here, Sir."

"Yes ma'am." Looking to Lizzie, he extended his hand to her, "I apologize Mrs. Macintyre."

"Thank you." She replied gracefully. Then, we went to the locker room as planned and she retrieved her personal possessions. I could tell she was rather shaken by the confrontation, so I didn't press her. Once we were finished, she handed me the silver key. "I don't know how to adequately express my appreciation."

Laying my hand over hers, I pulled her into me, hugging her tightly. "You just did. Take care, Lizzie." Pulling back, I walked away.

Now, sitting here with Lizzie, in the ladies lounge, the conversation is as clear as yesterday. Never could I have imagined, she and Jack would be together. It's amazing how fate intervenes, sometimes with nudging, and the good ones end up winning.

Lost in my memories, I initially didn't hear her question the first time. After gaining my attention, she repeated. "I was always so curious, how did you know my name while speaking to the Manager? Obviously, I knew who you were… you're an icon, but I always remained curious how you knew me?"

"Oh, I'm sure it was mentioned by the Manager."

"Well, interestingly enough, he didn't say it. So, it was a mystery to me all this time."

"Oh, Lizzie. I'm a mysterious person, what else can I say?" I smile and dismiss the question. Now, is definitely not the time for a history lesson. Realizing I don't want Jack to see her emerge with mascara marks, "You go ahead and freshen your pretty face up. I'll head on out, and leave you to it."

"Okay. Thank you for the kind words, Mrs. Loving."

Standing up, I bend down and kiss her cheek. "Mrs. Loving was my mother-in-law. You may call me, Sarah."

"Yes ma'am, Sarah. I'll be out in a bit." With a confirming wink, I leave her.

Returning to the table, my favorite men, stand upon my return. Jack, while pushing my chair in, whispers in my ear, "I was worried you'd scared her off."

Caressing his cheek, "No worries, Son. She's on her way. We were having a private chat."

He looks at me questioningly. "Please don't do anything to interfere, Mother."

"Me? Seriously, Jack! You have nothing to fear from me. In fact, quite the opposite. I approve of Lizzie. My inclination is she's a wonderful woman and would hold her own against you."

He chuckles, "Oh, she does, believe me." He glances back towards the door, and when he doesn't find her coming, "She's the one. On paper, it's the wrong time for both of us, but in my heart I know, I'll marry her."

"Jack, that's awfully soon." My husband quickly interjects. "You have only begun to really date her. There is no way to be sure, and you need more time."

Shaking his head at his father, "No, I've lost too many years not being happy. You two know more than anyone how I've always felt about...well, she makes me feel a unique connection. I've never felt it with another person and I'm *going* to marry her." Winking at him in support, yes, he's a smart man indeed.

"Be smart this time around, draft an agreement."

Feeling the air around me suddenly change, I look up to see that Lizzie has returned. Having no way to know if she heard the conversation, I jump in to salvage it. "Lizzie, you're back!" The men stand, as etiquette would dictate. Jack quickly assists her with her chair and kisses her cheek lovingly. "Would you like to take some dessert home for the children?"

"Oh, it would be lovely. Thank you."

The night comes to a close and was successful by all measure. My son is happy. Therefore, I'm over-the-moon. Nevertheless, I'll stay observant. Making sure their romance continues to unfold. Keeping tabs from afar... *just as I always have.*

Chapter Twenty-Nine

The Enemy Of My Enemy, Is My Friend

Victoria

I literally feel sick. At any moment, I will most certainly hurl. Needing to return my tennis pro instructor to the Country Club, after an afternoon of delight, I saw Jack's car. Not able to help myself, I decided to pop in for a peek. If even from a distance. Truly, it's shameful I can't seem to simply walk away. My heart is so broken, and I miss him enormously. You just do not realize how important people are in your life until they are no longer in it.

Desperate to catch a glance, or even hear a few words, I waited off to the side. When the coast was clear, I stood at a nearby staff entrance. Looking around the room, I first saw my in-laws, Jack, Sr. and Sarah. They were laughing and smiling, perfectly enjoying their dinner conversation. It was then, I saw my beloved, Jack. Mesmerized by him, I studied his face, his slightly overgrown hair, the new outfit he was wearing. Mostly, I was struck by the rapt attention he was paying to the person beside him. I would imagine, he was watching *her,* much the same as I was watching *him.* Staring at his lips, I remember so many times, they willingly gave me pleasure. *So, much pleasure.* Then, he moved closer to *her,* and those lips met hers freely. God, it ripped me open, and burned me straight through.

Someone approached their table, wanting to make small talk—I used to hate those interruptions, now I'd kill to be a party to them. Sarah looked annoyed but chatted for a moment, then her visitor left. Stuck to the floor, I couldn't seem to make myself leave the hurtful scene in front of me. Maybe I needed this in a strange way. Especially because those lips aren't meant for me anymore. Then, Sarah stood, glass "tinging" away. As only Sarah could, she addressed the room: "I know all of you have more important things to do than talk business with me and my family. It's after office hours, and I'm enjoying my son's new girlfriend. So, please… quiet down the whispers and table talk. They're happy, and I'm over the moon. Her name is Ms. Lizzie Macintyre, *yes…* she's a former member here, and we should embrace her return. I look forward to witnessing everyone's warm welcome, extended to our sweet girl."

Now, here I sit, in the Country Club bar, drinking a Long Island Iced Tea. I don't think I could drive, even if I wanted to. When Sarah made that announcement, everything went partially black. Grabbing for the wall, I held on waiting for it to pass. But… really, it won't pass. Jack has moved on. He loves her, and it's written on his forehead. Seeing them together, absolutely pulverized me to bits. Truthfully, this is the last place I need to be because this is their turf. Home to all their rich friends and business associates. Even still, here I am. I don't want to go home. Even the children don't want anything to do with me. I guess they blame me for our divorce. Oh, well, it's nothing I can do except have another drink. Wait… I do have something… money. Lots of money. I spent my entire life thinking money was the most important possession. My parents made me feel like shit about myself all the time. The only time I received their approval was when I gave them money. Now, I'm loaded. No matter what… they won't see a penny of it.

"That was a train wreck to watch. Wasn't it?" A lady sits beside me and comments. Looking at her like she has lost her mind, I turn back, completely ignoring her. "You don't know me, but we have a common enemy." She announces with certainty.

Slamming my drink down, "Excuse me, but can you please move along?"

She smiles and decides to ignore me. "I don't like her either. She's a conniving manipulator, who uses sex appeal to attract men. They're blind to her, but I know what she really is."

Terribly pissed off at this nosy bitch, "I don't know who the hell you're moaning on about, but I could care less. So, please… just… leave me alone."

"Lizzie Macintyre." My head twists immediately. "She's evil and she took what was mine. She took my man, now she has yours. I want to destroy her."

Now very interested, "Who are you?"

With a sarcastic smile, "Oh, now I got your attention. My name is Cindy Hall, and I'm about to become your new best friend."

Not really knowing if this woman is a head case or just full of shit, I give her my attention. "I don't care who Jack's seeing."

"Bullshit!" She laughs loudly. "I saw you, watching as his mom issued the royal proclamation. Don't lie to me, that fucking shit hurts like hell."

"Doesn't matter anyway. We're divorcing, he has a right to move on."

"Yep, but with gutter trash?"

"What do you mean?"

"I know a lot about Lizzie Macintyre. Here's the highlights… she's a paid escort who turned tricks with Mark Chesney. After gaining his trust, he gave her free access to his checking account. I believe she stole his money working on so-called charity projects. She never told her husband*anything*. I saw him the day he died, we spoke at length. Lizzie was out of control, and I believed it was wrong to lie to Jeremy, who already had his own set of problems. She trampled that man. It's her fault he's dead. She'll break Jack, too."

Fuck. *What the hell?* I'm in total shock right now. Thinking back, I remember seeing them together at charity events. Mark said she was working at his Endowment. Now, she has set her eyes on Jack? *No fucking way!* If she is an escort, is she Jack's escort? Is all of this for show? Is he playing a game to hurt me, or get back at me? Maybe his parents don't know anything about this. Now she wants his money. It has to be his money she's after.

"I want you to tell me everything you know about Lizzie Macintyre. Don't leave anything out." I implore her.

Shrugging her shoulders, "No problem, but in exchange we come up with a plan to take down the whore. I want her to know, it was me who played a part."

Considering her suggestion carefully, I know I have to help Jack. "Deal."

For the next two hours, we sat drinking coffee, planning ways to expose the woman who has captured my husband's heart. By the end, everything was set. "I'm coming for you Lizzie," I said into the night sky. At that moment, it began to drizzle, yet I oddly captured a shooting star. Taking the opportunity to make a wish, yes—it's a good sign indeed.

Chapter Thirty

Tight Vaginas Lead To Breaking And Entering

Lizzie

"It's tight!" Marianne announces to our tight-knit group.

"It's tight?" Janice asks skeptically.

"Well, it's tight-er ish, it's not like I'm twenty-one again, but Derek says it's tight."

"I'll be damned," Jenny chimes in.

"My girlfriend at work, said she used them after pregnancy. She's Asian, and she claimed the East widely uses them post-pregnancy, to tighten your vagina back up," remarked Marianne.

"Seriously?" Janice questions, still unsure about any of this.

"Yes! That's what she said, so I figured I had nothing to lose. I went out and bought a set. Apparently, it's cultural, and I'm here to tell you, it's a smart idea. Ben Wa balls honestly work. You have to buy several different sizes though. Starting with the largest size, they're generally plastic and come two on a string. They're hollow, but when you shake them, you can feel there's something inside rolling around. You insert it, then you squeeze your Kegel muscles… tightly."

"Doesn't it fall out?" Jenny bursts out laughing.

"No. I tried wearing them for fifteen minutes, several times per day, then built up the time gradually. Then, I began using the midsize plastic balls without the string and timed them the same way. Now, I'm using the smallest metal balls."

"What will they come up with next?" I asked.

"I don't know, but I can't wait to discover it," said Janice.

"Damn, who would have thought you could tighten the 'ole vajayjay!" Jenny comments rather too loudly, causing fellow patrons at The Boathouse to turn and stare. Ah hell, here we go again. Why do we always seem to become the center of attention among the customers, on girl's night?

"Well, I sorta found another benefit, I wasn't expecting." With baited breath, everyone moves in closer, waiting for Marianne's discovery. "Once, I wore them for longer periods of time, I started noticing they were… ya know." The girls shake their heads "no."

"Stimulating you?" I asked her.

"Yes! They were stimulating me… from the inside. Not enough to bring me to orgasm, which was the maddening part of it all. It's like I was constantly on edge, and all I thought about… was sex!"

"R-really?" Janice asked excitedly.

"Oh, yeah! The second I got home, I jumped Derek's bones. So, be aware if you keep them in for long stretches of time, make sure you have your man nearby."

"Or a tall, dark and sexy, dressed in all black, commando-type, if you're lucky." Jenny mumbled under her breath.

We couldn't seem to help our wails of laughter. Luckily, the customers that hang out often have come to expect our silly behavior, and simply ignore it. Others, for some reason, always seem to move nearby once we arrive. Oftentimes, the real show, is watching them… while staring at us. They think we're crazy wild women!

Approaching almost midnight, I have consumed far more alcohol than I needed to. The girls all know about my relationship with Jack and my security detail. Being the overprotective man he is, we changed the transportation plan several months ago. Now, they drive me to The Boathouse and bring me home. It's not just my welfare, Jack is concerned about. The girls receive the same treatment. They are picked up and returned home safely. I'll never forget, the first time Jenny met Seth. Her jaw dropped open, and he had a moment of stuttering as well. Now, I tease her relentlessly about what's taking place in the car after he drops me off. They're amongst the gene pool of the beautiful people, so I've already announced they would make beautiful babies—*and I best be Godmother!*

Walking over to Seth, who doesn't normally work evening hours, although suspiciously never seems to miss girl's night. Upon plopping in a chair, I'm wearing a huge smile, but remain quiet.

"Yes, ma'am. May I get you something? Water perhaps?"

"No… I received the three glasses you already sent my way earlier. I'm good with hydration."

"O-kay."

"I have a plan, and I need your help."

Narrowing his eyes at me, "What exactly is your plan?" He asks cautiously.

"I want you to let me in Jack's house tonight, without him knowing it."

With a sarcastic chuckle, "Ah, I don't think so."

Tilting my head and jaw dropped, I'm sure I look like a petulant teenager. "Seth...," I whine. "Look, I don't want to spell it out for you, but I guess I'll have to. If you tell him you've delivered me home safely, he'll go on to bed. Because you and I both know, he keeps tabs on me during girl's night and won't go to sleep until you call him. He won't expect me at all. I'll slip in, tiptoe my way through the house and give him a very special surprise."

"You'll get me fired if I go along." He says confidently.

"No... you'll get fired if you *don't* go along."

Sitting back abruptly in his chair..."You fight dirty."

"No. I'm just horny."

"Fuck." Shaking his head, he has *that* look—the one men have when they know the woman gets her way.

"Gather your crew. I'm texting the boss you're heading home."

"Thank you, Seth!" I jump up excitedly.

"Yeah, yeah."

After we drop off the girls, with lots of hugs and kisses, of course, we head toward his house. He told me where he lives, but I've never been before. The closer we get, the more nervous I become. Maybe I didn't think this through very well? Looking up, I realize it's too late for second thoughts as we turn into his driveway. Seth turned the headlights off, as to not arouse suspicion. Going through the security gate, we go around a curve and finally the house comes into view. Dear heaven, it's massive! Never in my life have I been in a house this huge. With large white columns that frame the center section, and brick bookends, it's gorgeous. *Shit how will I find his room? How will I get inside? What have I gotten myself into?*

"You ready?" He asked.

"Ah... I probably didn't plan this well... actually, I don't know how to get inside?"

"Gotcha covered." He stated calmly. Walking around, he opens my door, gesturing me outside. Then, he proceeds to explain a general floorplan of the house. *Damn, I hope I remember everything.* "I'll input the code, then you're good to go. Let me tell you if I get fired over this—."

"You won't! I promise."

"You better promise." Then he muttered under his breath, thinking I didn't hear him, "Wish I had a good looking woman slip into my bed late at night just to surprise me."

I smirk knowingly, and I can't help but recall the weird look he and Jenny gave one another, just a few minutes before. "Thanks, Seth." Then, I walk inside, scared as shit, but very excited.

Chapter Thirty-One

Without You, There Is No Me

Jack

Warm, wet lips go up and down my shaft several times. Lost in the realness of my dream, my body goes along unwittingly, and my hips gyrate slightly. Moving from my side to my back, I begin to dream about Lizzie. Her body, her mouth, her hands, and her smell. Incredibly tired from a long stressful day, I am completely exhausted and my mind is playing with me. When the warmth leaves my cock, it is replaced with a firm hand, pumping up and down. Then, I feel the same warm feeling enclose around my balls while stroking me. Damn, it feels so good. *Too good... shit!*

Forcing my eyes open, I sit up in bed quickly while reaching for the lamp. When the light floods the room, all I see is the top of Lizzie's head moving towards my dick. The wet heat resumes its ministrations of enclosing me with pleasure. Scared out of my mind, my heart rate is so high, I cannot even speak. Forced to lay back against the headboard, I focus on getting my breathing under control. With my eyes closed, I gather my wits, and reality sets in to enjoy the surprise of a lifetime.

"Sorry to scare you, but I was craving your cock." She pauses to whisper.

With a deep breath, "Ohhh... baby... the way you make me feel right now is worth the heart attack you almost gave me."

"Good, but I'm selfish."

"How's that?"

Sitting up on her knees, she gifts me with the sight of her beautiful body, covered in a sexy multi-color bra and G-string. "I had a reason for getting you good and hard." Removing her panties, she climbs over and straddles me. In one precise movement, she impales herself quickly. Watching me, we become fixated on one another. It takes a few seconds, for her body to adjust to my girth. Until then, we are both in the sort of pain which only hurts so good.

I grab her hips and begin to guide her up and down. Realizing I'm missing out on the perfect view of boobs-in-motion, I reach around her, pulling her bra away. "My god, Lizzie. I'll never bore of seeing your body." Raking my fingers along her side, I cup each breast in my hands, squeezing them, planting my face in her overflowing mounds. Instantly, panic strikes me wondering if the door is open or closed. Looking around her, I'm pleased to discover a closed door. Smiling largely, "I can't believe you're here."

"Honestly... me either. I guess too much alcohol left me horny and wanting you pretty badly."

Continuing to control her movements, I hold her in the down position. Leaning up, I hug her hard, "Then you made the right decision coming here. The last thing I want happening is you, out on the streets, needing a hard fuck."

Releasing her, allowing her to move, "Yeah, bad idea. By the way, if you fire Seth for going along with my plan, I'll never forgive you."

"Fire him? He's getting a bonus!"

"Good, but then again he may be getting a bonus just like this…" she speeds her upwards and downwards movements, "with Jenny."

Shocked with that piece of information, I decide to file it away for another time. Right now, I have more pressing matters to attend to. "My concern is not whether Seth and Jenny have casual sex, my concern is this gorgeous ass bouncing on my cock."

"Umm, it feels so good, Jack."

"Yeah, well, I need a taste. Grab onto the headboard, arch your back, and do not let go." Knowing I want to drag this out, I lift her hips off my cock and slid downwards until she's sitting on my face. Immediately, I'm hit with her scent containing our combined flavors, and I don't mind making it obvious how much inhaling it turns me on. Desperate to lap up her shiny wetness, I delve my tongue into her tight channel, long and deep. Reaching around, I place my thumb on her clit, flicking her piercing. Always so responsive, Lizzie moans with each new movement I make.

Her drenching wet pussy, easily opens as I slide in two fingers from my other hand, seeking the spot which is guaranteed to bring her total bliss. Her muscles begin to clench on my fingers, and her clit swells under my tongue. I'm trapped and confined by long sexy legs, now stiffened while she chases her orgasm, along with a face full of silky goodness… *yes, I could die right now a happy man.*

With laser focus, I flatten the tip of my tongue, determined to bring her ecstasy. Bending my fingers inward, I stroke her inner wall, feeling her folds becoming more engorged. Lizzie, lost in the moment, throws her head back and rides my face, seeking the exact pressure she desires. Just on the edge, her tiny bud swells, she gasps for air, and I gently nibble on her clit with a tiny bit of pain. Holding her pierced hood carefully in my teeth, I use the point of my tongue to flick across the sensitive nerve endings. Too many sensations at once, she shudders and screams the announcement of her orgasm. Thank goodness for thick walls, but at this moment all I experience is the fluids drenching my mouth and down across my face. My clamped fingers, begin to feel the post-orgasmic pulses strongly, as she continues to grind against them. Yeah, my baby, goes all out when she comes, and once is *definitely* not enough.

Sliding out from under her, I quickly grab the wedge from my closet. Even though she looks blissfully satiated, I want more from her. Positioning it in the center of the bed, I throw on a towel... *for obvious reasons*. Rolling her over to her back, she looks so peaceful with her eyes closed. She mumbles resistance while in her hazy euphoria. "No sweetheart, I want to hear more screams. Remember, I promised you multi-orgasms every time?"

"Yes, but I'm tired now. I'm good, seriously contented."

"Well, you're about to be great." Grabbing her legs, I roll her legs and hips upwards, pushing the wedge underneath her back.

"What the hell is this thing?"

"I'm about to introduce you to heaven." I tease lovingly. Rubbing my shaft through her juices, gets me iron-hard in seconds. Entering her, brings her instantly on edge again. Since I prefer to bring her to orgasm, back-to-back because they're more intense that way, I need to focus on hitting those deeply hidden spots.

"Fuck, Jack... it feels amazing. *So* good. I can practically feel you in my womb. *This...* it's different. I don't know how to explain it, but you feel so incredible. The area deep inside has always felt good when you hit it a certain way, now I feel like I'm on fire." Breathing heavily, she begins to run her hands across my chest in a fierce pattern. Flouncing her head back and forth, she is overwhelmed with the sensations never felt this intensely before. "Oh, Jack, fuck me harder, *please.*"

Plowing into her, it's hard to chat and breathe. My student, always starved for knowledge, will feel it more if she understands how I'm titillating her body. "It's all about positioning, babe, and missionary is by far the worst for hitting the best spots." I rotate between her legs widely spread, close together and against her chest. Thanks to the wedge, her hips are perfectly lifted to hit the other erogenous zones.

Spreading her legs, I reach down, applying circular pressure against her clit. Drawing a pert nipple into my mouth, I suck hard, sending her over the edge. "I-I'm com-ing… oh Jack. Oh, baby, fuck that feels good." A deluge covers us both, immediately sending me to the top of the mountain. Thrusting my hips, we are surrounded by the wet, sloppy sounds of our lovemaking. Each and every time, I think it cannot get any better. Surely, this occasion won't be surpassed, because the chills overwhelming my body, completely dominate my manhood.

Trying to catch my breath, I settle us and lay my head on her belly. Unable to look in her eyes because of the rawness I feel. With a voice barely above a whisper, "Lizzie, having the opportunity to worship your body, electrifies and rejuvenates mine. But, I have to tell you, I'm interdependent on you, and if there was ever an opportunity to cripple a man, it's now.

I hear her sigh, and she begins to run her fingernails through my scalp, sending chill bumps across my skin. "Oh, Jack. Never in a million years, did I anticipate feeling real love like you award. I'm branded in your shadow. Don't you see it? Do you feel me there? I'm with you, standing beside you, only us. I've relinquished my soul for safe keeping, Jack. I have *nothing* because I trust you... with *everything*.

Chapter Thirty-Two

Wake Up Baby

Lizzie

Laying in his arms, I'm struck with just how right this feels. There are so many reasons why we should not get involved so quickly, but right now, this feeling—trumps everything. When he speaks about our future, sometimes the resulting feeling seems to burn me. Therefore, I shy away from considering it. For a moment though, I push the burn away, and I'm left with a healing warmth. Not one that makes me want to run.

But, on the outer fringes of my mind, is the work Ms. Martin and I, are doing. I've come so far in an incredibly short period of time, my head spins. Never did I imagine when I first went to the interview, I'd end up running the place. Once she introduced me to the interworking of her business, all my negative impressions vanished. Very rarely do I think about the sex, affiliated with the money. What dominates my mind, is how to distribute the money to the neediest people. Then, the aftereffects of the media reports, bring a huge sense of satisfaction over the small part I played. My job is so fulfilling—my job is… vitally important to helping others.

Inasmuch as it brings me satisfaction, it also brings me fear. *If I'm exposed, what will Jack think? Will he understand? Can he be hurt professionally if connected to me?* I think the answers are all… *yes.* So, every day, I keep doing the same routine because I have no good solutions. Making a real difference in the world, while lying to my amazing boyfriend. A boyfriend whom already makes a tremendous difference locally. The difference between us: his charity is public, and mine is totally illegal and secret.

I've gotten so attached to this man. He makes me feel confident and loved. Moreover, I'm a stronger person because he pushed me, and I can't give him up. I won't give him up. There are so many ways he has shown his love, and I've come around at a much slower pace. He said he knew last year, we were destined to be together. Truly, I'm not sure how he figured it out so quickly, but I'm glad he did. Now, it's up to me to have his same faith. In him— *in us.*

Listening to his slightly shallow breathing, I can tell he's on the edge of deep sleep. Knowing, I need to get this out now before I lose my nerve, I go for it. Rubbing my palm over his entire bare chest, my fingers ripple along his muscled physique. Feeling enjoyment from my touch, he whimpers softly. Giving feather-soft kisses in random patterns, he begins to awaken. *Good—wake up baby, we have a future to plan.*

Eyes still closed, his hands lift, seeking my head and gripping my hair firmly. Moving my body to lay on top of him, I align our warmest places. Gently grinding against him, he twitches and I can feel his limitless vitality. Instantly, I am aroused as he hardens and provides the perfect spot for me to rut against. At this moment, I could easily tilt, taking him inside me… but I won't. I want this to be about us—our contact with one another. Freeing myself of the past and being vulnerable to him. Making my commitment for a new journey.

As the minutes pass, I control the pressure and speed necessary to get me there. Seemingly understanding my intent, he allows me freedom to do as I please. Almost breathless, I hold his face in my hands. Moving my thumb to the center of his mouth, I plunge it inwards, wetting it and moistening his lips completely. Just when I'm climbing the proverbial, glorious mountain, "Yes, Lizzie, give it to me baby."

And on command, I will, "I love you, I *really* love you Jack!" The rolling warmth and white stars fill my eyes, as my orgasm explodes through my insides, and I shamelessly masturbate using his body. Feeling his muscles lock beneath mine, perfectly still. Foggy from my overwhelming experience, I fight to stay aware, being present in the moment.

Staring at me with razor sharp intensity, he says nothing. The only sounds in the room, us fighting to regain our breaths. Then, a very strained look comes across his face, as liquid warmth spurts, covering my belly. His big arms move around me, as he squeezes our chests together. "God, Lizzie, how I have waited and daydreamed about hearing you say those words to me. Babe, I know I'm squeezing hard, but I just need to hold on to you. I need to make sure this moment is real, and you won't take them back."

Tears begin to fill my eyes, listening to his unguarded, vulnerability. This moment, laid open for us both, expressing our inner feelings for one another. It's now the prime opportunity, to give him more happiness. He's asked for quite a while, and I've resisted. But, I know, I love this man and my children will eventually love him too.

Pulling back from his hold, "I agree, it's time."

Looking at me with confusion, I can see the wheels turning furiously in his eyes. "Time for…?"

"Meeting our children. I love you, Jack, and I know my children will love you too."

Regaining the temporary loss of his hold, "Oh babe, I know you're nervous, but it's going to be fine. I promise we'll get through it."

Moving to stand up, I retrieve a warm washcloth. "Jack, we need to be realistic. We have four kids combined, with different personalities, similar in age. It's going to be stressful."

"I'm not wary of those facts. We'll need to make allowances when we need to. Here's what I believe: our children inherited the best traits of each of us. Focusing on that, we cannot go wrong."

Needing to make him understand, my children face different circumstances, now is as good a time as any. Especially, when he's in a happy, contented place. "I need to tell you something important, and it partially explains my reluctance."

"O-kay." He responds timidly.

"Even if we try to create the most positive situation, we cannot change the fact our children have very different financial backgrounds. They—"

"No, no—I refuse to entertain it as a potential problem, Elizabeth. No."

"Jack!"

"No, it will be fine. We'll make it fine for them." He stands up and heads to the bathroom. Upon returning, he has an irritated look, "I'm not going to let anything get in the way of us having a future. Not my kids—not your kids. Not. Going. To. Happen. You need to accept it, and they *all* need to accept us…" changing his expression from serious to elated, "We love each other. Nothing's getting in my way of having you. I told you before, *just hang on*, I'll take care of everything."

"Honestly, I have tremendous faith in you, truly I do. However, you must allow me to express my thoughts, without steamrolling me."

Looking dismayed, "What?"

"Yes. Picture this, my kids have been around a drunk. We were kicked out of our home because we were evicted. Many times, we scrounged for enough food to eat. Compare it to your kids who never had to worry about food, or leaving their home, and... the big difference... your kids are millionaires, mine aren't. That's conflict and jealousy wrapped in a nice package."

"Liz, here's what my kids lack: a mother who shows affection, knowledge she stole from them, and practically no interest in any of their activities. Furthermore, they're going through a divorce... yours didn't. They are shuttled back and forth, between their only home and a suite at the Jefferson while wondering if their home will be sold. Instead of a real mother, they have a nanny." Sitting down next to me, he grabs my hand, "I hear you about the money. My Trust is specific and I can't do anything about the situation. Just know, I'd never deny your child's financial future, Lizzie. They are from you... I could never turn my back on them. Never."

Leaning my head against his shoulder, "Jack, I'm not asking for your money. I'm comfortable now. We're perfectly fine."

"You'll be better, I'll see to it. Just go with it... have faith in me, we will together make each of them important and loved. It will be an adjustment, but we'll get through it."

Shaking my head, because I know this is a fight I cannot win right now. "Okay, sweetheart."

He kisses me hard on the forehead, "I love you *so* much, Lizzie."

With a bashful smile, hardly believing we're at this place now, "I love you too, Jack."

Chapter Thirty-Three

A Madame's Inside View

Lizzie

Totally exhausted. Yep, that's how I feel this morning. Coming into work, I essentially crawl to the coffeepot. Everyone else seems to love the instantaneous, single-serve coffee pots, these days. Nope, not me. I have to have the messy grounds (with my critically exact amount of coffee), and measuring water, followed by the endless waiting for enough to brew in the pot, I can sneak it out before it's fully ready. Best coffee ever! This morning... I may have settled for instantaneous, horrible coffee.

After my bright idea to crash into Jack's house last night, and following *amazing*, off-the-chain sex, I insisted going home to my apartment. It was the first time, I truly appreciated his wealth. The security staff—not Seth, because the man never sleeps anyhow, brought me home safely. Additionally, the on-call nanny, Jack insists I have especially for girls-night, was waiting at the apartment for me to come home. Totally cool to have those kinds of resources. Yep, wealth does have its privileges. However, it doesn't do a damn thing for regenerating my lost sleep. So, today I'm suffering through, therefore, the need for lots of caffeine.

When the outdoor alarm buzzes, I make my way to the security panel. Recognizing the visitor, I buzz her in. Moving to the front, "Hello Carol, good morning."

"Yeah, good morning." She answers exhausted.

"Wow, you look like I feel."

"Yep, long night. My client was extra motivated. He kept going strong for six hours. I thought I would die!"

"Six-hours? Not non-stop?"

"Oh, yes! He enjoys the little blue pill. I was all too ready for it to wear off, let me tell you."

"I'll bet." I chuckle. "What can I do for you Carol?"

"Well, I'm in a bind. I was hoping you could advance me for last night? I have some bills I really need to pay, and I'm the only income for me and my kids. So, can you help me?"

Thinking about her situation and knowing exactly how that feels, I know I need to help her. "Sure. I've been where you're at sweetie. I know the struggle."

"It's so hard. One of my kids has special needs, so I have to provide him with a nurse's aide during the day, and it's expensive. There's no way I could make it without this job."

"Carol, I only know my story… my struggles. I'm curious, do you feel you would ever find a job making the money this pays, in a traditional career."

"Oh, hell no." She immediately responds. "Ms. Martin saved my life. I owe her everything and if it weren't for her, we'd be homeless. She always takes care of me too. I've never had a bad client before, always respectful, never violent. The other people I know that work here, we'd kiss her feet because she's been so good to us. We'll never do anything to jeopardize our setup, and she's smart too. I wouldn't want to cross her. She may be small, but there's a lot of punch in that small package."

Smiling because it's exactly how I perceived her when we first met, "I completely agree. She's giving people jobs and allowing them to earn a living safely. Her screening process is intense. Hey, I'm happy to give you the advance."

After Carol leaves, I sit at my desk, looking at the records for the legitimate side of the business. Running a few calculations, I determine our net charitable amount, available for funding. Granted, it's in the millions, and huge by any standards... but, compared to the illegal side of the business, it pales in comparison.

Reaching for the folder on the corner of my desk, it's filled with articles. "Anonymous donor feeds homeless on Easter." "A local Lutheran Church in Richmond, was given money for desperately needed repairs." "The YWCA receives one hundred thousand dollars for funding emergency programs for victims of domestic violence." So many articles, I have begun collecting, from the work we're doing here. It's a novel concept, I know. The *most* unlikely samaritans, very true. I've considered walking away from the illegal side of the business, but the truth is, it's intoxicating to help so many people. Then, I think of Jack. *What would he say? What would he do?* He's a lawyer and legally bound to report us. Decades long worth of work Ms. Martin has done, all for nothing. All because of me. So, here I sit, caught in this circle of non-answers. Continuing on another day. Looking for more uses of the millions sitting next door, hidden behind the wall of books.

Shortly after lunch, I received a text from Mark. He said he was coming over later, wanting to confirm I'd be at work. So, nearing four o'clock, I hear the back door unlock, and he walks in. "Damn, you scared me. I didn't realize you had a key."

A strange look crosses his face, and he immediately sought to hide it. *Good try.* Leaning in towards me, "You look ravishing today, Birdie." He then kissed me sweetly on both cheeks and sat down in the chair beside me.

"Well, you look rather dashing yourself. Do you have big plans tonight?"

A beautifully bashful, half-smile appears. I've gotten to know him rather well, and I know something is up. "Who is she?"

"What? Who are you talking about?"

"Oh, I don't know. You look *really* fine and smell amazing. You only wear that cologne when you're going out. I don't have anyone on the schedule for you—who is it, Mark?"

Totally exasperated, "You're making too much out of this. Stop playing detective, babe."

"I will, *after* you dish. Tell me."

"Not happening sweetheart." He smiles that big beautiful white, all-toothy, smile, always making women swoon. But, I'm patient, and he's my friend, so I only want the best for him. So, I'll stay relentless, until I get what I want to know. With arms crossed over my chest, I tilt my head stubbornly, waiting for a proper answer. Even if it takes all day. "Dammit, Lizzie!"

My answer... one raised eyebrow. Then I cross my legs, "Yes?"

He exhales loudly, "Look, we've only been out twice. She's a nice girl, professional, attractive, and... you'd approve. That's all I can say for now. Please, I don't want to jinx it."

"Jinx it! You? Wow, you must be falling hard. My, my Mark Chesney!"

"Stop! I mean it. Stop."

"Okay, thanks for the hints. Keep me posted."

With a happy, sly smile, "Of, course. You'll be the first to know."

"I better be."

"Alright… moving on. I need to warn you about something. I'm worried there might be a leak here. Do you know of anyone that's been upset recently?"

A leak? What in the world! "No, absolutely no one. Everyone is happy as clams, picking up money along the way. Why wouldn't they be happy?"

"All I know, is something might be happening. Are you running everything based on Ms. Martin's protocols?"

"Yes, absolutely!"

"No paper trail?"

"None?"

"Okay. Look, I need you to be extra cautious. Don't take on any new employees, and be aware of weird questions from employees and clients."

"Mark, what do you think is happening?"

"I think someone has broken the no records rule. Either they are working with police or someone has found the records."

"Police! Mark, am I in danger?"

"Babe, there's only the records for the legitimate business, right?"

"Well… yes."

"Okay, we've been through police interrogations before, we will again. Ms. Martin is smart, you know that, babe. You don't survive being a Madame for thirty years, being stupid, and careless."

"True, but what if it's me? I've only been a Madame for a few months? Maybe I did something to get her and me in trouble!"

"Hey… stop! Follow the protocols, exactly. She and I both believe you're smart, and know what you're doing."

"Maybe I don't know what I'm doing! I have tremendous guilt, over not telling Jack. It's killing me actually."

"I understand. It's a problem, I admit. Look, I just wanted to tell you, I'm looking into a few things. In the meantime, be cautious."

Standing up, he moves over to me, and I notice a spot of dried blood on his neck. "Hey, come down here."

"Oh? Am I going to get a scandalous kiss? You know my dream is to have you for real, so don't tease me Birdie."

Swatting his arm, "Stop it! Be still." I grab a tissue and moisten it with water. Mark, looking totally confused, just stands there waiting and watching. "You have some dried blood on your neck. I'm trying to get it before your big date." I tease him.

He snorts lightly, "Yeah, probably during shaving."

Rubbing the blood away, I notice a horizontal scar. "I've never seen this scar before, how'd this happen?"

He pulls back suddenly, "Oh, nothing, stupid shaving accident. Nothing, really. I just hit it every time I shave, and reopen it. No worries."

Judging by his response, something tells me, it is something and he's hiding the truth. Before I can formulate a response, he's heading toward the exit. "Mark?"

Turning back to face me, "Yeah?"

"Your friendship is very important to me, you know?"

Winking at me, he looks down at his hands and wrings them tightly. Smiling largely, "Jack is a very lucky man. If he fucks up, I'll kill him because I don't have many close friends. Plus you're special, because you're a friend, that I wouldn't mind fu—"

"Alright!" I interrupt. "I get the picture, we love each other—enough already."

A serious look forms on his face. Before walking out the door, he states firmly, "Yeah."

Wow, that was intense. Reaching over to the top of my hand, I pinch. It's hard to believe my life has changed this much. My boyfriend is wildly in love with me. My amazing kids, who seem so well-adjusted, even though they have been through hell. Our children are going to meet this weekend. I have amazing friends like Jenny, who I dearly love and will always be like family. Of course, there're my other girls: Janice and Marianne. There's Ms. Martin, who was the conduit to saving my life, and who has entrusted her life's work into my hands. The work we do here every day, which is understandably a problem for many people, but if only they knew the good we do as well. Finally, there's Mark. I owe him so much. He identified my business skills, challenging me to believe in myself. When money was tight, he determined how much I needed and paid me. He put me on the path to Jack and was there for me when I fell apart after Jeremy's death. He's so special, and I'm proud to be his friend. These people are special to me and I love them all. My life is going so well, I don't want to even think about any negativity.

Packing up for the day, I leave the building. Invariably, my mind goes back to my conversation with Mark. A shocking thought crosses my mind... *is it possible?* So involved in my deep thoughts, I fail to notice the car, whose passengers are watching me.

Victoria

"Today, just like yesterday, I've watched her. She goes into the building in the morning and comes out in the afternoon."

"Have you seen Jack here?" I ask.

Shaking her head, "No, never. Occasionally, she goes to her apartment for lunch, and also an apartment in the new lofts at Pohlig's." When I don't seem interested, she chuckles "Oh, you don't know do you?"

"Know what?"

"Your husband has a bachelor pad?" She says flippantly.

Totally surprised, "What? What are you talking about?"

"Oh yeah, Jack Loving stays there. A lot. He brings Lizzie, and she comes and goes too. I think it is their... *place.*"

The thought sickens me. No matter how much time shall pass, I'll never mentally give him away to any woman. "I didn't know," I whisper

"She's an entitled leech who thinks every man is hers for the taking." She says angrily.

"I want to see his apartment building."

"No problem, let's go. I have a spare key." She brags.

"What? How did you get that?" I'm shocked to learn.

With a psychotic look on her face, "I make it a point to keep tabs on the bitch. That's not the only key I have." Shit, just how far is the reach of my new ally? Then, we're off to discover Jack's new pad and plan the final phase.

Chapter Thirty-Four

Revelations

Jack

It's been a long day dealing with clients, and I'm glad to finally get to the apartment. The kids are with Victoria tonight, so thankfully I don't have to be at the house. The Lindy case has dominated much of my work. It looks like time is nearing for search warrants. After that, I'm sure the press will catch on. Luckily, I have friends throughout the judicial system, so I'm kept well informed. In the back of my mind, I'm still very concerned about Mark. Thinking as an attorney, the details on the USB pertaining to Mark, are very different as opposed to the others. It drives me crazy wondering how he would be involved with a prostitution ring, in a way that's different to the others. Surely the man has many different kinks, so why weren't they listed? The only explanation I can come up with, is maybe she was meeting with him for investment advice? I know it's a stretch, but that is his line of work. Damn, I just really hate not knowing.

Also, I'm unsettled and anxious over Lizzie. We didn't get to chat much today. Each of us going in different directions. Thinking back to last night, when she slipped into bed with me, fuck that was great. Never in a million years would I have predicted her to do it. She was in a mood, and I was thrilled to comply.

Early this morning, I sent word for Seth to come see me. Walking in, I could tell he looked hesitant, which is odd because the man is normally cold as stone. Pointing to a chair, he sat down, waiting for me to speak. When he opened the envelope I handed him, he fingered through the cash. Looking up, he asked, "What's this exactly?"

"Bonus," I replied flatly.

He slowly shook his head once, and the only sign he allowed was a slight creasing in his eyes. Yeah… he gets it. "Sir, thank you, Sir."

"No, thank you for making the *right* judgment call. Lizzie must have lectured me five times already that if I fired you, she would cut me off. Since I don't intend to ever let that happen, I figured I would reward you instead."

As stoic as ever, I can see the desire to burst out laughing hidden just beneath. "I appreciate the job, Sir."

Lizzie has this way about her. She's not bitchy, or rude. There's genuine warmness in her personality. She's caring, giving, and concerned about people other than herself. I'm lucky to finally have her in my life. "Thanks for keeping her safe for me. She's an important part of my life, and I don't want anything happening to her."

"Not on my watch, Sir. Can I speak freely?"

"Absolutely."

"This job she has… are you more familiar with her work now? Has she spoken to you about her job? Because I'll be honest, I don't feel comfortable. There's too much security for a simple dating agency. I think there's something else going on there."

"Like what?"

"Well, with your permission, I'd like to investigate further. My gut tells me, it's a front for something else. No offense to Ms. Macintyre."

Thinking carefully, I wonder if he could be right. He wanted to pursue his gut feeling months ago, and I stopped his efforts. An unnerving thought crosses my mind, and I immediately push it back down. Maybe he's right... why the need for such high security? "Alright, go ahead."

Now that I'm home, having time to reflect, I think I made a big error not having Seth check out Lizzie's work. She was so proud of her job and asked me not to interfere. In hindsight, it was probably a mistake. I really hope he doesn't find anything.

Deciding to take a quick shower, after I spent almost two hours in the gym, I enter the walk-in and begin by normal routine. Invariably, every time I'm in the shower, I always end up thinking about Lizzie. Then, before you know it, I'm jacking off to her in my mind, doing every nasty thing I want to do to her body. Even though she has been accepting of everything I've suggested, I still want to pace things. There will be a day, I know, we will go places neither of us has gone before. And, we'll do it together.

Getting out of the shower, I try to reach Lizzie by phone and text. No luck either time. Deciding to try and work a little, I take my laptop to bed. Feeling my eyes getting heavy, I'm determined to stay awake because I want to speak to her. Reviewing a set of depositions for a new client, takes about an hour of my time and then... I... doze off.

A slight stinging bite on my nipple brings me out of the deep sleep I was enjoying. Still in the sleep zone, I'm fighting slipping back in and out, then I feel the quick titillation against my nipple again. Realizing, I'm not alone, I begin to wake more fully, lifting my head slightly. Feeling a hand, gently pushing me back down, I relax into the pillow. "Oh babe, I'm glad you came. I missed you today," I say lovingly to her.

Reaching down, I grab the top of her hair and tighten, just as she begins to fully take me, practically to the root, into her mouth. *Fuck that feels so good!* Not wanting to move because it feels so fantastic, it occurs to me how lucky I am to have these late night visits from my girl. Working me up and down in her mouth, while she massages my balls, she begins to tease my anus with her finger. "Lizzie, shit! Don't tease me babe, fuck that feels good. Unexpected from you—but damn I like it." Taking more of her hair in my grasp, I pull her upwards, desperate for a kiss. She resists with a slight growl, pushing me back down. O-kay, I'll let her have her fun since she's in such a playful mood.

Disappointed that I don't have any lights on in the room… actually, I thought I left the nightstand light on. She must have turned it off. I reach to turn the light on, and she pulls my hand back. Straining my eyes, I really want to see her body as she moves around me, especially her head as it bobs on my cock. Instead, I only have the slight streak going across the other end of the room, from the moon.

She repositions herself over my thighs, lowering her pussy over my cock. *Oh yeah, this worked really well the last time.* She pivots her hips, rubbing her wet warmth all over me repeatedly, denying me what I really want. Reaching behind her, I grab the tops of her shoulders, pulling her forward, bringing her lips to mine. Needing to taste her, I plunge my tongue into her mouth, desperate to control something, anything. She returns my kiss for a second, pulling back, and pushing my wrists to the sides. "Kiss me dammit," I implore her, but she denies me ruthlessly. Deciding it's time to change up the control, I move my hands to her bare stomach. Moving my fingers upward, I grasp her breasts and squeeze. "What the fuck?" I mumble.

The room fills with light, and as I try and jump up while she's pressing me down into the mattress, my eyes are filled with white and black spots preventing me from focusing. However, what is easy to hear is, "Jack?" The despondent sound of Lizzie's voice ringing throughout our room, but she's not on top of me holding me down. It's coming from across the room. *Motherfucker, this is not happening! God, no!*

"No, no, no, NO!" I stammer away to Lizzie, trying to push the woman off me. Looking at the person who is currently laying on me, "Bitch! Get the fuck off me, Victoria!" When she won't move, I finally lift her up and throw her off me, causing her to land on the floor. Bad idea… my erection becomes an ornament for inspection by the entire room. Lizzie bursts into tears immediately. Moving over to my dresser, I grab a pair of lounge pants, quickly putting them on. Grabbing my head with both hands, I know I'm facing a two-second window before Lizzie bolts, so I urgently prioritize my next moves.

Taking two steps toward Lizzie, she throws her hands up to block me, halting my advances. "Don't come near me!" She screams.

"Baby, I thought it was you!" I plead with her.

"Ha!" Victoria mocks me. "That's a crock-of-shit! You fucking well knew it was me. Don't lie to the girl. You missed me… your cock proved that point." She sneers.

This is not happening. This is not happening. THIS IS NOT HAPPENING! Turning to face Lizzie, "Baby, you need to believe me! I was asleep… totally out. I was exhausted after work, then I went to the gym. I even tried to reach you and couldn't. Then, I took my computer to bed while I waited for you to call me back. I fell asleep, Lizzie. I swear on everything that means anything to me. I love you so much—"

Victoria makes a pfft sound, "You're stupid if you *believe* this shit. This isn't the first time we've been in a bedroom together while you've been in the wings. *He is my husband, little girl!*" She sarcastically vents.

No fucking way! "In name only, Victoria! Shut… the… FUCK… UP!" I wail as loudly as I possibly can. "GET OUT!" But, she just stands there totally naked, winding her long hair between her fingers. God, no! The hair… she has long hair… just like Lizzie. I pulled on that hair. I thought it was Lizzie's hair. No, this can't be happening! I press my hands to my face, trying to keep restraint from killing my wife because she's hurting my girlfriend. This scene couldn't get any more bizarre.

"W-wait. W-what is she talking about?" Lizzie asks, practically hyperventilating.

Reluctantly, I need to explain, "She was in the bedroom—"

"We fucked. Behind your back. Get over it, you aren't the type of submissive Jack needs. I am, I know exactly what he needs." Walking over to face her directly, "Has he whipped you yet?"

"VICTORIA!!" I lunge at her, grabbing her by the arm and picking up some clothes I find scattered near the door. I begin pulling her out the bedroom door, and through the living room, when I see more of her clothes: panties and bra. Bending to pick them up, and still holding her, I'm about to throw her naked ass outside, when I come to a screeching halt. *What the fucking hell?*

Still firmly holding Victoria in one hand, and her clothes in my other, I'm assaulted with blown-up pictures scattered all around my living room. Poster sized pictures of Lizzie… and Mark. I'm going to be sick. Her face… it's her look of ecstasy that I've seen many times. So many pictures… so many things *happening* in the pictures. My thoughts are on overload. I can't process, what I'm seeing... what I'm told by both of them... didn't happen. My Lizzie... with one of my best friends. This. Cannot. Be. Happening.

The room is silent, totally, eerily quiet. In my periphery, I can see Lizzie standing dumbfounded, looking around the room at the poster-sized prints of her, in various erotic poses. My hands are shaking, my knees feel like they are about to collapse, and I'm struggling to breath. Too much... too much to comprehend in five minutes, because my brain wants to explode. My heart already has... on the floor between the floor of my bedroom, to the living room.

"She's an *escort*, Jack. Mark bought and *paid* for her body. Is that the upstanding woman you really want by your side? Representing your beloved family at charity events? She's trashy."

Lizzie's dramatic inhalation of breath, followed by her hand quivering over her mouth, tells me what I didn't want to hear. It's true. She looks at me with pain in her eyes and falls to her knees bellowing in pain. "Jack, I'm so sorry. It's not what you think. I swear it."

"Pictures don't lie. Once a whore, *always* a whore. Jeremy found out and that's why he was so mad at you at the Christmas Gala. Now, his blood is on your hands!" Victoria yells across the room.

Having had enough of her brand of destruction for one night, I yank her hard to the door. Pull it open and push her outside. Naked. While she's begging for my attention and consideration, I throw her belongings out to her, slamming and locking the door. Then, Lizzie and I are... *alone.*

I walk over to a chair and stare at the sofa before me. Instead of focusing on the dreaded pictures looking back at me, I choose to get lost in my memories. The first time we made love on that couch. I'll never forget it. The woman had me by the balls. I would have done anything she had asked, I loved her that much. She has been in my heart and in my mind… for *years*. Now, here we sit, surrounded by memories of us, and other people. This apartment, "the nest," as Seth affectionately termed it, was always supposed to be about me and Lizzie. Our start, to our new future, with no other lovers to taint it. Now, in the span of fifteen minutes, my ex-wife was on my dick while the love of my life… the woman I want to marry, is watching. Then, I discover the same woman, slept with my good friend, lied about it, and oh…by the way, she's a fucking escort. *Fuck my life.*

"J-j-aa-ckk," she says still in the midst of hyperventilating.

I look over at her, and she is still on the floor, visibly destroyed. Her makeup caked in streams down her face. Always attracted to her, my eyes float down, and I notice she's wearing a lightweight jacket. Odd for this time of year. Open in the front, I can see she's wearing a beautiful bra and garter set, with matching crystal encrusted hosiery. Just looking at her, I can feel my dick grow hard and begin to grow. It pisses me off royally, my body, even in the midst of the most trying of times, wants this woman more than any hardship faced. Unfortunately, my hurt heart turns cold. "You wear that for a client tonight? Did you fuck him hard, Lizzie?"

Her expression, evidence of my verbal assault, shows a woman battered with my viciousness. I may not have physically harmed her, but my words slapped her just the same. "Fuck you, asshole! You texted me to come, and I did. I dressed up to surprise you. I wanted YOU to think I was beautiful. Only YOU! Why did you text me knowing you were fucking your wife?"

"I didn't *intentionally* fuck her. I thought it was you… ya know… the woman I was planning to marry. The woman I'm building a massive-ass house for… *for our four children*. That woman! The one I found so *long* ago, committing to save and protect. That woman! Not the woman who fucked one of my best friends and lied about it. Not to mention… how many other men have you fucked

Lizzie? Ten, fifty, one-hundred? What's the number? I'm such a fucking fool."

"You're an asshole!"

"Am I?"

"Yes. I didn't fuck Mark."

"Bullshit. I see the pictures in front of me. I know when you come... I treasure that look. It's the look I want to see when I take my last breath on earth. It's engrained in my brain. I jerked off in the shower tonight, thinking about... that... look."

"Fuck you. You're disgusting."

"You call *me* disgusting? I don't get paid for sex. Now *that's* disgusting."

"I hate you!"

"Good, it'll be easy to get over me then," I reply coldly and flippantly.

She harrumphs and before I can blink an eye... she's *gone*. Out the door, not even bothering to shut it. And I didn't follow her. Sitting in the chair, it suddenly dawns on me, I'm covered in Victoria's stench. Going straight to the shower, I pour soap on a rag... and I scrub. And, I scrub and scrub... and scrub. I scrub so hard, my dick is red and welted, but I don't fucking care. Falling to the floor, I sit in the shower, allowing the hot water to pour over me. Alone in my pain, I recount the first day she came in my life... a day filled with tragedy. It was the day I swore I'd always protect her. She was so innocent, so beautiful, and very, traumatized. For some reason, she attached herself to me like a second skin always in my presence. Always in my arms. I was her healing salve, and it empowered and affected me greatly. Going forward, I think about our recent memories and how amazingly happy she made me. A happiness I never felt before. Yet here I sit, so filled with pain, the water masks my cries and tears, flowing down my face. I can't even imagine another happy day… just anger. And, Victoria… she may be the mother of my children, but now even it accounts for nothing. I hate her intensely, and it won't be good if I see her again. All of this is her fault. She *knew* I loved Lizzie, and still she was set to destroy it. *You won, Victoria—you won.*

Chapter Thirty-Five

Betrayal, Secrets, and My Forgotten Past

Lizzie

Walking out of Jack's apartment, my eyes so full of water, I couldn't hardly see. When I turned the corner, headed towards the elevator, I saw a figure there. Not wanting to be seen, I kept my head down, hoping to avoid suspicion. Major failure.

"How does it feel?" I hear a woman say.

Hoping to ignore her, I attempt to sidestep her, but it doesn't work. "Excuse me," I say annoyed.

"Are you hurting Lizzie? *Good.*" Raising her voice and sneering.

Now that earned my heads-up attention, straight into the psychotic eyes of Cindy Hall. Totally caught off guard, because I didn't expect to see her here, I'm befuddled for words. "Cindy?"

"Yeah, bitch! I gotcha, didn't I? How does it feel to have your world turned upside down since you do it so well for everyone else?"

"Get away from me. I'm trying to get on the elevator."

Beginning to walk past her, she pushes her arm straight out, she blocks my way preventing me to pass. "You're good at making me hurt, so it's time for a little payback. Mark was mine, and you took him!"

"You're insane! Mark didn't want you, because you're an annoying leech who is completely transparent. Maybe if you didn't try so hard to trap a rich man, you'd have one by now."

Slap! My head is thrown to the side, my cheek burning in agony. "Haahhh… you bitch!"

Just as I am about to lunge in her direction, I'm pulled from behind by a wall of arm-candy muscle militia, dressed in all black. "Stop!" Seth barks deeply, causing both of us to instantly cease all movement. "Not another word. Both of you," he orders. Next thing I know, he's hauling me out the back exit of the apartment, which I've never used before. An SUV speeds up, and he pushes me and himself, into the back. Seconds later, we're off to my apartment.

Staring out the window, I say nothing. Actually, there's a lot to say, like: "Thank you for covering my whohaa so it wasn't seen getting into the SUV." Then, there's: "Thank you for saving me from a brawl with a psycho." Of course, there's: "Thanks for taking me out the back exit so the lobby staff won't see me in a total state of shambles." Finally, there's "thanks for the transportation back here because I *really* couldn't drive. After all that commotion because my heart is split open." Problem is… I'm so shredded right now, if I say anything, I'll surely fall apart on poor Seth. Who—doesn't really strike me as the "lovey-dovey" type. So, when I finally reach my apartment, he walks around to my door, like usual, and helps me out. Without giving me an option, he pulls me into my building and drags me up to my front door. Using a key I didn't know he had, he opens the door, pushing it open for me. I take two steps in, turn around, and just as I open my mouth to say something…."

Holding both hands up, "I know." He reaches in, quickly squeezes my hand, and pulls the door shut behind him. I'm standing at the closed door, mouth open, when I hear, "lock it."

Complying with his order, I do as he says, locking the door. Then, I'm *really* alone. Having just left here less than one hour ago, this is not how I planned my night. Knowing I can't wake up the children, I tip toe through the apartment headed straight to my shower. Turning on the taps, I get in. Fully dressed. *God, what have I done?* I've lost an amazing man. One I didn't go looking for, but found me and latched on… hard. Playing the odds, I got caught. Never did I believe a rich man, an uber-rich, mega-millionaire, would understand the struggles of the poor. There was a time… we were very poor. No food, no place to live… dire straits. I didn't trust him to believe in my desperation, the way Mark and Ms. Martin did. Now, I'll never know.

After the water runs cold, I strip away my jacket and beautiful new lingerie, I bought just today. Drenched with water, I leave them on the floor of the shower. I don't even bother brushing my long hair, which will surely be knotted by tomorrow. *Just fucking great.* Walking straight to bed, I dive in, soaked and completely drained, mentally and physically.

The last thoughts on my mind, for some odd reason, was a sentence Jack said: "The one I found so *long* ago, committing to save and protect." Feeling shaky tremors that oddly overtake me, I tighten the covers around me. Maybe sleep will give me some peace and clarity.

The restraints are binding my legs and arms. I cannot move and my breaths are waning. The shrill sounds of someone screaming, are incredibly annoying: Oh—that's me screaming, but I can't stop.... "Stop! Please stop screaming!" I hear from someone nearby. Is that Mark Chesney? But, I continue my wailing. Then, I vaguely hear a man's voice, "Birdie, please honey, I beg you. You're really scaring me." Something is activated, deep in my memory, and it causes me to become more afraid. I'm very confused as images pass through my mind very quickly. Two completely different accidents—I'm involved, and something has triggered my night terrors again.

An accident on Interstate, 95, horrifies me. Small car versus tractor trailer: no survivors. The small car burst into flames, trapping the occupant inside. The jack-knifed tractor trailer, flipped and mangled, a tree impaling the driver. A series of unfortunate events: ice on the roads, speeding, but none more significant than driving while intoxicated. Mangled metal, fire, and the smells of gas... and death.

Someone is rocking me, trying to soothe my pain. "Get away! Don't touch me! You're the reason this happened!" "Oh, Birdie, don't say it. He did this to himself, we know this to be true." Gentle shushing and light kisses on my cheek, try and calm me, but it only upsets me more. Suddenly, I'm moving. Carried like I'm an infant and presented across the bed with luxurious linens. The room is a flurry of sudden activity. There're people all around me. Anxious male voices, sounding very concerned. The doctor who came to my hotel room at the Jefferson? Is that Jack Loving's voice? One other—a female, who is that?

I thrash in the bed—I must get away! I'm picked up from the bed, held again, like an infant in someone's arms.

They're different—the smell of unique cologne permeates my nostrils. For a brief moment, I curl into the comforting arms. Home, it feels like... home.Wait—have these arms held me before? Why is this so familiar to me? Calming sounds spoken to me, attempting to settle me. For a moment, I'm at peace—it feels, good. I know those arms... Jack... I'm so confused!

Then, an image flashes before me of an angry Jeremy. He's calling me dreadful names, judging me. Jack's soothing voice tries to negotiate my renewed screams. I become more uncontrollable, unmanageable. To no avail, I'm held down on both sides. "Doctor, hurry!" The sharp pinch in my arm is quickly followed by a burning pain in my veins. Then, there is nothing but blackness. I'm alone, except for my thoughts, and the terrifying screams that never end.

In the deepest, darkest recesses of my mind, I'm taken to a place, a very long time ago, I'm not supposed to go. An image of a medicine bottle. A place my mind has protected me from. I'm convinced: all is surely lost. Left with only the confusing memories, and the constant, unending screams plaguing me, I focus on saying goodbye to those most important to me. I think of my babies: Hope and Ethan. My daughter, so strong willed and beautiful. One day, she will be an amazing mother, I'm sure. The giving and compassionate, Ethan, who no matter what, always has a smile on his face. Oh, how blessed I am to be honored with the privilege of loving them. A memory of Mother's voice rings in my head, "Be good to one another, my dear babies! Always be friends—never allow senseless feuds to split you. I will watch over you from above. My love will always guide you. Goodbye..." "We need you! I love you, Mommy," I hear them scream. Shredded from the thoughts of losing them, my mind goes to my own mother. Why do I have this memory of my mother speaking, so vividly in my mind? And, when did it happen?

In searching for answers to my Mother's words, my brain quickly moves pictures along at warp speed, and I'm transported to an earlier time. Something about the comfort of Jack's arms which seem so relevant, along with hearing my mother's words, incites deeply rooted memories. Ones that for some reason, I'm not supposed to remember.

My chest hurts, my breaths are labored. Bright flashes of light appear, then disappear. Trying to focus on them, I see oranges and reds. It's fire! The smoke suddenly fills around me! Oh, God, PLEASE SAVE ME!

I can't breathe! Too much smoke… I can't see either. My eyes are open but it's black everywhere and my eyes are beginning to hurt. Rubbing them, it feels like there's sand inside. A faint flash catches my attention so I focus hard on it. Oh no! "FIRE! FIRE," I yell as loud as I can. No one can hear me or if they can, they aren't answering.

Trying to move, I feel something heavy laying across my legs. Pushing with all my might, I realize it's a… it's a person. A body, a heavy person. No! It's my daddy. "HELP!! Someone, please help me!" Rolling out from under the weight, I climb through towards the fire, hoping to get a better look.

Our car, we're in my mom's minivan. Looking beside me, I see her slumped toward the window. Shaking her, "Mom, wake up! You have to wake up!" She cries out once in pain. "Elizabeth," she says weakly. "It's all up to you now. Be strong baby and save them. I-I can't." "We need you! I love you, Mommy," I beg her in reply. With a big breath in, she squeaks out, "Be good to one another, my dear babies! Always be friends—never allow senseless feuds to split *you. I will watch over you from above. My love will always guide you. G-goodbyyyyye...."*

No! Unwilling to leave my mother, I settle in to accept my fate. Moments later, I am pulled from the burning car, moments before it explodes like a bomb. "I have you, Lizzie! You're safe! You're safe, sweetheart!" A man, with arms like small trees, smelling of cinnamon, carries me like a feather. He whispers warm, loving thoughts into my ears. I cannot understand what he's saying, but I feel his strength rocking my body back and forth. Please, I vow, I'll never forget the way I feel in his arms... those I imagine feel, like home, would feel.

Then I hear screaming, high-pitch screaming, so loud—it's piercing. It doesn't stop... the screams prevail... they never stop, they live on into the dark night. Watching the minivan from afar, I see a woman who has stopped alongside the road. "THERE, OVER THERE!" I yell to her, begging her to do something for my parents. Then, their piercing screams... just... stop.

The mystery woman, and her son, my savior, took me to their home and cared for me. Filled with medications to help me cope, I stayed there for days. Eventually, Jenny's family would come for me, and I had to leave. But, my savior and I spent non-stop time together, trying to cope with the tragedy, within the comfort of his arms. Then, when I left their home, for reasons I don't understand, he disappeared completely and became faceless to me. A coping mechanism maybe? All I know for sure, is this person who I became so connected to, would become yet another person, I lost.

My flashes of memories push forward to the present quickly again, and I'm once again at the Jefferson, on the night of the Christmas Gala. Laying here, coming out of a medical fog. Opening my eyes, I find I'm on the bed of luxurious linens, in the arms of the mysterious Jack, who knew nothing about me, but gave so much of himself tonight… so selflessly. Pulling away from him, I lean back and try to see his face, but it's distorted. My mind knows it's him, but my eyes are playing tricks on me—a faceless man. I'm at the hotel, but feel my eyes are filled with soot. How bizarre? The basic structure of his face, appears, and for no reason which I can explain, I place my hands on each of his cheeks. My thumb gently touches the center of his lips. He kisses the pad and I spread the wetness from one corner back to the other corner, stopping in the middle. Leaning in, I gently lay my lips against his. He's caught off guard, but immediately pulls me into his chest. Heat fills my body, wanting to be closer, needing to feel more. He greedily attempts to deepen the kiss, and I let him. It's… that familiarity, the way he holds me, the way he tastes of cinnamon gum… it's… him. "No, it can't be." Jumping out of his lap, I stand up, feeling very dizzy. "Sweetie, do you remember me? Sit down, now." He orders me. "No, you saved me years ago. It was YOU! I know it! Your touch, it was you. You pulled me out of the burning car, then you healed me for days, and threw me away… you let me go. YOU! I remember now, we related because of your loss. Your brother died—your twin. Everybody leaves me, even YOU!"

"No, I never forgot you. Not one single day, Lizzie. I've been waiting my entire life for you to remember. You were very sick, and the doctors felt it was best if you forgot the accident… and me." Hands circle the back of my head, pushing my mouth closer, his tongue enters mine. The taste of cinnamon fills my taste buds, and I want more of it. I need all of it, all of him. Anything he wants, he takes. This is so different than what I'm used to and I really like it. My body craves the anticipation of this newness… please teach me, use me, help me heal. "I will take care of you, Lizzie. You'll see, you're stronger than you realize." He forcefully returns to kissing me *and the passion is dizzying. My body completely relaxes into him. The more he takes, the more I give.*

I don't know how long I laid in his arms, but the final memory was the doctor returning to give me another shot. Then… blackness, again, followed by the vicious cycle of unending screams.

I'm awakened feeling like I may choke, my body begins to cough violently. Sitting up in bed, I'm drenched with sweat. My nightgown, the bottom sheet, my pillowcase, soaked. Finding it difficult to breathe normally, I place my hand on my chest, and my heart rate is pounding.

Moving to the side of the bed, I turn on my night table lamp, and the room is cast with a soft glow. Looking in the mirror, I'm shocked to see my appearance. Just under the mirror, my eyes catch on a picture of Jack. That's when everything floods back to me.

For years, I've suffered from night terrors following my family's accident. Luckily, I never remembered them. Jenny's family took me to a therapist, at VCU Medical Center, diagnosing me with PTSD. Over time, they improved. I blocked out the accident scene for many years, but following Jeremy's accident, I started having dreams again. Problem is, much of it didn't make sense. It was like a movie film, but with all the frames out of order. This time, the movie made sense.

As I sit on the side of the bed, I struggle to catch my breath. I grab a nearby notebook and pen, needing to get these thoughts out, I begin to frantically write. The night of the Christmas Gala, Jeremy showed up and made a scene. He and Mark fought. *Yes, Mark was in my dream.* I remember him carrying me, and I yelled at him over our dating. Then, I was yelling again and Jack got there, and he consoled me. He held me closely and it felt familiar. *Every time, it feels familiar!* The cinnamon gum he always chews; it's his vise. It's always comforted me to chew it too. Now I know it was my memory of him. Running the memory in my head, carefully, and slowly, I make my notes. Feeling like I'm coming out of a dense fog, I immediately drop the notebook and pen, as if it may burn me. Suddenly, the room depletes of oxygen. *They were there.* Jack saved me from my parents burning car. *Sarah was there, too.* They took me to their house, and a therapist came—my therapist! This is the secret he was keeping from me from the night of the Christmas Gala. He has said repeatedly, after that night, he wanted me to remember the night of the Gala, on my own. He has also been clear, he would have me, and I belonged to *him.* What he neglected to say—*he already had me and threw me away.* After all these years, he found me, and the Loving's— *they knew it the whole time.*

My stomach begins to protest, and I race to the bathroom, emptying its contents. I feel so betrayed, so lied to. Gathering the strength to stand, I wash my face and stare into the mirror.

Why didn't he just tell me we knew each other? He saved my life! Now, everything comes into focus. This is why he took a keen interest in me. *Was it pity? Has his savior complex gone too far? Am I a distraction from the betrayal in his marriage?*

Stumbling and moving to my depressing, reflection chair next to the window, I stare out into the night sky, seeking answers. And, of course, it would be raining. My life is in shambles. I've destroyed the trust of a man I absolutely love. In my effort to save him, I've ruined us. So many raindrops… so many memories. They all flow together as dots, and when it gets too heavy, the rivulets just… roll away, hitting bottom. My life, similar to the little dots, gets heavy and it runs and rolls away too.

"Oh, Jack, will we ever get our happy ending?" I say to the window, into the night sky, begging for answers.

"I honestly don't know." A pained voice, sitting in the dark, whispers behind me.

The End

I hope you enjoyed, The Unlikely Samaritan, as much as I have enjoyed writing this series.

If so, PLEASE take five minutes and leave a review on the retail website. Thank You!

Stay Tuned for Book Three, in The Good Samaritan series by Jolie Mae Miller.

Due for release Summer, 2015

Acknowledgments

These last few months have been life changing for me. The moment I hit "publish," I didn't know whether to dance a jig, cry out in fear or get sick. When you make the decision to self-publish, it's so scary but it has opened my world to incredible new possibilities. As an avid reader, I loved learning those tidbits of information from my favorite authors. Now, I have fangirl moments when those same authors message me and wish me luck on my new series. It's truly mindboggling!

To begin, I'd like to reiterate my book's Dedication, and explain it more in detail. I owe so many people, but I would be terribly remiss if I didn't take everyone back to a series of events which occurred during the production of book one, The Good Samaritan. After the manuscript was complete, acknowledgments written, the process of uploading the file to various sites began. Faced with an impending deadline, and my newbie status, my formatter Deena Harrison Schoenfeldt had mercy on me and stayed up throughout the night assisting me. When I say throughout the night... I'm not exaggerating because it was five o'clock in the morning before we finished. These last minute, late night difficulties, turned out to be quite literally life saving.

Shortly after finishing, Deena finally went to bed. Within thirty minutes, an intruder broke into her home and entered her bedroom with a knife. Thankfully, she was still coherent from our late-night work and was able to fend off her attacker. She sustained multiple stab wounds and literally fought for her life, causing the assailant to flee down the street with Deena chasing behind him. This fiery redheaded cowgirl is a warrior. She fought to protect herself, her child sleeping nearby, her property and I am in awe of her. Never, ever, in a million years, did I imagine my little book of erotic romance fiction would be the difference in her surviving or not surviving. Had Deena not given her time to help me throughout the night, she would have surely been in a deep sleep, unable to defend herself. The thought of a different outcome horrifies me completely. This experience has bonded us, and she knows we're friends for life even if I need to trek to Texas to find her. Deena has written an amazing blog entry about her attack. Please take the time to read about this amazingly cool chick at http://smarturl.it/DRS-Crime.

To further expand on how critical Deena has been to my team, she was the person I immediately thought of if I had a question. She's a tech goddess, so anything and everything I didn't understand…all roads led to Deena. So much so that I've felt guilty because the woman has a business to run! She's an amazing book formatter and I'm privileged when she shares her wisdom and creativity. If you are an aspiring author, you need a professional formatter. So e-bookbuilders.com is who you should use! Whether it's website questions, social media questions, graphics design, anything A-Z, I trust her. She has been one of my biggest advocates and through her I've met some amazing people in the author and blogging community. She administers a group, Badass Book Bitches, and as my Dedication states, Deena: You're the baddest of the BaBB, and we all think you're amazing! I'm honored to have you on my production team and every day I'm thankful that fate put us together. You constantly pimp my books to anyone who will listen and I owe you so much. Our frequent late night conversations where I'm left laughing hysterically with tears running down my face, invigorate me. Thank you for being a sounding board when I needed it and offering sage advice. More importantly, I love you for being my bestie. Thank you, Deena. ♥

New to my production team is my editor, Laura Tepedino Hampton with Editing For You. She is also a book reviewer for the blog, Swoon Worthy Books. I'm incredibly jealous of her scenic Utah views. Lucky girl! And, I just found out she manages the leading St. Bernard kennel in the country. (My Saint is a rescue, and I'm obsessed with them! Eeekk!!) I've enjoyed working with Laura and hearing her enthusiasm for the series. Not every editor has to like our books, but it's very refreshing when you hear her excitement for the series. I remember asking her if she wanted to know my plans for the third book and she sounded like a child at Christmas. Deciding rather to wait for the surprise, it was nice to hear her appreciation for my unique approach to writing this series. Thank you very much, Laura for editing my "baby" and understanding why this series means so much to me. ♥

Now, on to my cover designer, Laura Hidalgo with Bookfabulous Designs. Laura designed the original book cover for book one, The Good Samaritan. Since I'm still a new indie author, and really wish I had paid more attention in marketing class, I rely on professionals to guide me on major decisions. The book cover is critical. In some ways, it's more critical than the story inside. If an audience does not respond well to a cover, they will not pick up a book. In book one, I was determined to match the cover to the authenticity of the story. In that case, the iconic stairs of Jefferson Hotel, the site of the Christmas Gala. Unfortunately, as beautiful as it was, audiences did not respond. When I went to Laura about book two, I explained my vision. In fact, I wanted Lizzie's building at 111 East Main Street to be the cover—she *is* the unlikely samaritan. After going through countless stock photos looking for the perfect storefront, Laura said, "Do you want it to match the story, or do you want it to sell?" That question led to hours of debate—push and pull between us. Finally, she told me my concept was totally wrong and should trust her to come up with the right cover for Lizzie (whom I didn't want on the cover). When I opened the file and saw her design, I literally was paralyzed for a few seconds. I was totally blown away. Realizing how beautiful the cover for book two was going to be, it was a no-brainer to have a new cover for book one. Yes, Laura Hidalgo was right...Jolie Mae was *wrong*. Moreover, her mockup for book three is outstanding! So far the response to the new covers as well as the amazing accompanying graphics, has been amazing. Thank you Laura...you were right!♥

Before a manuscript is sent for editing, it's reviewed by beta readers. For this book, I had four: my mom, Kathi Bowers, Tammie Taylor and Christy Pritchard. As I've stated before, some people find it odd that I would ask my mom to review, considering the content. She's the most avid romance reader I know. Regardless of content, I trust her candidness. She has a strong attention to detail and hands down...my biggest fan. Thank you, Mom for your support and unending love. I love you. Kathi Bowers and Tammie Taylor came through again for me. They were excited to read the new book and both were incredibly helpful. Kathi reads A LOT, so she brings a wealth of knowledge, helping me with finer details of plot development. Tammie's strengths are attention to detail and I can rely on her to make sure there are no inconsistencies. When you look at a manuscript for many hours, your eyes just automatically glaze over. Therefore, their roles are very important. Thanks again Mom, Kathi and Tammie, I really appreciate your help.♥

   This time around, I added Christy Pritchard to beta as well. From Ohio, I met her when she sent me a message after reading The Good Samaritan. Before I even realized it, we texted for hours! I just love Christy and her enthusiasm and support for the series has been amazing. Christy is actually a blogger for Crickette's Bookshelf. Her support for indie authors is incredible. She has pimped my books far and wide and was the reason why I ultimately formed a street team. I'll never forget when she messaged me in the middle of the night (I'm always up anyway), after finishing the book. "I have to have book three now!" That led to a two-hour conversation whereby we laughed and chatted about finer plot points. She was the first person to finish reading, so it was fantastic to finally be able to talk to someone. Christy is a such a well-rounded reader, blogger, confidant, and friend. She is co-sponsoring my Release Day Event, and I'm incredibly lucky to have her on my team. I can't wait to meet you in person, thank you, Christy!♥

   Erin Spencer, Lifesaver. That's her new permanent title. Typing this, my eyes are full of tears because this girl is the real deal. Promotions for an indie author can be very overwhelming. It's time consuming and there's so much that goes into promoting today's books. For indie authors, you cannot underestimate the value of blogging. Specifically, there are cover reveals, blog tours, release day blitzes and so much more. I had the great fortune to meet Erin Spencer, with Southern Belle Promotions. She is quite possibly the nicest, most generous person, I've ever met. Also, her ability to multi-task is astonishing. She performed a tremendous amount of work for me while cooking dinner and taking care of her children, all at the same time. The woman is crazy good, and very well respected within the blog community. Fate keeps aligning me with amazing people and Erin is a keeper for sure. My only wish is that we lived closer because I just know she's one of those people that you would love to have as a close girlfriend. Thank you, Erin, for everything you have done to help make The Unlikely Samaritan successful. As I keep saying to you, I don't know how I will ever repay your generosity.♥

Jolie Mae's Sexy Samaritans, AKA my street team, is made up of a great group of women. Small in number, we are strong at heart. For those of you who don't know what a street team is, it's a group tasked with promoting the works of an author. Since promotions on social media is hugely important, no author can do it alone. Street team members are volunteers, who post graphics on behalf of the author, anywhere and everywhere on social media. When Christy suggested I finally needed to organize one, she came up with the name for the group and I think it's perfect. To all my lovelies: Alex, Amanda, Carol, Christy, Deena, Hellie, Jennifer, Kara, Kathi, Laura, Michelle, Pamela, Tammie, Tiffany, Tina & Verna...THANK YOU!!! Thank you for your support of these characters and most especially, thank you for helping me. Words cannot express the joy each time I see a new notification pop up, with your names listed. Your time is precious and please know I appreciate your dedication. If you love the series and interested in helping promote it, please let me know!♥

To the Badass Book Bitches: I consider it a privilege to be amongst you. Your knowledge of various issues constantly amazes me. Thank you for accepting this newbie the way you have. In addition to the technical support, the laughs we've had, have lifted me on some really dark days. I'm truly looking forward to meeting many of you in person someday.♥

To my best friend Jennifer Greenwell: I owe you for saving me in my frustrating hour, trying to name this book. Jenny and I have an uncanny way of knowing just what the other needs. I spent countless hours trying to come up with the perfect title to no avail. When I shared my frustration, within minutes, she came up with three choices. The interesting part was she had no clue where I was going with the series, so to suggest The Unlikely Samaritan was ingenious. Lizzie is the *most* unlikely samaritan of all. Who could imagine her being a Madame? Or when would you ever expect an escort agency to be in business for the sole purpose of philanthropy? Yes… "unlikely" was the perfect word. Thank you, Jenny!♥

To Tamo Sein: When you need a personal recommendation for incredible local musical talent in Richmond, Virginia, who better to ask but the totally awesome, amazingly cool, DJ from XL-102! She's fun to hang out with and generous with her time. I wanted to highlight bands who are right on the edge and her suggestions of Those Manic Seas, Snowy Owls, and Cosby & Against Grace, were perfect. Thanks Tamo!♥

To the bloggers who have supported me, you have my loyalty forever. I'm hesitant to list names because invariably I'll miss one. However, there are a few I must recognize. Crickette's Bookshelf, E-BookBuilders, Southern Belle Book Blog, Like a Bump on a Blog, Swoon Worthy Books, and Eye Candy Bookstore. Thank you for supporting my recent cover reveal and my series. It means everything to have your support!♥

To fans and the nearly 3,000 Facebook friends: Words cannot express how you have changed my life. I keep saying it because it's very true. Never in a million years did I expect just one year ago, to meet so many interesting people. Except for Antartica, I routinely chat with people from every continent. History and cultures are fascinating to me, so to have this opportunity is extraordinary, and I don't take it lightly. So, thank you for inviting me into your lives with my words. I love to hear from fans concerning the series and hope you will contact me. Your support of an indie author is vitally important in continuing our writing. Most people never publish anticipating wealth, they publish because they love to write. So, thank you for supporting my dream!♥

Last but certainly not least, my family. I've intentionally withheld their pictures, their names and their stories from social media. Not because I don't care about them, or choose not to brag on their accomplishments. I'm Mom—my job is to protect them. In this world of social media where we've seen author's lives hacked and ruined, it's too scary to publicize them freely. If you see a post about my family, it will be on their terms because my choice shouldn't affect them. They know I love them immensely and there is no way I could write without my family's support. It takes a special family to support an author of erotic romance! So, I love you all very much and I apologize for the craziness that goes along with my schedule. Thank you for your sacrifices which allow me to chase this wonderful dream of mine. Don't forget to always follow your dreams too!♥ ♥

Independent (AKA Indie) Authors, really need your reviews! PLEASE! Take five minutes and return to the site where you purchased from, and leave a book review. It is incredibly important for us to know what YOU think.

All my unending love and appreciation from my home in Virginia to you, I am,

Very truly yours,

Jolie Mae

P.S. Stay tuned for Book Three, coming Summer, 2015!

About Jolie Mae

Jolie Mae Miller is an independent author, living in Prince George, Virginia, with her loving husband and amazing children. Her busy home also includes a Yorkie, a Poodle, and a St. Bernard. Her favorite job is being a Mom and Meme (because she's too young to be a "GRANDMA!").

She grew up in Powhatan, Virginia, working in her family's auto parts business for many years. After her sister received a life-saving transplant, she pursued and was hired by Richmond-based, non-profit, United Network for Organ Sharing (UNOS). She enjoyed thirteen years working in the Accounting department managing various functions. Today, she has the best job, Mom.

In her free time, she enjoys reading and watching baseball. Whether it's her husband who umpires, her son or the Orioles. Additionally, she's an ancestry junkie, knowing quite well it's a never ending project. Jolie Mae is incredibly blessed to have a supportive family behind her while she pursues her love and passion of complex-themed writing. She credits her amazing parents for continuing to be positive, guiding forces in her life. Her love of reading definitely came from her Mom and is constantly inspired by her Dad's outgoing personality and knack for great storytelling.

Contact Jolie Mae

Jolie Mae absolutely loves to hear from fans! To learn more about Jolie Mae, please feel free to contact her as follows:

Official website: www.joliemaemiller.com

Email her directly: jolie@joliemaemiller.com

Marketing, Autographed Books or other
inquiries: info@joliemaemiller.com

Newsletter requests: newsletter@joliemaemiller.com

Facebook: Jolie Mae Miller-Author
 www.facebook.com/JolieMaeMillerAuthor

Twitter: @joliemaemiller